ODD MEN OUT

Matt Betts

DOG STAR
BOOKS

Odd Men Out © 2013
by Matt Betts

Published by Dog Star Books
Bowie, MD

First Edition

Cover Image: Bradley Sharp
Book Design: Jennifer Barnes

Printed in the United States of America

ISBN: 978-1-935738-46-6

Library of Congress Control Number: 2013936667

www.DogStarBooks.net

Dedication

To my wife, Mackenzie—Your support and encouragement made this possible.

And to Calvin and Miles—My two best characters, ever.

Acknowledgements

Odd Men Out had a lot of help on its way to print.

Thanks to The Naked Wordshop for the critiques, advice, barbs and support on this book and many other pieces over the years. Big love to each and every one of you. The Pit Crew was unbelievably helpful with their astute last-minute panic critiques, and special thanks to all of the other amazing beta readers who shaped the early versions of the book.

Huge thanks to all the top dogs at Raw Dog Screaming Press and Dog Star Books. I'm grateful to Deanna Lepsch for the wonderful edits and kind words. Jennifer Barnes's continual encouragement and insightful suggestions were instrumental in making this novel fly. An airship or two full of appreciation to Heidi Ruby Miller for believing in the book. Her hard work, sage advice and amazing patience made everything seem easy. I look forward to the next time we get to work together. Soonish, rather than laterish, I hope!

Thanks to my boys, Miles and Calvin, and my wife, Mackenzie. It would never have worked without you.

Finally, thank you to my parents for, among other things, giving me a love of books. See if you can find room on the shelf for this one. It should probably be listed in alphabetical order by author's last name.

FOREWORD: ODD MEN OUT
by Liz Coley

Matt Betts could have been my little brother—maybe he is in an alternate universe—judging from his self-described journey to adulthood. Like my this-universe brother Matthew, Matt's younger days featured Dungeons and Dragons, comic books, *Star Wars*, *Mad Magazine* and *MST3000* monster movies. I suspect that I am not the only one to have enjoyed *Zontar, Thing from Venus* or *Them* or Godzilla versus Fillintheblank on Saturday mornings when I should have been outdoors. My early B-movie habit was hosted by Moona Lisa, a local predecessor to and foreshadower of Elvira, Mistress of the Dark. Her trademark signoff wished us a sultry voiced: "Happy hallucinations, honeys."

Now, I'm not saying that Matt suffers from hallucinations. But his inner vision is clearly a simmering stew of many influences and ingredients, beginning with this admitted youthful nerdery, supplemented by his father's determination to train him in circus arts, seasoned with his jaunt through both radio and stand-up comedy, and sprinkled with his insatiable appetite for books and blogs. And then there's The History Channel, cable TV's alchemist of the past, which imbued him with a passion for the forces that shaped the American story. Out of this savory cauldron rises the creature Matt—to become a poet, a storyteller, and a novelist.

Matt's poetry has been widely published in such venues as *Escape Clause*, *Ghostlight*, *The Book of Tentacles*, the *2010 Rhysling Anthology*, *Vicious Verses and Reanimated Rhyme*, and *Kaleidotrope*, but most importantly in his 2012 collection *See no Evil, Say no Evil*. The voice is clever, wry, humorous, and never far from zombies and the horror themes of yore. He has also stamped his mark, not unlike an oversized mutant dinolizard, on the short story market in horror, fantasy, and science fiction with numerous stories anthologized in *Arkham Tales*, *Ethereal Tales*, *Triangulation: Taking Flight*, and *Bizarro Fiction!* among others.

In your hands, you hold his debut into the wider scope of a novel, and it is with anticipation that we enter the big screen version of Matt's imagination. The sweeping tale he has pulled together, *Odd Men Out*, follows several bands of fellows through the alternate history steampunk setting of a Civil War temporarily on hold while we get control of the little zombie problem. The Midwest is already uninhabitable, and Europe has quarantined the U.S. The young country struggles to deal with chaos as the characters struggle to define their roles. There's a North-supporting insurgency masquerading as a circus, a self-appointed peacekeeping group masquerading as the government, a Turtle transport captain and his loyal girl Friday, a mysterious super-weapon, and a very, very large bipedal reptile with an uncanny resemblance to you-know-who. Matt makes it all seamlessly plausible as he gradually reveals the invisible ties between these seemingly disparate elements. By the end, it becomes apparent that the title *Odd Men Out* works on multiple levels, taking in all the people who are trying to find their way alone or together in this strange new-old America.

Matt's world and character building are so persuasive, this novel opens the doors to—in fact demands—both prequels and sequels. Let's hope they are forthcoming soon. Congratulations on this release, and now get back to the keyboard, Matt.

Liz Coley, author of *Pretty Girl-13* and *Out of Xibalba*
January 2013

Liz Coley's short science fiction has been published in Cosmos Magazine, both online and in print, as well as in several print anthologies, including *The Last Man, Strange Worlds,* and *More Scary Kisses*. She is the author of young adult alternate history novel *Out of Xibalba* (self-published under the LC Teen imprint): the story starts when the world ends. Most recently, her debut novel with traditional publishing, psychological thriller *Pretty Girl-13,* is being released in at least ten languages on four continents. Visit her online at lizcoley.com or on Twitter and Facebook as Liz Coley Books.

1

Cyrus Joseph Spencer spied another insect on a pile of crumbs near the edge of the table and ground it beneath his palm. *"Lester,"* he mumbled. He braced himself against the bulkhead as the Turtle lurched with another giant step.

"Lester!" He enjoyed the way his voice echoed in the tight halls.

Lucinda stood in the center of the washroom as he walked past. Without a word she used a soapy hand to point farther down the hall toward the outer hatch.

Cyrus grunted and continued stomping down the rattling metal deck.

He shoved the rusty hatch open and stepped out into the bright sunshine of the observation deck. "Lester! What in hell did I say about eating in the goddamn navigation room?" He shaded his eyes and scanned the deck, seeing Lester Lomak with his face pressed against the telescope. "Lester, I've half a—" The ship lurched again and he grabbed the rail. Cyrus looked down at the land far below them. He could see one of the massive legs bow out as it went back down to the ground with a rumble and crunch. "I've half a mind to toss you over the side and let things happen as they will." He was perturbed that the boy wouldn't even look at him. "I'm talking—"

Lester interrupted. "There's an airship."

"What?" Cyrus moved toward the kid.

"On the horizon. An airship."

Cyrus nudged Lester out of the way and looked through the telescope. "How long's it been there?" Cyrus turned to look at the boy. He'd finally gotten to the point where the teen's face didn't make him cringe. His cheek and jaw on the left side were a dark scarred mess—the victim of an exploding boiler when he was younger. It hadn't healed well.

"Noticed it a few minutes back," Lester said.

"Any idea what it's doing?"

"Sittin' there. Far as I can tell." The boy shrugged.

"That's almost due north?"

Lester nodded. "That would probably mean they're over Sacramento."

"Mmm." Cyrus put his eye back to the scope. "They can have it. That town's a hole anyway. It ain't nothing but another zombie lounge now. If they think they can salvage something there, good luck to 'em." Cyrus gave the dot on the horizon another hard look. He envied whoever was onboard for their freedom. An airship could go places that the five-story six-legged Turtle couldn't. "Any markings?"

"Not that I can tell."

The hatch opened and Lucinda stepped out onto the deck. "Crew meeting I wasn't informed of?"

Cyrus hiked his thumb at the boy. "Our lookout actually saw something. Tell 'er what you found, kid." He started walking toward the hatch.

Lester put his hands on the telescope and looked down at his feet. The high-pitched sound of one of the Turtle's massive iron legs rising and then plunging to the ground invaded the silence.

The boy had a crush on Lucinda, it was plain to see. Cyrus did nothing to discourage it, and completely understood the power she had over any number of men they'd encountered. He himself had let his mind drift to thoughts of her long legs and dark hair. She'd made it clear that none of the crew was on her agenda, but it never stopped them from considering it. "Found himself an airship."

"Whose?" Lucinda asked.

"Don't know," Cyrus said. "Keep watching, Lester. Let me know if anything changes." He opened the hatch and held it for Lucinda. His hand came away with flakes of rust, and he wiped the red-orange residue onto his vest.

As Lucinda entered, she spoke up a little to be heard over the vibration and rattle of the Turtle's movements. "Gibson says the passengers in the cargo hold are bitching," she said.

It was dark in the hall, with only the sunlight streaming through the occasional porthole to guide them. Still, Cyrus made a show of looking at his watch. "Six days already? Right on time. Let me guess. They're hot and hungry and want fresh air? Did anyone mention to these people before they got aboard that they'd be traveling cross country in a giant, slow-moving metal box in the middle of summer?"

"With three hundred other people..."

He'd heard the same complaints on every trip he'd captained for the last two years. A three-week journey from one civilized and safe coast to the next and less than a third of the way through, everyone wants to go home. They hate the food, can't stand the smell of their fellow human beings and the metallic grey and green walls are nothing to look at. "Is this meant to be your daily report?"

"No. Gibson was getting shit. I thought I'd pass it along."

Cyrus opened the hatch to his quarters. "I'll make a note."

"Oh, there is something else. I hate to mention it," Lucinda said.

Cyrus turned back and raised his eyebrow. She never mentioned anything unless it was important.

"Gibson got a note from the administrator down in the hold." Her face was hard to read as it fluctuated from skeptical to grim. "Probably nothing."

"Go on."

"She seems to think one of the passengers is infected."

2

The crowds moved along at a pace just slow enough to take in all the sights and sounds of the boardwalk, but just fast enough not to be drawn in by the barkers trying to take their money at the games of chance or freak shows. Colorful balloons and streamers waved from the booths, nudged aloft by the breeze coming off the Pacific. The breeze also carried the underlying oaky aroma of smoke from the vendors that made foodstuffs—gingerbread cookies, bread and other overpriced treats.

Thomas Preston moved easily through the people, not allowing himself to be slowed or blocked by the looky-loos. He'd stopped staring at the sights years ago, and the barkers knew they had no chance to gain his interest. From the day Tom had gone to work for Umberto Cantolione, everything had changed. People started treating him differently. They knew the influence and power that Cantolione held and by extension, they gave it to Tom. They assumed that a pillar of the community such as Cantolione would only surround himself with like-minded people.

Tom was fine with that.

At first it seemed logical to Tom that Cantolione had to be a criminal mastermind, but it became obvious in the early days that he was just a good guy that made his name and his money by hard work. While Tom admired the ethic, it certainly wasn't his own style. Cantolione was naïve and trusting and took Tom at his word on every matter from his work experience to his family name. It was easy to insinuate himself into the business.

He rounded the corner of the last block to the familiar sounds of the steam organ belting out "The Frog in the Well" as it did with infuriating frequency during the day. It was at this corner that the stench of the main boulevard hit Tom every day. The heavy fragrance of the sea air mixed with the accumulated history of the bodily odors of thousands of visitors to the area. Even when there was almost no one there, it seemed the street remembered and spat their smells back out. It was almost as bad as the fragrant dung of the animals that populated Tom's workplace.

The sounds of a barker were louder here, amplified by a megaphone to make them heard above everything else on the boardwalk. Tom stopped to take in the spectacle of the business that his boss had constructed here. It wasn't a pathetic wooden stall like everyone else's property—it was an experience.

While he wasn't the brightest when it came to human nature, Cantolione was a natural showman and promoter. He had put together a destination for the people of the West to flock to for entertainment, and he'd named it after himself: The Cantolione Family Hall of Amazement. He had constructed a small zoo, complete with an elephant, bear, alligator. The other animals were ones anyone could encounter in the nearby woods and trails. There was a fox, some raccoons, common birds and even a dog that one of the workers had picked up as a stray. Cantolione posted a sign on its cage claiming it was a highly sought-after European breed. When people got to the elephant and the major attractions, they generally forgot about their disappointment at the other animals.

The sprawling compound included a circus-like big top in the middle of the buildings. Here, his boss acted as ringmaster, introducing acts from clowns and acrobats to dancing cats and trick-shot gunmen.

Just a block away from the Hall of Amazement, casting a shadow over the rest of the boardwalk, was the airship tower called Cantolione's Launch. He charged passengers a minor pittance for one of his pilots to fly them down the coast for an hour and serve them stale cheese and watered-down drinks. The tower was also the departure point for Cantolione's cross-country flights. Pilgrims who wanted to head for the East in comfort sat in the spacious lobby and waited in style. That morning, the dirigible *Pride and Joy* sat moored and ready for the influx of tourists. They could get from point A to point B in almost a month via a Turtle and its squalor, or take an airship and get there comfortably in a week. Luxury cost a bit more though.

At the steps to the Hall of Amazement, Tom looked up to the barker's stand. The man hawking the zoo and the tours was his boss, dressed in a colorful topcoat and matching red top hat. It didn't surprise him—it happened a couple of times a week. Cantolione liked to be involved in all areas of his company. Tom nodded and waved, but Cantolione didn't even slow his pitch to acknowledge Tom's existence. Not that Tom minded—he was a little embarrassed by the atmosphere and the day-to-day antics of the company's public persona.

Tom walked through the always-open doors of the lobby, winking as he passed Janine, the ticket seller, and continued down the hall plastered with bright posters announcing past and upcoming exhibits—the Ying Sisters of China, the two-headed giraffe, the Belgian plate spinners. In the lobby proper, he strode past the permanent oddities behind the glass: jars with strange fetuses, shrunken heads. There were the innards of strange animals, malformed skeletons and an enlarged brain preserved in a green fluid. He had gotten over their novelty and grotesqueness quickly after he'd begun to work for Cantolione—especially when he'd found out they were fake.

The door to the main office was blocked by the shabby figure of Kendal Liddy, the company book keeper, fumbling with his keys while trying to keep his briefcase under his arm. His shirt was half-tucked in and his tie hung loose at his neck.

"Can I get that door for you?" Tom asked.

Kendal was startled, but managed to end up with a smile. "Thanks, I'm trying to do too much today, I think." As Kendal stepped back, he dropped the briefcase and a small stack of papers slid out. "Dang. Just isn't my morning."

Tom shook his head and unlocked the door. Kendal was a buffoon, but he knew his numbers and that made him useful in so many ways. "Brother, you just can't win, can you?"

Kendal looked up and flashed a wicked smile. "No, brother, I just can't." He returned to gathering his files. The man hid a secret like a child—the smile on his face gave away too much. Tom was beginning to think the idiot would spill his guts if only someone asked him the right questions.

The two of them had something in common, which was the only reason why Kendal was still around. "How are we doing on that front?"

Kendal looked to make sure they were alone, and then whispered his response. "Close."

"Excellent, let me help you up." Tom extended his hand and pulled.

Cantolione came through the hall just as Kendal was back on his feet. "Good to see everyone working so well together." Cantolione twirled his top hat on his index finger as he went. He passed it off to Tom as he moved into the office. "But I don't pay you people to stand around holding hands. Let's get to business."

They followed their boss and dropped their things in their respective areas. It was a tight room that housed the small desks of Tom and Kendal. The walls were barren and the single window was dirty and didn't close all the way. Opposite Tom's desk was a door that led to Cantolione's private office, which was adorned much more brightly, with colorful posters of acrobats and a window that extended the length of the wall and offered a view of both the crowds on the boardwalk and the line-up to the air tower.

Tom trailed his boss into the inner room to join him for their morning meeting. It was these gatherings that Tom enjoyed. Here they talked about real business matters, leaving things like lions and snakes for another time. They ran over the finances, reviewed the previous day's take and looked at the rest of Cantolione's massive empire.

"I think I'm going to have to let Cappy Marks go. He's a horrible barker," Cantolione said.

Tom hung the boss's hat on its standard hook by the door. "Aw, that's too bad. He's an excellent clown—a crowd favorite." A shiver ran up Tom's spine as he thought about what he'd just said. Even the real meat of the business often involved clowns and wild animals. He watched as his boss hastily moved over to the window and opened it.

"Listen," Cantolione said.

There was a faint shouting that Tom couldn't distinguish from the rest of the noise.

"He's terrible. He's got no banter, no…"

"Repoire?"

"Exactly."

The image of the lanky man in his full clown makeup and clothes brought a smile to Tom's face. "So find someone else. Let Cappy do what he does best."

The room was filled with the sounds of crowds and popping balloons, and the faint staccato sound of Cappy trying to draw in the early morning drifters.

"I don't know who else to get." Cantolione rubbed his chin.

"We'll work on it. We'll find someone," Tom said. He sat at the small table in the corner and took out his notebook. He made a note that was barely legible about

Cappy. He never intended to follow up on it, so it didn't matter what he put, as long as it looked good if Cantolione glanced over. He watched his boss fiddle with his jacket as he sat behind the oversized mahogany desk.

"I got a wire that some of our equipment up north got damaged in a pretty bad rainstorm yesterday. The air tower up there got some lightning strikes that knocked out the guidance lights. They're expecting more weather today."

Tom was aware of the situation. He'd had someone send the message. "Will they be able to continue the crossings on schedule?" Tom knew very well what sort of condition the airships were in—he'd had one of his best people oversee the maintenance. He wanted them in top shape when his own men took them.

"Nothing launching for the next couple of days up there, but one of our others should be landing this afternoon, hopefully. It may've been set back by the storms, too. We'll see what we get today."

"If it becomes a problem, maybe I should go up there and help out," Tom said.

"Not a bad idea, I'd say. Maybe someone needs to get up there and remind our contingent who they work for." Cantolione stopped as voices came from the outer room. Someone was talking to Kendal and after a moment there was a knock at the door.

"Mr. Cantolione? There's a man here says you'll want to talk," Kendal said.

Tom and his boss exchanged a glance. "Were we meeting with someone today?" Tom asked.

Cantolione shook his head no.

"Well, then. I guess you should tell him he's wrong," Tom said.

"He's very insistent." Kendal lowered his voice. "And large."

"Good God, Liddy. Show some backbone and toss him out." Tom saw the reluctance in the accountant's face. "What's his name?" he asked.

"He claims his name is Moose," Kendal said.

3

Cyrus unbolted the steel door and pulled the rough handle. The door stuck and he gave it two great tugs before it creaked on its hinges and opened for him. Lucinda stood behind him with a hand on her sidearm and a rifle across her back. They were always leery that the passengers would try to mutiny and bust through the security checks to storm the command and crew section of the Turtle.

The heat and stench hit him in a wave. It was hot on top of the Turtle, but down below it was absolutely sweltering. The body odor and sweat was nearly a thing you could taste. The lower part of the Turtle was ventilated, but two levels with hundreds of perspiring travelers made for close quarters.

Cyrus's footsteps on the metal stairs echoed as he made his way down. Lucinda slammed the hatch and locked it, then made no sound as she descended.

The landing was surrounded by wire, forming it into a cage with a large reinforced door opposite the stairs. Through the wire, a second cage was visible on the other side of the door. A pale light hung from the ceiling and swayed with the Turtle's strides. The traveler's administrator, Genny Pickerd, stood in the small circle of the bulb's glow with her arms down in front of her. She held a bulky bag in her hands that hung down to her knees. Cyrus found her attractive when they talked at the boarding plank. Now, like everyone else, she'd stopped caring about her appearance and Cyrus was put off by her. Every passenger got an allotment of water each day, and few used it for regular bathing past the first week.

"Mrs. Pickerd, thank you for coming," Cyrus said.

She smiled weakly. "I'm actually enjoying the breeze that's trailing in."

Cyrus didn't notice—he only felt the heat rising from below. He walked back and forth, looking through the wire to inspect the cage that Pickerd was in just to make sure no one had come in with her. Seeing she was alone, he examined the door behind her to make sure it was locked and barred. "Sorry to drag you up here like this." He pulled the bar up and opened the door. "Those are the records?"

"They're all in there," she said dryly. "Is there a problem?"

"Let us have a look at the records and we'll go from there," Lucinda said. "Probably nothing." She began to dig through the bag.

"I understand that you're getting complaints from the passengers," Cyrus said offhandedly. "Absolutely normal. Happens every time."

Her voice steady and low, nearly a whisper. "How should I handle it?"

"First trip, ma'am? We'll hit the river tomorrow. We stop there to take on fresh water and we open the loading bay doors to let a little air in. That tends to cool things down and dampen any fires that might be popping up." He winked at her and smiled. "After we reach the river they'll all come around."

"Mrs Pickerd?" Lucinda asked. "Aren't these the passenger's identifications?" She held up a fistful of folded papers and held open the bag to show Cyrus more like them.

He sighed as he felt the air flow out of him. "Did anyone discuss with you what these papers are for?"

"Of course, they're the passenger boarding papers."

Lucinda waved them. "Which each passenger must keep with them in case of emergency."

"Or if the government needed to identify them," Cyrus added. "It cuts down on fraud and stowaways."

Still in a quiet voice, Pickerd replied, "But I have many children onboard. They'd loose the papers…"

"Then you give them to their parents, grandparents, neighbors or nearest semi-responsible person you can find." Cyrus raised his voice and grabbed the bag from Lucinda. "If all the goddamn papers are in your bag, how do you know who anyone is?" He shook the sack in her face. "Whatever possessed you to keep them?"

Pickerd seemed unflustered. "It was a madhouse down at the dock. They stretched around the building." She looked down at her feet.

Cyrus rolled his eyes. One more thing to go wrong.

4

Tom hustled Moose to the outer room for a word. "We agreed to meet outside the office, if you remember?" Tom said.

Moose leaned close. "I know, but I have something your boss will like as well."

Tom looked at the envelope that Moose had handed him. "You're sure this is where the weapon is currently? No wild goose chases?"

"Outpost Two Thirteen. I swear it."

Tom gave him a hard look.

"Can I just talk to your boss?"

"Five minutes, no more," Tom said.

The large man pushed into the room behind Tom. He held his tattered bowler in his hands in front of him and nodded respectfully. Cantolione's face remained stony, but he returned the courtesy and pointed to a chair across the table from where Tom sat himself down. "I understand you have something terribly important to tell me. At least I hope it's terribly important."

The bulky man spoke as he sat. "Yessir. My name is Joseph Perez, people call me Moose."

Tom immediately regretted letting the man in. It was bad enough that he was just talking about clowns, now he was taking a meeting with a man calling himself Moose, who wore a dirty undershirt and a torn jacket to meet with a well-respected man like his boss. "Mr. Cantolione's time is valuable. Surely you know that."

Reaching into the pocket of his coat, Perez extracted a long envelope folded in half, much like the one he'd given Tom. "I have something that I think might be valuable to you, sir. I know how you like to know about certain things, what with your line of work and all." Perez slid the packet over to Cantolione. The wide desk could've held a dozen people, but Moose seemed to fit it perfectly. Cantolione took the envelope and slid the folders and papers inside it onto the table.

Tom leaned down and sorted through them to array them in some sense of order for Cantolione. They were ships logs, map sections, manifests and rough photographs.

"Worthless photos and shipping lists? Nothing new here," Tom said. "If you're trying to get money out of Mr. Cantolione for some old garbage, I don't think you're going to like the reaction you get."

Cantolione raised his eyebrows but didn't speak.

Tom knew the situation and was authorized to speak for his employer. "A lot of people bring this man their trash in hopes he'll give them a few dollars for it. We rarely get anything worth a nickel."

"You look at them pictures closer, you'll see something new." Moose folded his hands in front of himself. He looked pretty proud of whatever it was he'd brought, but there was definitely an underlying fear, which is what Tom liked. He absently picked up the material and started looking in earnest, while Cantolione gazed on. They were blurry, for the most part, though some had identifiable shapes within. Most were of strange lizards.

"What's this?" Cantolione asked.

"Tell us, and don't talk shit," Tom said. He looked at one picture closely, bringing it up to his face.

Cantolione looked bored. "Tell me more about this picture." He held up another photo of a lizard.

"Let's hear what you know about these little monsters here." He tried to smile and forced himself not to roll his eyes. Typical of Cantolione. There was no game with him. He only cared about drawing in more rubes to the business. All that mattered was the few coins it would put in his pocket. As Moose began talking about the lizard pictures, Tom looked toward the door and thought about the accountant on the other side. He thought about that accountant and the money that he was currently stealing for Tom and his cause.

"I used to work for a man named Dr. Poley. I was one of his lab assistants." Moose sat back but continued to smile.

Tom kept his face stoic but wanted to shoot Moose on the spot. He'd just given Tom important information for a good amount of coin and now Cantolione got his for free? "You worked in a lab? What exactly did you do?" Tom asked, forcing a wary tone. He looked Moose over and decided the man's sausage-like fingers weren't meant for delicate work.

"I mostly assisted with heavy things, when they needed moving."

"Tell me more about the big lizards. People will pay to see a big lizard."

Dr. Poley's device could play a big role in what the cause could do next.

"Men've been bringing these lizards in every once in a while, but they die quickly. They're usually pretty sickly and slow when they cage them up," Moose said.

"Any of them survive at all?" Cantolione asked.

"Not longer than a day or so."

"Any of the men that have captured them know a thing about caring for animals?" Cantolione was still looking back and forth between pictures.

"Where are these lizards from?" Cantolione said.

"There're all over the damn place on an island out there. Hundreds of them. Poley's lab was nearby, so he could do experiments on them," Moose said. "I guess he grew some to be enormous. There's supposed to be a mighty huge one out there that the sailors call the Dragon, or some damn thing. Never seen a picture of that one though."

Moose's words were a jumble of nonsensical sounds as Tom thought about the envelope in his pocket. Nothing Moose or Cantolione said mattered now, he no longer listened. It was like when Tom rode a train and the chugging and rocking sounds eventually faded once he got used to them.

Tom fingered the smooth paper. Inside were exact directions to an incredibly important machine, one that could change the course of history in the Americas, and he sat around talking about lizards.

Tom's group had destroyed small targets to get attention, but if this new device were powerful enough, it would make more than a statement, especially if the Sons of Grant turned it loose on the capital of the Confederate States, Richmond, Virginia. Without their leadership, the Confederacy would be thrown into chaos and the North could easily reclaim what was rightly theirs.

Yes, the destruction of Richmond would spell the end of the divided country and the beginning of a new United States, with Tom Preston leading it.

5

Cyrus was startled awake by Lester's voice. "Sir?"

Cyrus opened his eyes, looked at the boy and glanced at the still-locked hatch then back to the boy. "Mm?" He didn't feel the need to be particularly articulate and wasn't ready to inquire how the kid kept getting in.

"Problem."

"Problem?"

"Maybe."

"Maybe?"

The boy shuffled a little. "I think something's coming. The airship released something and it's coming our way."

Cyrus wiped the sweat from his brow and stared at the boy. "Is that a cracker in your hand? Are you trailing crumbs around my ship?"

The boy shoved it in his pocket.

Cyrus took a minute to get himself together, then headed up to the deck. He rubbed the sleep from his eyes and leaned close to the scope. "I don't see it."

"It's a small one-man thing. A little west of where you're looking now. A bit more." Lester reached out and nudged the scope.

"Hands off," Cyrus said. He focused until he found the small shape in the sky in the direction of the airship. "Looks like a Goose. One of them damn flyin' bicycles." He could make out the outline of a pilot laying back and kicking. Cyrus had seen one of the craft before and thought it was a crazy way to fly. The pilot pedaled, the chain made the wings flap and kept the craft aloft. "Those things don't have much range. I doubt they'd try to fly it all the way here." Cyrus folded his arms and stood a moment, unsure whether to wait it out or wander back into the hot belly of the gargantuan machine.

"It seems to be sweeping low over the river between us and the dirigible," Lester said.

"There's a dam and some gold sluices up that way. Not much else."

"Should we change course?" Lester looked up at Cyrus for a reaction.

Cyrus looked at the small craft dipping low over the water, then stared at the larger craft beyond it. "No. Steady on the course we've set. Whatever's going on down there has nothing to do with us." It was a moment before he had another thought. "You're sure that's the only one of those things? Have you checked everywhere for another Goose sneaking up on us?"

"I checked."

"Did you?" Cyrus scanned the sky over the squat, gray dome that housed the crew quarters and gave the Turtle its shell, but found nothing in the air. He took a quick look over the side nearest the telescope and then stomped to the opposite side and surveyed the area there as well. Below, all he could see was the rhythmic motions of the fat legs carrying the craft forward. Leaning over the side, he heard the familiar shriek of gummed-up gears that weren't happy about doing their task. It sounded like a knee joint, but could've easily been closer to the hip socket that connected the legs to the main body. Cyrus tried to remember which crew member's turn it was to hang by a rope from the belly of the Turtle and scrape out whatever detritus had collected in the unhappy works.

Cyrus was startled to find some of the crew had walked up behind him as he was assessing the situation.

Jansen nodded toward the airship and spoke up. "Could be dangerous. Let's just hit the emergency blow and ditch the whole cargo bay, passengers included. No reason to put ourselves in danger here."

"That's your answer to everything." Lucinda hit Jansen in the back of the head.

Cyrus sighed. "Let's not talk about dropping our passengers, please. We have a job to do for them." He had stopped counting the times Jansen joked about running away from the slightest hint of danger, leaving the passengers behind. Jansen was never serious, and they'd never come close to doing it.

"I think we should just stop the Turtle and find some way to communicate with the airship," Lucinda said.

"Did you learn some kind of signaling code when I wasn't looking?" Cyrus asked.

"No, but there's got to be a way to talk to them." Lucinda looked more than a little exasperated with the situation.

"I can't think of any. Besides, they are pretty far off our course. Let's keep an eye on them and see what they do. Give me an update if they head in our direction, but there's a good chance we won't even come across them." Cyrus didn't really believe it, and from the crew's faces he saw they weren't taken by the possibility either.

6

Walking through the back alley toward the airship port, Tom led the way. "Moose? I think what you've handed me is well worth your pay. You've provided a valuable service to both me and my boss. Telling him about those big creatures surely made him happy." He slid his hands through his hair before replacing his brown bowler. "I'm having a party on *The Moon and the Stars*. We'll be taking a little pleasure cruise and I insist you come along." He stopped walking and he turned to Moose for an answer.

The big man looked around. "Well, I don't...I'm expected at..."

"Nonsense, we'll be out for the rest of the day, back just after dark. What's the harm?" Tom asked.

Moose paused again. "It's just that..."

Moose stopped as Tom stepped close and wrapped his arm around Moose's shoulder.

"Look," Tom said. "It'll take me a bit to get your money for you. Accept this as an apology for not having that pay on hand. You have a knack, my friend. No, a gift for finding information where it cannot, should not be found. I would very much like to talk to you about coming to work for us on a more permanent basis. Surely, you can take a day out of your busy schedule to talk to me about that, right?"

The crowds of shipmen and passengers continued around them. Tom liked playing the big man, though it was hard to flex your muscles when your boss was such a pussycat.

Tom raised an eyebrow and Moose caved in right on cue. He smiled and reluctantly nodded his head.

"Good man. Good man," Tom said as he patted Moose on his beefy back. "Let's get going."

"Will Mr. Cantolione be joining us?" Moose asked.

"Soon, soon," Tom said. Cantolione hadn't exactly been given an invitation.

The men walked next to each other down the promenade toward the launch towers of the port, crowds parting for them, nervous hellos offered to them at every instance where a passerby couldn't look away fast enough. Shopkeepers waved and offered a glimpse of the produce and other wares. The smart ones offered easily portable foods that passengers could take on the journey with them like breads and cured meats. With the ocean so close, a number of the shopkeepers offered smoked fish, the process of which caused the thick stench of salmon and black perch to overpower the pleasant buttery smell of fresh bread loafs for a block or more. There were few people in the market area that Cantolione's organization hadn't touched in one way or another. Tom was happy to be loved by so many even though it went against his better nature.

At the base of the tower, Tom paused and looked up at the lone dirigible docked there. It was Cantolione's favorite pleasure craft, *The Moon and the Stars*. He'd had it built with his first influx of money from the pilgrimage business he'd started. Cantolione had it painted a pale blue to match and sky and the red letter "C" of his company was scrawled across both sides of the huge bladder that carried the craft aloft. It only took three trips across the ever-widening dead lands to be able to afford it. He'd purchased many things before and many since, but it would always hold a place in his heart. Staring at the sleek undercarriage, Tom wondered how his boss would react when it didn't return.

The doormen nodded and pulled the wide doors open as the men stepped across the room to the elevator. Tom tipped his hat to the girls in the revealing, red, clothing with the gold piping who hawked cigarettes, flowers and newspapers. At least Cantoline had listened to Tom on that point—pretty girls could sell anything to men, and judging by the low inventory in their baskets, sales were good. One young girl with her blonde hair stacked high on her head caught his eye and as the elevator doors slid shut, he made a note to buy a rose from her when he came back this way.

The short ride was hot as the elevator jerked and shimmied its way up to the top floor. "Ever been up here before?" Tom asked Moose.

"No sir," he answered.

Tom raised his eyebrows. "Big day out for you then. Riding an elevator."

The big man's face reddened. "Been on an elevator plenty. Just never this one, and never up to the dirigible port."

An attendant pulled the doors open at the top floor and the duo exited onto the landing. The berths were all open, letting a cool breeze drift through the whole of the floor. This waiting area had six rows of chairs in the middle and was just as lavishly decorated as the lower lobby. There were silky, sky-blue banners pinned to the center of the dome, flowing out to the wall. Cantolione paid to have them made by one of the finest artisans in Baltimore. The paintings of airships and airmen hanging on the walls were done by George Peter Alexander Healy, the same man who painted portraits of Lincoln, Buchanan and Jim Bowie. Airships weren't Healy's subject of choice, but Cantolione made it worth his while.

Four men in pressed waiters' uniforms stood in a line with carts and dollies full of drinks and food. They each took their place on the loading ramp as a spot became available.

Another line, a much more lax arrangement, waited at the passenger dock. There were eight men laughing and carousing with a dozen or more women. Tom recognized one or two of the girls as regulars to Cantolione's parties, but the others were new. He scanned them quickly to see if there were any he'd desperately miss were they not to come back and he came up empty.

He held his arms wide and smiled. "Welcome, welcome," he said. "I hope you are looking as forward to this as I am. Let's get underway." Tom's announcement was met with more excitement.

Another attendant slid the doors aside so the passengers could embark. Tom patted Moose on the back heartily. "My good man, here we are." He pointed to *The Moon and the Stars*.

"Aren't you coming?"

Tom nodded. "In good time. I have to make sure everything and everyone gets aboard safely. Go, go. I wouldn't miss this."

With a single glance back, Moose stepped onto the walkway and disappeared into the airship.

Another man bumped into Tom. Kendal Liddy. Bumbling his way through life, as usual. "Kendal!" Tom said, just a bit more exuberantly than he'd meant to. "I was afraid you'd miss out."

7

As Lucinda, Gibson and Cyrus looked on, the airship closed quickly to within a mile of the Turtle and paralleled its course west. Jansen was at the controls and the boy had gone to his bunk for some sack time. Cyrus squinted and strained his eye at the telescope but couldn't make out any details of the airship that would officially identify it. "Hell if I know," he said.

"We checked it too," Lucinda said. "Nothing."

"Sounds like one of them government ships we've heard rumors about," Gibson suggested.

Cyrus laughed at the reference. "Why would the government skulk around in grey airships?" He rubbed his chin and pointed to the airship in the distance. "It's probably just one of our competitors. Cantolione has plenty of airships, could be him. Might have dammed the river to keep us from continuing. We can't make it without water, that's no secret." His finger shifted to point at the two crewmen before him. "Whoever it is, I want one of you watching that bastard at all times. Take turns, whatever, but I want a pair of eyes on it constantly. Right?"

Lucinda and Jansen nodded reluctantly.

"Right." Cyrus turned back for the hatch.

"I'll grab a rifle and be right back," Lucinda shouted to Jansen over her shoulder. She didn't wait for his response. "This is getting to be a busy little trip, sir. I'm not sure I like it," Lucinda said.

Cyrus nodded. The two of them stood outside Lester's tiny cabin and waited for him to answer their pounding.

"Ever consider knocking it on the head and finding a new career?" Lucinda asked.

He pounded again and laughed. "Like what?"

"There are other things. More—"

"Respectable? Safe?" Cyrus interrupted.

Lucinda raised her eyebrows. "More fulfilling."

"More lucrative would be nice," Cyrus said.

She was right, though. There was nothing at the end of the day that made him feel like he'd done real work.

The door was unlocked and Cyrus cranked the handle and pulled.

"Lester?" He looked around the room and pushed his way in, with Lucinda behind him. The room was just as stark as all the others, with metal bulkheads and rivets for wall decorations and a cold steel floor. The only difference visible in Lester's room was what was hanging from the ceiling. A taut hemp rope had a dozen or so large water bladders dangling from it.

Cyrus looked at Lucinda. "Is the boy stealing from our supply and hoarding water?"

"I don't think so, he told me once that he always bought a little extra water at each port just for safety sake, but…" she looked around the room. "This has to be a bathtub worth or more. This could sustain the crew for a couple of weeks if we ever got stranded."

Cyrus stepped around the hanging bladders and scanned the rest of the room. There were also empty ones lying nearby. He looked from the full ones, dripping sweat off their leather hides, to the dry ones on the floor.

"Check the hall." Cyrus pointed to the door and Lucinda leaned out. She shook her head as he slid one of the boy's foot lockers out from under his bunk. He had a suspicion.

The locker was filled haphazardly with a hodgepodge of items, which seemed unlike the boy. On top was a large box of fine salted crackers.

"I think I know the source of the crumbs now," Cyrus said. "Those look a bit expensive for what I pay him, don't you think?"

Other items lining the top included a white shirt with fine ruffled cuffs, two pairs of goggles, what appeared to be a hand-crafted wooden whistle and a peacock feather pen.

"Is he stealing from the passengers?" Lucinda asked.

Cyrus extended a finger toward the water bladders. "More likely bartering. Sneaking down to the passengers somehow and trading with them."

He moved aside a few of the topmost items and dug down a bit. He'd seen something that caught his eye and he needed to confirm it was what he thought. He tugged the flowery cloth out and held it up for Lucinda to see. "Looks like he's trading for all kinds of things."

"Are those women's underthings?" Lucinda wrinkled her nose and stepped back to the door to check the hall.

"Looks like."

A shout came across the intercom. It was Gibson. "We're approaching the river."

Cyrus threw the garment back into the foot locker and slid the whole thing back under the bed. "Find the boy," he said. He left her in the hall and made his way up onto the deck. He joined Jansen, who stood at the forward rail. They stared at the great muddy expanse before them that used to be the Sacramento River. There were still large puddles of standing water, a few trickles that ran like veins down the river bed and everywhere were bodies that had been washed away by the water.

Cyrus took the binoculars and focused on debris in the river bed. Some of the bodies he saw were moving and he sighed at the ubiquity of the undead. "Is there enough water out there?"

"I don't know. It'd take forever to collect it. We'll be moving around, starting, stopping, restarting. Puddle to puddle. The boys downstairs'll be busy," Jansen said.

Cyrus stared out over the river bed. "Check the maps. There's a good-sized lake on the other side of the river, if I remember right. We'll drain that. To hell with this mess." He handed back the binoculars and went back inside to help Lucinda.

Gibson poked his head out of his quarters. "Sir?" He disappeared again.

"I assumed you'd be asleep," Cyrus said. "You've been driving this thing for hours."

"Hard to sleep," he replied.

"Why's that?" Lucinda joined them in the doorway.

Gibson put a finger to his lips. "Shhh. Listen."

With the Turtle idling, the crunch and stomp of the great legs was silent and the engines were quieter. Cyrus heard nothing at first, and then a sound he thought was a hose with a slow, intermittent leak. He stepped forward, careful not to make a noise. He paused to listen again and then moved to the nearby bulkhead. He waited for the sound again and knelt on the metal floor, where the sound was slightly louder.

"What...?" Lucinda asked, but Cyrus held her off with his hand.

He got on all fours and put his face near the floor. The sound was closer. He paused to listen, to try to identify the sound, and he realized it wasn't a leak, or a hose or steam escaping—it was someone crying and sniffling.

"Boy?" he called through the lines of the grated metal floor. The word echoed in the ventilation system. "Lester? Is that you?"

Lucinda knelt down and listened with Cyrus.

"We know what you did," she said. "And it's ok, you don't have to be scared. We just want you to come out. It's dangerous for you to be about without the rest of us."

As Lucinda spoke, Cyrus felt a wave of relief. He had a hard time speaking with Lester in calm tones. From the time they'd taken him on as part of the crew, Cyrus had spoke to him severely, as a gruff captain. It was a joke at first, trying to make the boy uncomfortable with life on the Turtle in an effort to see how far he could push the lad. The tone had stuck when Lester became a model crew member under Cyrus's command. Or so Cyrus thought. Profiteering, possibly theft, and now the boy lay crying in the ductwork.

The boy's sobbing was accompanied by a sliding sound and both noises slowly became fainter. "I'm sorry, I'm sorry." The sounds ended with the boy's apology.

"Lester!" Lucinda called. "Come out." She got no answer.

Gibson cleared his throat. "What the hell?"

"Our Lester had a business of selling water to the passengers," Lucinda said.

Cyrus nodded. "He must have stumbled upon someone who was infected."

"What?" Gibson stepped toward the threshold of his cabin. "Christ. What the hell do we do?"

There was a clatter in the hallway as the outer hatch was slammed shut. Footsteps of someone running reverberated throughout the deck. Everyone turned to see Jansen run past the open door before sliding to a stop and coming back. "The ship's changing course to intercept us."

One more thing. Cyrus thought. *In an ever-increasing pile of things I don't need.*

8

The moonlight reflected white off the ocean as Tom made his way down the boardwalk. The festive lights had all been dampened and, except for the occasional street lamp, the moon was all Tom had to guide his steps. The crowds had long gone at that late hour and the majority of the stalls were shut except for the ones that specialized in things that adults might fancy—dancers, beautiful women, illegal substances. He listened to the boards creak beneath his feet and the waves crash against the pier as he passed the last of the open shops and made his way into the warehouse districts off the docks. Here, the lights were dimmer and fewer, and some carried lanterns to see what needed to be seen. Tom didn't need the light. He had it all memorized.

The buildings still looked relatively new, though the sea had already begun to take its toll and yellow what started as pure white paint. When San Francisco became uninhabitable, Santa Rosa developed quickly, flooded with refugees from the former port city. Santa Rosa grew from an inland town to the main port on the West Coast, complete with a naval yard and ship works. The train yard was built long before Santa Rosa was done with its growth spurt, and the rail works ended up being closer to the center of town than most would like. Still, it made unloading goods from the ships and onto the trains that much easier.

He stopped at an unmarked door and rapped on it twice, waited a beat and rapped again. The door swung open slowly and he stepped in. A large man with a gun stood behind it, but Tom didn't stop to talk. He stepped toward another doorway inside with a tattered blanket hanging in the frame and light streaming from underneath it. He took time to pull his handkerchief from his pocket and tie it around his arm.

When he pushed the makeshift curtain aside, his eyes were assaulted by the bright lights of the multitude of lamps lit there. He tried to keep his composure and not look away from them, to keep his entrance grand—something he learned from Cantolione—because he knew everyone would be looking. He was purposely twenty minutes late.

He moved his gaze around the room, trying to look like he was assessing the gathered men, but really he was giving his eyes time to adjust. As they did, he made out a few of the regulars, like his right hand man Ian Potts. There were new faces, most of them dirty and disheveled, former soldiers who never quite made it to the life outside the military and still sporting parts of their dark blue uniforms. In the back he barely recognized Cappy Marks without his clown make-up.

All of them wore white handkerchiefs around their right arms in the tradition of an elite unit of the Union army called the Jennie Scouts. Those brave men made their way behind enemy lines wearing Confederate uniforms with only a white piece of cloth tied to their arms to show their loyalty to the North, and prevent themselves from getting shot by their own allies. Tom felt it was only fitting that the Sons of Grant wear them, since they were spies in their own country. He, himself, moved about in his normal life without one in order to escape detection. But he made sure to wear it when he addressed the men.

They all sat loosely on the crates and supplies wrapped in burlap and stacked about the warehouse. The assembled were calm, but looked at Tom as if he might say something profound at any moment.

Potts came forward first and extended his hand. "Good to see you, Tom. How're things?"

"I'm well, you?" It was awkward to Tom that anyone was looking to him for leadership or waiting for him to take charge. The men gathered in the warehouse were his peers, his countrymen. He'd fought with a few of them against the South and the undead alike, but he'd never been a leader. He was just another soldier with a gun back then, and he took his orders from someone else.

Potts smiled nervously. "Just fine." He nodded a couple of times. "You ready for this? You seem a little unnerved."

"Not unnerved. Not in the least. Invigorated." He patted his friend on the shoulder and walked toward the table at the center of the gathered men. Tom thought about what he was going to say as he looked at each of the men's faces and gave a slight smile. He thought again about Cantolione's theatrics and the antics he used to flog his business. The idea of leading by falling back on his own experience in the theater made him happy.

He searched each face until a glimmer of recognition gave him a place to start. Sitting on a crate with one leg tucked underneath was a somewhat familiar face. Tom pointed in his general direction, but made sure not to single him out distinctly. That way, one man might think Tom was pointing at another and Tom could be as free as he wanted to make shit up. "I remember you. You were at the Battle of Culp's Hill, right there on the front line, about six men down from me, weren't you?"

Everyone turned to see the man's reaction. Truly Tom didn't know the man—he was just pulling random facts about his own service and applying them to whoever was convenient. Before the man could say anything, Tom continued "I remember it distinctly, because by the end of the day, we weren't six men apart, we were right next to each other. The goddamn Rebs mowed us down like animals that day with those fire bombs they dropped from the sky."

A number of men grunted their agreement from the crowd and Tom paused long enough to let them.

"And over there, over in the back." He pointed to the back of the crowd in the general direction of a number of men standing next to each other. "When we were pinned down in the mud near Gatlinburg, the filthy Southern army raining bullets down on our position with their muskets, you risked your life for everyone on that line and everyone in our country that day. What did we get for it? Did we win that war?" He paused to let the mumbling begin. "Hell, did we even lose that war? No one won, but we were the ones that had everything taken away."

More mumbling and agreement from the crowd.

"The Treaty of Cleveland? More like the Treaty of Convenience, am I right? President Lincoln didn't have the guts to use the means at hand to give us the victory we deserved, so he shook their dirty hands, gave them a hug and started calling them friends again."

The murmurs of the crowd got louder and more adamant. Some laughed at the mention of the president's actions.

"Right now, some of your friends and fellow soldiers are striking another blow for our cause. They are preparing to take out the dam in Sacramento as a show of what we can do." There were nods and half smiles. "As luck would have it, we'll also have the opportunity to show a group of Southern sympathizers the error of their ways." He thought it best to keep the last part cryptic. Some of the men in the crowd might not take too well to the murder of more civilians, no matter how wrong those citizens' beliefs might be.

"And I have bigger news for us. Gentlemen, I've been handed information that one of the Union's greatest minds has left us the means to strike back. All we have to do is seize it," Tom said as he produced the picture. "This is a photo of a device created by the infamous Dr. Simon Poley, the brightest and best inventor the North had working during the war. Rumor has it, that this very device was under construction to end the conflict just as the President tucked his tail between his legs."

The mumbling ceased and it got quiet in the warehouses. Tom took his time in continuing, letting the information sink in for the assembled men.

"We have it on good authority," Tom said. "That this very device is housed in a secret UNA facility not far from Santa Rosa. All we have to do is strike at their base and take this for our own."

He waved the photo to the assembled men. They remained silent. He'd expected cheering.

Tom raised his voice a notch. "We have the funds, we have the mission and it would seem that the means is just within our grasp. Today, we begin to set our purpose to motion. Today, the Sons of Grant strike out against the forces that have been holding our beautiful Union down."

Tom Preston felt the energy of his words spread through the room. Men were finally nodding, pushed by this summation and statement of intent.

"With this device in our possession," he continued. "We will level the Southern capital and render their leadership useless. With our actions, brothers, the North shall rise again!"

Tom watched the crowd get to their feet and raise their fists in excitement. Their cheers filled the room, and he waved his arms along with them.

Potts came over and said something that Tom couldn't hear. He bent down so his own ear was closer to the shorter man's mouth.

"You sure about this?" Potts asked.

"Leave it to me," Tom said. "You just get these men and equipment in order and head north toward the mountains. I'll send instructions as I get them."

"There are too many people involved here," Potts said. "Someone is going to trip us up by opening their damn mouth. Times is hard, a man will do anything for pay."

"Not to worry, the only people I'm concerned about are going to have a very nasty accident soon enough."

"More killing? Tom, you know I'm with you, but a lot of innocent people have lost their lives. We aren't winning any supporters to our cause." Potts looked around and smiled wanly at a few men that shouted to him.

"Innocent?" Tom asked.

"The train. Those people had nothing to do with the war."

"They were sympathizers," Tom said. "Or traitors. There is no in-between anymore."

Potts lowered his voice. "There were kids on that train. What political leaning do you think they had?"

"Trust me," Tom told him. "It's all within our reach."

"It's nothing if we can't win over the people." Potts stopped talking and walked away when Geraldine Yardley approached.

One of the few women who made it into the inner circle of the Sons of Grant, Geraldine was handier with gadgets and weapons than any of the men milling about.

"You got a new gadget to tinker with?" she asked.

"I'd tinker with it carefully," he said. "I want you to look it over and let me know what it does."

"I'm hoping it is something that explodes and leaves a big mess afterward."

"I'd count on that much," he said. "Let's just find out what kind of mess we're looking at."

She stared with him out over the crowd. Handshakes and back pats made their way around with bottles of whiskey.

Tom grabbed ahold of Potts's arm. "You put together some good men for this. We want to get this device and get it back here quickly. We'll only be able to surprise these people once."

Potts nodded his understanding.

"And," Tom said. "Let me know as soon as you hear anything from the dam."

9

"Get down, get down." Staff Sergeant Trent Lowell knew it was redundant to yell it to the other men once the gunfire erupted, but he said it anyway. Most of the men had been with the Office of Military Operations for years, Northerners and Southerners tasked with keeping the tenuous peace between their two nations. They were well-trained operatives with copious amounts of combat experience, but Lowell felt useless to offer any other guidance at the moment. Their O.M.O. squad leader, Emmett, wasn't quick with any other solutions, either.

All six men crouched behind the rocks along the bank of the river. Each man readied his weapon and waited for a break in the shooting to return fire. They looked to Emmett for their next move. No one said anything, but Lowell knew they were cursing their leader. In Emmett's haste to get to the dam quickly, he'd blindly led his team into a trap set by the Northern splinter group called the Sons of Grant. Lowell and the others were pinned down by riflemen on the high ground.

"Wait for your shot, men," Emmett said.

Lowell pulled his rifle to his shoulder and quickly caught a glimpse around the rock to find a target. One of the shooters saw Lowell and began firing wildly in an attempt to kill him. Lowell took a breath and drew a bead on the man, ignoring the unfocused shots that exploded on the rocks around him. After a moment he released the breath and pulled the trigger. His target slumped forward, his face resting on the log he was using for cover. The weapon fell from the man's hands and a white cloth was visible on his shoulder.

"It would help a little if we knew how many of the Sons of Grant's men we were facing up there," Corporal Sykes yelled. "Any ideas?"

Emmett stammered. "I only caught sight of three. But there must be more than that."

"Christ, there's more than three up there," Lowell said.

It had happened so quickly that he hadn't gotten a good count. "I hear at least eight guns firing at us. But that doesn't mean nothing." He'd seen the movement before the shots rang out and his thoughts had gone instantly to getting the men to cover. "Plus, there's gotta be a group somewhere setting the explosives while these Grant boys keep us occupied."

Emmett tried to look like he'd known that before Lowell said it.

Lowell got all the men's attention. "There's one of them up behind a pile of shrubs on the left. Everyone concentrate your fire there when I give the word. Sykes and I will try to keep the others busy while you do."

Everyone tensed their bodies to pop up when it was time.

Lowell counted quietly to Sykes and they popped their heads up over the rocks just enough to keep cover but still fire.

"Now," he yelled.

The other O.M.O. soldiers fired at the man Lowell had indicated. The bushes in front of the man disintegrated in a hail of gunfire, and the body rolled out after a moment. Everyone returned to cover, happy to have one less opponent.

But Lowell had taken a second to get a count. "I'm afraid I still see ten up there."

"Did you count the man lying flat by the old oak on the far side?" Emmett asked.

"I did," Lowell said.

Another of the men spoke up. "You see that skinny bastard over on the left a bit?"

"Got him," Lowell said. "Anyone else see one of them being sneaky? If you do, speak up."

He looked around. His attention fell on another large rock closer to the dam. It was only twelve or fifteen feet away, but it seemed like a continent with the continual volley of gunfire. "I'm—" He thought about the chain of command before he went on. He wasn't really in charge here. He turned to Emmett. "I'm thinking of trying to make a run for that group of rocks. It looks like some good cover that I can use to get up closer to the dam a bit. What do you think, sir?"

Emmett looked over at the proposed route. "You really think you can do it? Seems like a long shot with ten men firing at you."

Lowell nodded.

"All right. Get to it." Emmett waved the men into position.

Lowell gripped his rifle tightly as he waited for the men to provide cover fire and allow him safe passage to the next rock. He vaguely heard Sykes yell "Go" as the rifles roared to life.

Lowell was running a moment later. The wet ground gave way slightly as he dug his feet in with each step. He could hear the enemy rifles come to life as well, returning fire on the others and targeting him. He stared determinedly at the rock ahead, zeroing in on it like nothing else existed. Halfway there, he paid for his blindness when his foot slid on the pebbles and mud and he fell to the ground. He quickly got himself up but dropped his rifle as he did. A bullet tore up the ground at his feet, and he ran without the weapon, leaving it in the muck. He dove down the last few steps and found himself safely behind the rock.

Sykes looked over at Lowell and motioned for him to stay put, to which he agreed. He hadn't planned on going too far. He reached to his side and pulled out his pistol. He flipped open the chamber and made sure the weapon was fully loaded. That was something to make him feel good, at least.

He looked up the hill and braced himself against the rock. Once he got to the top, he might be able to flank them—if the enemies didn't realize he was only one man with a revolver and limited ammunition. He stepped up to go, but stopped when a new barrage of fire broke out. He turned just in time to see Sykes running across the gap. He wasn't fast and he slowed down momentarily, as if he were actually going to grab Lowell's rifle as he passed it, but the rapid fire convinced him otherwise and he kept moving. Lowell didn't have time to warn him off.

When the next shot rang out, Sykes took a bullet to his gut and stumbled sideways. He fell forward just feet from where Lowell stood. He bent down and grabbed the man's arm even as more gunfire rained down. Lowell got the man to safety, while his fellow soldiers frantically tried to provide cover for them.

"Sykes?" Lowell asked.

But it was too late, the man was gone.

"Jesus," Lowell whispered. He looked back over at the other men—each of them wore a hard expression. Except Emmett. He stood behind the rest, and his face showed nothing but terror at the death of a man under his command.

Lowell had always feared that Emmett's inexperience would cause the mission to fail, but he hadn't expected it to happen so easily.

He looked down, knowing Sykes's sacrifice might be for nothing. Not only had he failed to pick up Lowell's rifle, he'd dropped his own as well. It lay not far from the first one in the wet muck. Under his coat, Sykes still had his revolver snapped into its holster. Lowell checked it, found it loaded, and tucked it into his own belt. He needed to get moving before one of the militiamen got wind of Lowell's idea and came around to greet him. He took a last look at Sykes before signaling the others that he was on his way up. Emmett's face had returned to normal, exchanging the fear Lowell had witnessed with the usual blank stare. Hopefully the others hadn't seen Emmett's fear—their confidence in the man was shaky enough.

With a tight grip on the pistol, Lowell scrambled up the incline, still hidden by rocks and the trees that grew up next to them. His path took him farther away from the others than he'd planned, but it got him to high ground.

As he made it to the area where the ground leveled off with the top of the dam, Lowell came face to face with one of the shooters. They'd surprised each other, thinking they were alone until they were ten or so feet apart. The man turned his rifle, but it took too long—Lowell's pistol was already in front of him and he pulled the trigger twice, sending the man to the ground. The noise of the shots would surely bring more of them.

Back down the path to the dam, Lowell heard footsteps of someone coming to a stop in the crisp leaves. Lowell edged along a fallen tree trunk until he almost stood on the dam. Ahead a few more paces, a dirty, disheveled man clutched a box to his chest. A long T-shaped plunger protruded from the top. Cords came out of the top of the box and led back toward the center of the dam. A piece of a crude handkerchief blew in the breeze at his elbow.

"Don't move, mister," Lowell said.

The man's fingers flexed on the plunger.

"You don't want to do that," Lowell said. "You press that, and not only does the dam go, but it takes all your men with it." He neglected to mention that it might just sweep the both of them away as well. "Put it down." He pulled back the hammer on his pistol for added incentive.

"Ain't nothing you can do here," the grimy man said. "We are taking this country back. Ain't nothing the U.N. or anyone else can do about it."

Lowell didn't figure reason was going to stop the man, so maybe authority and force would knock some sense into him. "Right now, by the power instilled in me by the United Nations of America, what I can do is order you to put that thing down, sir. Or I will shoot a hole in you. Maybe two, if the situation warrants it."

Some nearby branches parted. Emmett slowly stepped out. The demolitions man was unaware of the development.

"Why the hell you going to blow it up anyways?" Lowell asked. "We get the picture, you and your Sons of Grant buddies are blowing up shit to prove you can blow shit up. Am I right?"

The man smiled, exposing his yellowing teeth. "This is just the beginning."

"Then tell me about it. Explain it to me in small words, please," Lowell said. "You know, so I can follow it." If he kept him talking, maybe Emmett could get closer and the two of them could get the detonator away without the explosives going off.

"Come on, let's hear it." He stole a glance at Emmett, and was dismayed to find that instead of working his way forward, Emmett was drawing a bead on the man with his rifle. There was no way to signal Emmett without giving away his leader's position.

"How's this for explainin'?" the man said as he took a deep breath and tensed his body. "The North shall rise again!"

"Wait," Lowell said, holding up his empty hand. "Just—" He didn't even know who he was really talking to, or who he hoped to stop, but it didn't matter—the crack of Emmett's rifle disrupted the words coming out of Lowell's mouth.

The scruffy demolitions man jerked immediately and he stood still for a moment on his feet. Lowell stepped toward him, but couldn't cover the ground fast enough to catch him. The man's knees buckled and he fell forward, landing on the plunger and forcing it down.

"Christ! Emmett. Get over here," Lowell shouted.

A second later the middle of the dam exploded, sending wood and rock and debris into the air. The ground shook with the vibration of the explosion and both Emmett and Lowell fell to the ground.

Water surged through the opening, taking more of the dam with it. Lowell could see at least two men from the enemy group go over the side, obviously surprised by the sudden acceleration of the timeline of their plan. The remaining sections of the dam creaked with strain.

Lowell stood and reached out for Emmett. "Come on, before the rest of this thing goes."

Emmett took his hand. They scrambled for the relative safety of land. As they both sat on the muddy ground catching their breath and taking stock of themselves, Lowell heard the sounds of footsteps crashing up the hill from the direction he'd come. He leveled his pistol at the sound and was relieved to see it was one of their own.

"Jumping Jesus on a Tuesday," the corporal shouted. "What in hell happened up here?"

"We…" Emmett stopped and looked back at where he'd shot the man, but the body was gone, as was the section of shoreline they'd been standing on. "We didn't make it in time."

He was floored by the man's explanation, but Lowell wasn't ready to contradict his superior officer just yet. He knew he wasn't all right with the version Emmett offered, but he chalked it up to the chaos of the situation and let it go in hopes of a future correction.

"What're you doing here?" Emmett asked. "Where's everyone else?"

"They're all down below. We captured a couple of them and the rest backed off, regrouping, we figured. I thought you could use some help here."

Lowell scrambled to his feet, suddenly alarmed. "They were all still around the area with the rocks?"

"No, they moved up toward those bastards a bit."

The hill made it hard to keep his footing as Lowell made his way down toward the rocks where they'd taken cover before. He grabbed his rifle as he passed the gap where he'd dropped it. The area nearby was entirely swept away. It was obvious that anyone who'd broken cover to make their way up the hill would've been swallowed when the dam went.

The other men walked up behind Lowell.

"Christ," Emmett said. "Blum?" he shouted. "Anyone?"

Down in the valley, the airship *Leonidas Polk* swooped low toward the Turtle standing in the middle of the low river as the water rushed at it.

10

The Turtle moved again, slowly stomping across the riverbed. Cyrus stood behind Jansen with his eye to the periscope, watching the airship.

"Can we go any faster? I'd like to be out of this muck so we can maneuver if we have to," Cyrus said.

"It's damn slippery."

Across the debris field, Cyrus caught a glimpse of one of the many small streams that made its way down the river bed and thought of how strong the current used to be in this area. He'd scouted out several locations over the years and this was the best crossing he could find. It was shallow here. They could traverse it with relative ease.

"Doesn't the river wind through Sacramento?" Cyrus asked.

"It did," Jansen replied. "Why?"

"When we first saw that black ship, it was hovering over Sacramento for some reason," Cyrus said.

Without looking up, Jansen said, "They couldn't have dammed the river could they?"

"Then what were they doing if they weren't damming the river?" Cyrus watched the stream trickle down the river bed. He could see the danger adding up.

"Get yourself ready to leave." Cyrus turned in the cramped control room and started to climb the metal ladder. He stepped into the main corridor. "Lucy?"

"Down here."

He followed the passage toward his own quarters and found her outside his door. She had a tool belt around her waist and a steel pry bar in her hand.

"I was just going to see if I can find the boy in your quarters," she said. "I've been pulling all the panels off the floor but none of them lead anywhere. The air ducts are pretty small most places. I can't imagine he crawled through them."

"This vessel is pretty patchwork and modified. The previous owners used some mismatched, odd-sized innards." He motioned for her to open the door. "Listen, if that airship is with the government, what where they doing up around Sacramento? And why was that Goose of theirs flitting around?"

Tugging on the handle to Cyrus's quarters, Lucinda heaved as hard as she could. "What're you thinking?"

"I just don't know who to trust. Maybe it is here to help us."

Just then, a loud explosion rang out in the distance and the Turtle shook unsteadily for a moment.

"I think your government ship just shot at us," Lucinda said.

Cyrus wasn't sure, but if they were, his whole theory was out. He turned to make his way back to the deck hatch.

A figure lunged out of the darkness of Cyrus's cabin and grabbed Lucinda, knocking her to the ground. It was Lester, snarling and drooling as he pushed his face toward her. Cyrus had only a second to see the boy's chest was torn open in several places and his leg was shredded. Lucinda still had the metal bar in her hand and she swung it hard at Lester's head, connecting twice. The boy tumbled off her but immediately got back up and started after her before she could make it off the floor.

"Lester!" Cyrus yelled. The boy turned and revealed that a good portion of the scarred side of his face was missing. Bits of flesh hung below his eye. As Lester was distracted, Lucinda scrambled to her feet.

Cyrus didn't allow himself time to think about it. In one fluid motion he pulled his pistol and shot the creature in the head. It fell down on its knees and landed propped up by the bulkhead.

A rustling sound came from Cyrus's quarters.

"Come on," he said. "There's more of them. They followed the boy." He was too far away to safely close the door and lock them in his quarters.

He and Lucinda ran to the hatch and stepped out on the deck. The airship was about to pass over their head. Its engines roared as it maneuvered into place. Cyrus marveled at how large the craft was. He could tell from his vantage point that it had four air bladders keeping it aloft. He'd seen airships before, but this one was double the size of most and menacing in its black and gray coat. There were bits of white streaming down from the belly of the craft and it took a moment to realize they were ladders the ship had extended.

There was a high-pitched squeal from the craft, followed by a bellowing voice, clear as anything, even over the strum of the engines. "This is the United Nations of America ship *Leonidas Polk*. **You must evacuate immediately. Use the ladders and make an orderly withdrawal.**"

Cyrus had never been much for the U.N., but he was glad to hear from their people now. He ran to the intercom and shouted into the mouthpiece. "All hands evacuate to the upper deck. All hands evacuate." He lowered his head to the earpiece, but couldn't hear anything over the roar of the airship. He put the mouthpiece closer and shouted again. Lucinda grabbed his arm and tugged him toward one of the approaching ladders.

"Let's go!"

He shook his head. "Jansen, Gibson."

Lucinda pointed to the turret to show Gibson hastily extricating himself from the gunner's seat. He stumbled the last step and sprawled on the deck. They turned back to see the ladders and ropes from the airship about to come in contact with the edge of the Turtle's deck and saw why Gibson was in such a hurry.

The river was coming.

A great wall of water frothed and rolled down the empty river bed. Someone had blown the dam in Sacramento. The airship engines had covered the roar of the river as it came.

Cyrus grabbed Lucinda's hand and ran toward the nearest ladders. He shoved her onto one and heaved himself at another. He gripped the ladder, locked his arm around a rung and tried not to panic as the ladder swung out into open air. He looked over to see Lucinda clinging in a similar fashion. Behind them, Gibson ran hard and leapt at a rope just as the ship started to pull away from the Turtle. He got a hold but immediately started to slip.

"Hang on," Cyrus shouted, though he doubted the man could hear anything but the roar.

The Sacramento River claimed the Turtle as they were looking back at Gibson. The craft was bowled off its legs by the wall of water that was just as high as the vehicle. It rolled and disappeared with its legs in the air.

Cyrus turned away and concentrated on Lucinda, as if he could keep the last member of his crew safe through mental power alone.

The airship turned and headed back over land, the direction Cyrus and his crew had come. The ladders slowly ascended. Two figures in dark uniforms pulled Cyrus and Lucinda into the ship.

11

"Are there meals on the flight?" The gray-haired man asked.

Tom kept from rolling his eyes. *You're crossing the country on an airship for a week or more. No, you should've packed all your own meals.*

"Of course," he said. "The dining hall serves breakfast, lunch and dinner. Even opens up for the occasional snack, my dear man. You've paid good money, after all."

The man smiled and moved off toward the stairs to board *The High Road*, one of Cantolione's overland ships. Tom's ancillary duties included shaking hands with the travelers and seeing them off on their journey with a warm, friendly goodbye. He also picked up the receipts from the ticket counter once the ship was off and then carried the money back over to the office to personally ensure its safety. Tom looked around at the crowd and quickly estimated there would be another full ship, no empty cabins.

A lovely young woman stopped beside him. "Hello, my dear. How can I assist you on your journey?" He saw her ticket sticking out of a dime novel she was hugging to her chest, so she wasn't just seeing someone off. "On your way to the other coast?"

She leaned close to him. "I've heard I can catch another vessel to Europe, once we land. How much does that cost and how do I reserve a seat?"

Tom turned on his charm as much as he could. "Oh my dear, you must be very careful. You didn't buy a ticket for that journey, I hope?"

She shook her head warily.

"Good. I'm so glad to hear that. You see there is no such flight. Not from my company or any other," Tom said. "Europe is…well, Europe is closed to Americans. They have patrols that keep everyone out, by sea or by air."

"Oh, surely that's just a tale."

"I wish it were, miss. There's never been a ship come back from the old world. That is all I know for a fact. As for rumors, I've heard they shoot anything they see, no questions asked."

The young lady looked shocked at the idea. "That has to be made up. If no one has ever made it back, who told you the Europeans kill everyone that approaches them? There would be no survivors, right?"

Tom gritted his teeth, but kept his smile. "You are quite right, madam. Very astute. Yet, that doesn't explain where all the travelers have vanished to, does it? It's my understanding that is how the continent deals with our problem with the undead. They keep everyone out."

The woman smiled. "Are you having a joke on me?"

"I assure you, I am not. I am a very serious man and you would do well to believe each and every word I've said." He reached into his coat pocket and pulled out a slip of paper. "To make up for your disappointment, I can offer you this. It's for a complimentary drink at the bar onboard. Use it in good health."

The woman placed it in her book next to her ticket and walked to the entry plank without thanking him. Tom watched her go and wondered what she'd be like in bed for a moment, then blocked the thought out because she was getting on an airship and crossing the country and he'd never get to find out.

Across the room, Cantolione was handing out candy to all the children that passed within ten feet of him. On other days he'd hand out pin-on wings with the company logo. It was yet another example of what Tom saw as a waste of the company's funds on some ridiculous folly.

He smiled at a family passing by and tipped his hat to them. It occurred to him that if he weren't about to launch an attack on the government, selling fake tickets to Europe wouldn't be a bad confidence game. The people would be long gone before they realized they'd been duped, and they'd be too broke to come back to California and attempt to get some sort of reimbursement. He nodded at another couple passing by and decided to keep that idea tucked away, just in case.

12

Cyrus sat with his back against the wall in a small cell on the airship and grit his teeth to keep his composure. He felt tears coming on and didn't want to show that weakness in front of the men who'd saved him. The uniformed men had ushered him to this holding area immediately after bringing him onboard. He scratched at the dried blood from a tiny cut one of the men had inflicted. He said it had been to test Cyrus for the illness that turned men into chewers.

The thrum of the engines vibrated his cell, and the noise was loud as the ship maneuvered back and forth. His chest ached as he thought about those people trapped in the Turtle—his crew, the old man, the little girls and all the other faceless people that he'd taken under his protection.

Cyrus used some water they'd left him to clear the blood from his face.

He got up and tried to get his grief under control long enough to pound on the walls again and shout. "We have to go back." He took a deep breath. "Those people are helpless back there." He stuck his eye up to the tiny slot in the door where light streamed through. "Hello?"

With no reaction, he paced back and forth before he struck his fists against the wall again. He was in control of nothing and he could protect no one. Not even Lucinda, though he knew they'd pulled her aboard as well.

"Lucy?" he shouted. "Lucy?"

13

Onboard the *Polk*, Lowell went through his evening ritual with less enthusiasm than usual. He laid out his pistol and holster on the blanket and pulled his cleaning kit out from under the bunk. He sat down and started by running a brush through the cylinder, slowly and carefully. By the time he got to the last step, he was polishing the weapon until it shined like the first time off the factory across the sea. The gun's blue hue was unique to the world of weapons, most barrels being gray or black. The English Kerr revolver came to him through a man he'd met in the war, Travis Crosby, and where that old hick got his hands on a weapon made in London, England, Lowell had no clue. Still, he'd gladly accepted the gun as payment for a debt and then hung on to it like it was gold. The gun got him through the war, through his time as a lawman in a tiny Ohio town called Chagrin Falls, and was acquitting itself well during his tour with the O.M.O. and the U.N.A.

Once the weapon was in perfect shape, he set it in the holster and hung the whole set over a peg he'd fixed in the wall. Then he replaced all the ammunition in the tiny holders around the belt, looking at each individual bullet, inspecting it for imperfections, before putting it where it belonged. When he was done, he turned away and forgot about it. It was all part of the routine. He cared for his weapon at every opportunity, so that when the time came for a fight, he didn't have to worry about it failing him.

He took off his uniform shirt and hung it in the small closet, at the back of a row of similar shirts. The ones near the front were the fresh ones and he brushed some lint off the next shirt and hung it on the outside of the door. A welcome hint of starch hit his nose as he closed the storage area. He walked to the small sink in the corner of his quarters in his undershirt with his suspenders hanging at his side. The water was piss warm, but he splashed it on his face and underarms, using a fresh towel to dry himself.

On the wall, a picture of Lowell's regiment from the war hung slightly askew. He fixed it offhandedly. Next to the picture was a shelf with a set of nesting dolls that

Lowell had found in the wreckage of a tiny town up the coast. There were six red dolls in all, a tiny one, then a bigger one and so on. Whatever tilted the picture had upset the dolls as well—the middle two were lying on their sides.

Lowell reached up and put one back on its bottom. He picked up the next largest and righted it as well. As he walked away, he heard a slight plink as the smaller doll fell over again. He walked back and set it the little toy upright. It wobbled for a few moments and toppled.

Lowell sighed and closed his eyes. He grabbed the troublesome thing and hurtled it against the door behind him. The sight of that toy splintering against the door made him both sad at the loss of a souvenir and excited at the release of tension.

He reached for the tiniest doll and smashed it on the door as well. Then he did the same with the next and the next and the next until there was only the largest left.

He moved it to the center of the shelf, stepped back and checked the symmetry, then nudged the doll to the left a touch. He felt stupid for letting his anger get the better of him, but he was glad he didn't lose his composure in front of anyone else.

Goddamn Emmett. His heart was in the right place, but he didn't know shit about military tactics, which left Lowell to wonder how Emmett ever rose to a position of authority in the O.M.O. or anywhere else. Not only had they lost the men at the dam, but Henry McMasters was shot a few weeks before that. And the two Jims died just a month prior. Emmett commanded every one of those deadly operations.

Lowell walked to the locker and brought out a dust pan and hand broom to clean up the splinters of the toys he'd shattered.

Goddamn Emmett.

14

"We can't keep this charade up forever, Emmett," Cashe said.

Emmett stood in front of Cashe's desk with his hat in his hands. "Maybe you need to quit bringing people onboard this ship. You ever think of that?"

Cashe and Emmett had gone around about this a number of times since they'd started onboard the *Polk*.

"And do what?" Cashe asked. "Wait till all our crew is dead? What then? We sure can't keep pretending to be the flagship of the goddamn O.M.O. if it's just you and me."

Emmett looked as if he'd been shot and over-acted his injury at the perceived insult. "I don't know what shit Lowell fed you, but those men died at the dam because of the Sons of Grant. We all did our best to stop them, me included."

"I know that."

"Then quit pissing in my goddamn ear about it." Emmett tossed his hat down on Cashe's desk. "You don't think I feel bad enough?"

"I'm not saying a word about that," Cashe said. "I'm saying we lost some good men at the dam. We were at a skeleton crew before that and now we're running light on resources. If we want to continue to do the work we swore we'd do, we need men."

"So you're going to ask them to join?" Emmett asked.

"I'm thinking about it."

Emmett shook his head vehemently. "You don't make all the decisions here. We are a team, you and I. We are in this together here."

Cashe had known that from the beginning. From the first day they'd decided to fake their ranks and begin using the *Polk* as they saw fit. "You mention that from time to time. Maybe you should have made yourself the leader in this scheme when we were hatching this little plan."

He pointed to the door and ushered Emmett out. "Now if you'll excuse me, I have to go tell that man about all the people on his vessel that we couldn't save."

Emmett stood his ground, waiting at the door.

"Unless you want to do it?"

Emmett turned and left.

Cashe closed the door and swallowed hard. He told himself the same thing he'd been telling himself since the beginning: *We're doing some good for this country.*

15

Cyrus attempted to get someone's, *anyone's*, attention. "Tell me how my friend is," he yelled. "Is she all right?"

With no answers, he settled on being peeved and perpetually grumpy. Besides, he was in no position to actually demand anything, and he hoped by their military uniforms that they had some sort of affiliation with a government—he just couldn't be sure which one.

Some hours later a man in uniform brought food, but wouldn't answer his questions. Then Cyrus heard new footsteps. These were more solid and purposeful than the first. A stranger appeared, dressed in the same type of uniform as the man who'd brought the food, but he had more medals and badges. Cyrus knew little about military structure, but the new guy had an air of authority. His graying hair was longer than Cyrus would guess was standard for an army man, though.

"Are you here to explain what's going on?" Cyrus asked. "Or are you just bringing more water?"

The man leaned against the wall opposite the cell and folded his arms. "I'm sorry for the inconvenience. We need to know you aren't going to turn into a chewer and try to eat us all."

"I don't have any bite marks, do I?"

"You had several scrapes and cuts we couldn't identify."

"I've never been bit," Cyrus said. "Never come close."

"We had to be sure."

"Am I a prisoner?" Cyrus was glad to get some information from someone in charge.

"No. Just a precaution. Again, we are terribly sorry. We couldn't be too careful unleashing one of them chewers on our vessel. You understand."

"Yeah."

"Our people checked and rechecked your blood and your friend's. Didn't find anything unusual."

"So, we're healthy?" Cyrus said as he stepped to the door of the tiny holding cell in the bowels of the ship.

"Yes."

"You going to let me out of here?"

The man on the other side of the slot paused. "I need to tell you…"

"What?"

"I need to tell you, and you have to believe that we did all we could, but we couldn't save your Turtle. We circled and circled, trying to catch it with a winch, but it went under."

Cyrus stared at him for a moment and then retreated back to the darkness of the cell. While he was waiting in the cell, he'd resigned himself to that very possibility, but the confirmation shocked him back to the reality of it.

He heard the door open behind him, but he didn't walk out or turn to look at the man.

"Cyrus?" It was Lucinda's voice and it sounded thick with the same grief he was experiencing. Her footsteps came close and he saw her bare feet as she stepped next to him. She leaned down and grabbed him in an embrace that only made things feel worse.

"I'll give you two a few moments to talk," Cashe said.

They were there for hours.

16

"I'll see you in the morning?" The young circus ticket-taker asked.

Tom waved her off with a flick of the wrist and took another drink of whiskey. He didn't turn as the door slammed upon her departure. He'd been thinking about the young lady who'd asked about Europe and couldn't get her out of his head. After *The High Road* departed, Tom took the ticket receipts and walked the money back to Cantolione's office himself, minus a small dinner stipend. As he departed, he saw Janine at the front booth and, after finding someone to cover for her, invited the girl back to his room. She didn't say no and after a snort or two, they both got undressed.

A persistent knock at the door forced Tom to put his pants back on and walk to open it. He grabbed a pistol he kept behind some books on the shelf in the hall.

"Who is it?" he called from a safe distance.

"Potts."

Tom opened the door and tossed the gun on the kitchen table. "Come on, then."

Potts followed him back to the living room that doubled as a bedroom. "We found a good spot north of town. We had some of the men set to clearing brush and start making some lean-tos and tents."

"Good," Tom said. "There's room for airships to land?"

"Yes. That was your main requirement."

"All right. We'll use it as a staging area for our next job. That'll keep down the time we have to spend here in town."

"You want us to bring all the weapons and gear from the warehouse in town?"

Tom poured a drink for his friend. "Nah. Not yet. Let the men make camp. There's no one snooping around here. We'll leave it be and use an airship or a boat when the time comes to get out of here." He held up the glass to Potts.

"I'm not really ready for a drink, Tom."

Tom gave him a sideways look. "Come on. Don't make the future president of the United States drink alone." The idea of becoming the leader of the country had stuck in his craw and wouldn't let go.

Potts took the whiskey and stared at it for a moment. "You really think you could become president?"

Tom noted how Potts wrinkled his nose as he asked.

"What do you think we're doing here?"

"I guess I never thought that far ahead," Potts said. "I assumed we'd reunite the country…."

"And?"

"I don't know."

"Why shouldn't I be the president?"

Potts put the glass to his lips and took a half-sip. "No reason."

"Goddamn right, no reason." Tom put his glass up in a salute and swallowed the dark liquid in a single gulp. "No damn good reason, at all."

17

When they'd collected themselves, Cyrus and Lucinda emerged from the cell. The graying man waited down the hall.

Cyrus spoke first. "I think we've been more than patient, Mister…?"

"Cashe. Lyle Cashe," the man said.

"Cashe, are you the captain of this ship?" Cyrus wanted to find the man who could give him answers in the shortest order and Cashe looked to be the one.

"I'm in charge if that's what you're asking."

"Then what now?" Cyrus asked.

Cashe motioned down the hall. "The crew is assembling for dinner. What say we join them? You've been cooped up in those holding cells for too long."

They walked down a fairly stark metal hall where the thrum of the engines was less pronounced the farther they moved away from the small brig. No other crew members were visible as they went. Cyrus found that strange for such a large vessel.

"How do you manage this thing without a lot more people on board?" he asked. "Seems you'd be overwhelmed and short-handed."

Cashe laughed and adjusted the collar of his uniform. "Cyrus, my dear boy, did I not mention it was time to eat? When that dinner bell rings, it's every man for himself."

Cashe's tone was uneasy, clearly not sure how to handle the two who had just lost so much. He tipped his head at Lucinda. "And every woman. Hopefully it'll put you at ease to know you aren't the only female onboard."

"Wouldn't be the first time I was the sole representation of the fairer gender," Lucinda said.

Cashe nodded. "Good to know you're not easily intimidated."

They took a few more steps and stopped in front of double doors at the other end of the hall.

"Here we are," Cashe said. "I warned them about company but who knows if they'll be on their best behavior or not." He slid the doors apart and revealed a large room with wide windows on the other side.

The smells of the meal drifted out of the room and Cyrus wondered how long it had been since he'd eaten anything substantial. This wasn't salted pork and pressed potatoes, it was something that took time and effort. He scanned the table quickly before he looked at the faces of the people in the room. Down the center of the room was a thick wooden table surrounded by chairs with soldiers sitting around it. Most of the people stood when Cyrus and Lucinda entered. The men nodded to Lucinda. A quick count told Cyrus there were just half a dozen dinner guests, with one of them being a woman. All of them wore similar uniforms of black shirts without any rank or name designations.

Cashe pointed to the right half of the table. "These are the Confederate troops— Zeke, Holt."

He indicated his left next. "Over here's the Yankee side. Here's Bethy, Emmett and Daniel. The man on the end is the Union liaison, Lowell. Maybe it's not obvious to you, but I sit on the side of the Confederacy."

Cyrus nodded to the men and looked them over. The only identifiers were small rectangular patches of blue or gray on the upper arm of their shirts, which Cyrus assumed showed their loyalty to country. He also noted three letters stitched on their breast pockets—*OMO*.

There were empty seats on either side of the table.

"Should we pull out a chair for either of you on one side or the other?" A wave of Cashe's hand showed them their options.

Cyrus knew the implication of the question, but had no idea whether it truly mattered who he stood with during the war. Since the treaty, he'd considered himself a man of dual citizenship, even if neither government agreed.

"Any chance you have a chair that straddles the middle?" he asked.

Lucinda laughed and moved to a chair next to Cashe's with the Confederates. No one else at the table showed a sense of humor about it.

Cyrus planted himself in a Union chair across from Lucinda and continued to assess everyone.

Lowell cleared his throat. "Uh, are we going to get to know their names? Or should we just call you ma'am?"

Bethy sighed and rolled her eyes as Lowell pushed his way forward to shake Lucinda's hand across the table. The lone crew woman was a short, thin thing, who was dressed just as everyone else, but kept a pair of eye coverings hanging around her neck. A couple of the men around the table wore their hats while they ate, but she kept her head uncovered, though she wore her shoulder-length brown hair in a ponytail. Her face was smudged on one cheek with some sort of grime or grease, but otherwise she was well-kept.

"Sorry, how careless of me," Cashe said. "This is Mr. Spencer and that is Miss, ah…"

"Just Lucinda," Cyrus said. "Her name is just Lucinda and mine is just Cyrus."

Lowell fell just short of kissing the back of her hand as he took it for an unusually long amount of time. "Pleased to meet you."

Everyone murmured at Lowell to sit down and he did after lingering another moment.

"This is the closest thing this vessel has to officers, I guess," Cashe said. "I exaggerated a bit—this isn't really everyone. There are a few of the crew missing here. You'll meet them soon enough, I suppose."

The feast before them was modest, but welcome. There were several small birds cooked a dark brown scattered throughout the table. They were served with field potatoes with butter and biscuits. It took Cyrus a few moments to decide whether to accept the hospitality or hold out until he got some answers. Moreover, he wasn't sure he could eat with the news of his lost crew weighing on him.

Lucinda had no such qualms. She grabbed the nearest roll and slathered on a thick pat of butter.

"We have already said grace, and a few words about the men we lost," Bethy said. "But we can take another moment, if you'd like to remember your crew and the others."

Cyrus shook his head. "Thanks all the same, we'll remember them our own way."

Lucinda looked around, obviously interested in breaking the silence that followed Cyrus's statement. "What is it you actually do, Mr. Cashe?" She was already pushing bits of the roll into her mouth as she spoke. "Surely, fishing people from floods isn't in your general job description."

"Our group is part of the O.M.O.," Cashe said. "The Office of Military Operations for the United Nations. We're officially an international peacekeeping force by definition."

Lowell jumped in before Cashe could swallow a piece of white meat. "The United States and the Confederate Territories of America thought it would be smart to find ways to work together, considering the current crisis that affects the whole of the North American continent."

Cashe swallowed his food and spoke up. "We were tasked with sort of an intermediary role not long after the peace accord. I'm sure you know how high tensions were after that. It was like the war never ended."

"'Cept we couldn't be everywhere at once," Zeke said.

Lucinda grabbed a leg from the bird nearest to her and held it up. "Is this chicken?" Zeke shook his head. "Nope."

Carefully taking a bite, Lucinda shrugged and attacked it more fully.

"For a while there," Emmett said, "they had us going around to troubled areas to show them how well we were getting along, encourage everyone to work together till the whole tiny problem with the chewers went away." He poured Lucinda a tall glass of ice water from a gray metal pitcher. "But the undead problem got worse, 'stead of better."

"So the governments slowly started giving us less to do with keeping things calm and more mundane tasks," Lowell said. "Transporting prisoners and cargo, scouting out towns to mark off maps, rescuing settlers. Nothing that one country or another couldn't do on their own."

After Cyrus sniffed a chunk of potato, he pointed around the table with it. "And yet here you are. Someone must've found something for you to do."

"We kind of found our own work," Cashe said. "Made our own opportunities."

"We like to say the O.M.O. stands for Odd Men Out." Lowell passed a bowl of corn down toward Cyrus. "Kind of an appropriate name for a company of men making it up as they go along with no governments and nowhere to call home."

"We used to work out of Sutter's Fort," Cashe said. "Until it was overrun with chewers. Since then we've stayed more mobile."

Lucinda sipped her water and looked at each person, then back to Cyrus. "And you're all right with working together and doing your own thing even though you're all from different sides? Some of you might've been shooting at each other back at Vicksburg or some cherry orchard. There's no animosity there? No occasional considerations of payback?" Her eyes flared playfully.

Emmett passed her the butter. "We all ain't forgotten anything if that's what you're asking. But we've all seen enough on this ship to know how bad it is out there. A Northerner can get to be a chewer just as easily as someone from God's Confederacy. Once we put this whole menace down, then we'll see about settling debts. I'm not sure that'll happen in my lifetime, though."

Zeke raised his voice and cut into a roll. "I hate every goddamn Yankee that ever picked up a gun."

Everyone at the table stared at Zeke waiting for a qualifier to his statement, but none seemed forthcoming.

"But?" Cyrus said.

Zeke looked around and saw that everyone was staring and seemed puzzled. "What?"

"You hate them but?"

"Oh, I hate 'em all, but I know these fellas are trying to do something good and right." Zeke scraped the remaining crumbs onto his fork and shoved it in his mouth.

"Most of us were plucked out of dire circumstances and made crewmen," Lowell said.

"Keeping the peace between the nations while everyone fights the chewers is a fairly easy job," Daniel spoke up for the first time. "Everyone's still looking over their shoulder and giving each other the eye, but we know how much we have to rely on each other now."

"Originally, the O.M.O. was a temporary thing," Cashe added, "until the threat of the undead was brought under control. Who knows if that will ever really happen?"

"You could say we have job security." Lowell raised his glass, but no one returned the gesture.

There was a shuffle as Daniel left and Cyrus looked up in time to see a man step through to the dining hall. He was the blackest man Cyrus had ever seen in his life. Tall, muscular and bald, the man stepped around to the side of the Northerners and patted Cashe on the shoulders as he passed.

"I think that engine's just fine," the black man said. "The intake valve had some rust forming. Filed it off, shouldn't give us trouble again."

"Thank you, Alek," Cashe said. "Have you met our guests? This is Cyrus and that is Lucinda." He indicated them with a wave of his fork. "This is our ace mechanic, Alek Marshal."

Cyrus stood and extended his hand to Alek slowly. When they began to shake hands, he could feel the strength that coursed through Alek's frame, could see the veins exposed on the man's beefy arms. "Pleased to meet you, Alek."

"You seem surprised to see a Negro," Bethy said.

"No, I'm still getting used to the way this crew works. I have to say not much is surprising to me at this point," Cyrus said.

"Just stopping in for some chow," Alek said. "We want to get this thing running as best we can in the next day or so. We don't have much opportunity to come across spare parts made especially for this ship, so we have to make do with what we can."

Across the table, Zeke grumbled but didn't make an actual comment. Given the ideals the South was fighting for, Cyrus was suspicious about just how easily the people on that side of the table were taking the fact that a black man was on the crew, no matter how good he was with repairs.

18

The animals were settled down for the night. The horses that the acrobats used in their act buzzed their lips from time to time, and straw swished as the bear paced back and forth in its cage. Tom hated that his good waistcoats always smelled like wet straw and zebra dung. He had a standing weekly order to clean his clothes with the best launder in town.

Tom followed Cantolione, sliding between a cage with a pudgy badger and another holding an anemic bobcat. The moonlight shone in from the overhead windows, illuminating their way without the need for more lights that might disturb the animals. Tom knew Cantolione was in no hurry. The night would end like all the others, with the two of them sitting in the office counting the day's receipts.

Tom had had Cantolione followed and knew his boss had a routine that he rarely deviated from. He would use some of the petty cash to stop on the way home and buy some dinner, maybe a bottle of wine. He would follow the same route home, step into his mansion alone, eat his food and be in bed an hour later.

After that, Tom would get to the business of stealing everything the man had, paying close attention to making it look like nothing was happening.

"Maybe we should go out and grab something at that little tavern down by the water before they close for the night," Tom said. He knew full well his boss would not accept the offer. He never did, but Tom always asked. Just to seem sociable. "What do you say?"

Cantolione stopped in front of the elephant enclosures, though the beasts were somewhere in the shadows around the back of the cages.

"I... don't think so," he said. "Thanks just the same."

They walked on, checking the main show area. Here, the acrobats did their acts on the high wire and rode the horses. Clowns ran around spraying the crowd and each other, and the trainers trotted out their animals. Even though the performers and assistants had already done it, Cantolione went around and inspected each rope and ladder, looking for wear and tear, fraying, any problem.

Tom walked the stands of the little arena, picking up the odd piece of trash that the crew may have missed, but his attention always came back to his boss, walking from area to area, testing ropes and props.

"He do this every night?" A man stepped out of the shadows and walked down the steps toward Tom. It was Cappy Marks.

Though Cantolione had been in this routine for a year now, it was a fairly new ritual. But Tom didn't feel like getting into every detail with Cappy.

"Every night," Tom replied.

"You ever help him check that stuff, so it doesn't take so long?"

"Wouldn't matter," Tom said. "He has to be sure of all it himself. Even if I said it was fine, he'd still have to verify it. His son died in an accident up on the trapeze a few years back. He takes responsibility for the safety of his performers nowadays."

Cappy nodded. "You said you wanted to see me about something?"

Tom had nearly forgotten his conversation with his boss that morning. "Cantolione wants to move you back to clowning full-time. He thinks that's your strength, and we should play to it."

Cappy didn't seem terribly shook up. "I think I was starting to come into my own as a barker. I drew a few big crowds on Wednesday and Saturday."

"There's always a crowd on Saturday. Four-year-olds can draw crowds on Saturday. We need the barker to draw *every day*."

Cappy shook his head and grew quiet.

"Look, Cappy. Mondays are dead. You can pull a shift roping every Monday until you develop a good pitch and then we'll try you out on another day to see how you do. What do you think?"

Cappy nodded, a smile forming.

"But the rest of the time," Tom said, "you're either out front or in here, in full makeup. Deal?"

They shook hands, and Cappy faded back to the shadows where he came from.

Tom turned his attention back to his boss in the center of the arena, testing the podium where he himself introduced most every performance as the ringmaster. Tom pulled his pocket watch and sighed, preparing for forty-five more minutes of the same routine.

19

The door shut with a thud. Cyrus listened to Cashe's footfalls on the deck as he walked away. Cyrus didn't quite know what to say to Lucinda. The Turtle, the men, all those passengers. Then there was this new business with the airship and the O.M.O. It was all too much to deal with and the future wasn't looking quite as he'd planned it.

"Don't say it," Lucinda said.

"Say what?"

Lucinda took off her vest and hung it over the only chair in the room. "Anything. Whatever it was you were thinking of saying about our current situation—don't. I don't want to hear it. I don't want to know. I don't want to think about it." She sat on the bottom bunk and smoothed out the thick woolen blanket there.

"Lucy…"

"I'm exhausted. I'm not thinking right. Let me sleep and we'll talk about it when we wake up."

It wasn't like Lucinda to defer a problem. Cyrus had only known her to face a problem head on and stare it down. She forced everything to bend to her will when she could, and admitted when she couldn't, but she never ignored things.

"We did have a rough time of it," he said.

"No. It was a beautiful day. The river was beautiful. It was fine." She relaxed and her body went limp. Easing down onto her side, she sighed and closed her eyes. "In the morning, Lester will come round the cabin with some weak tea and a leering glance at my cleavage and all will be right with the world."

Cyrus left it. No reason to argue and prolong the situation. Besides, he figured she was asleep by the time the last word escaped her mouth.

He stepped across the room, stopping to pry his boots off as he went. He pulled a ragged curtain aside and looked out the porthole. Outside, wispy clouds floated by, illuminated by the moonlight. The land below was an indistinct dark mass, too far away to judge where he was, how high, what direction. Wasn't all that different from life up till now, except the vehicle for his aimlessness was under someone else's control, not his own.

Of course all the rest of the responsibility belonged to someone else now. He was only in charge of Lucinda and himself—if anyone else died, it wasn't his fault. In the morning he'd talk to Cashe and find out where he intended to leave them off, and then he'd start formulating a plan for what to do next. Not having the Turtle and the income it assured was a blow to the plans he'd made. Not having the potential income from selling the Turtle was even worse. The vehicle would've fetched a decent price on the open market on the East Coast.

There was a sudden sharp noise behind him. Lucinda was snoring. Cyrus smiled for a moment and walked to her side. He grabbed the blanket she'd smoothed out, covered her gently. He stopped short of running his hand through her hair, but pulled an errant strand away from her face.

20

"I want your version, Lowell," Cashe said.

He'd already heard the long drawn-out statements from both Zeke and Emmett. He'd been smart to have them each come in one at a time. Had he not done so, he had the sneaking suspicion that Zeke would've taken the head off his fellow soldier.

"Things went bad," Lowell said. "There wasn't anything we could do."

"That's the extent of your report on how half a dozen men died? Things went bad?"

It was obvious Lowell didn't want to talk about it. He'd been evasive about the whole thing since he'd returned.

"Zeke seems to think it was all Emmett's fault," Cashe said. "He says Emmett is a disgrace and shouldn't be leading the squad in the field like that."

"I don't know," Lowell said.

"Don't know, or don't want to speak ill of Emmett?"

"Don't know."

"You're a good man, good soldier," Cashe said. "You've probably had more time in the field than Emmett, if you count your stint as a lawman. You don't think he's much of a leader, do you?"

"I'm not trying to evade you, just don't know what to say. It was chaos," Lowell said. "Emmett could've done things differently. It isn't the first time he's had trouble in the field. He's got the best of intentions, but yes, I'd say he's not a terribly effective leader of men."

"Six good soldiers are dead," Cashe said. "That's a little worse than not being effective, wouldn't you agree?"

Lowell shrugged and looked away. "I tried to help. I tried to push him in his decisions, suggest ways to go about things, but it didn't help."

Cashe felt bad for Lowell. He was a good soldier mainly because he could follow orders and respected the chain of command. It was hard for him to get past the flaws of his immediate superiors.

"Thanks," Cashe said. "I appreciate your candor. Emmett and I need to sit down and discuss things again. He and I go back a long way, you have to understand."

56

"There are worse things in this country than loyalty," Lowell said.

"Yes. I suppose so." Cashe nodded to the door, and Lowell excused himself.

The old chair Cashe had salvaged for the office squeaked as he rotated himself toward the window behind him. It was a small pane of glass, but he could still see the nighttime sky and the thousand points of starlight that shone on the field of black.

He and Emmett had come aboard the *Polk* together, had worked on her side by side for years. They had grand visions of what the O.M.O. could do, what it could become, but Cashe wasn't sure how Emmett would handle the idea that Lowell should take his place. He certainly knew what kind of man Zeke was. He worked well with everyone, but his temper scared Cashe.

He extinguished the lights, walked over to the wall, and slid his bed out of the closet. The covers and blanket were already on it as he hadn't bothered to fold them or put them away in a few weeks. He just left the bed made and fell into it night after night.

He always had trouble falling asleep. Counting stars was a big help, but sometimes he read. That night, he thought of the people that were lost that day and the others that were found and couldn't figure if one outweighed the other.

21

There was a light rapping at the portal. Cyrus shifted with every intention of getting up and responding, but as he did, he heard the soft padding of Lucinda's naked feet on the metal floor.

"I'll see what they want," Lucinda said.

"Mmmmff…" It was the closest thing to a profound statement Cyrus could come up with. He watched Lucinda move across the room but shut his eyes at the light of the door creaking open. There was a low exchange of voices—Lucinda talking to Cashe from the sounds of it. The portal closed again.

"Apparently, Cashe wants to speak with us before breakfast," Lucinda said. "And breakfast starts soon." She held up a bundle of clothes for Cyrus to see. "And they must think we smell, because they gave us something to wear."

Cyrus walked to the sink and started washing up as best he could. "Do you think we should have our talk now?"

"Let's meet Cashe and get some food in us," Lucinda said.

Cyrus wondered if the delays were a coping device for her or if she already felt comfortable in the new environment. She'd slept well, ate well and she was so far off the ground that no one could touch her.

She changed, then opened the hatch to meet Cashe in the corridor.

"Good morning," Lucinda said with an enthusiasm Cyrus hadn't heard from her in all the days since they'd met.

Cashe nodded and indicated the stairs leading up. He was a little nervous about her outfit, judging by the way he continually averted his eyes, but he seemed to recover quickly. The stairs led to a wide room that was considerably brighter than most other areas of the ship. The entire front wall was glass and the sun shone through brilliantly. Cyrus stepped forward and put his hand lightly against the glass, then pulled back.

"It's ok. You aren't going to fall out," Cashe said.

Cyrus forced himself to look annoyed but put both hands firmly on the glass after a moment. He leaned his head forward and looked down to see the ground. There were tree tops and hills far below. He couldn't gauge how high they were, but the view of the land was spectacular.

"We were tipped off to the Sons of Grant's plan some days after you left," Cashe said. "The business at the dam was all we knew about, though. They've been destroying things across the region and we just assumed they'd blow the dam and be done with it. We had no idea they'd intended to target you as well. One of our operatives tracked his men to the area but by the time we figured out they were lying in wait for you, it was too late. We rushed to try to save you and your passengers. I lost a number of men at the dam," Cashe said. "Believe me, I wish I could've done things differently."

"Lot of trouble to put me out of business." Cyrus watched the clouds that disappeared in the wake of the *Leonidas Polk*.

"Not sure what you mean," Cashe said.

"Umberto Cantolione. He has a vendetta against us and this was a vicious attempt by that bastard to destroy us. We've been waiting for this," Cyrus said. He looked over at Lucinda, but she didn't react.

"We're working on theories," Cashe said. "I don't think Cantolione is the real threat. We're eyeing another man in his organization." He sat in the chair next to

Lucinda. "This group has been hitting important structures all over the West. It is conceivable you were caught up in their chaos accidentally."

"How so?" Lucinda asked.

"You were taking passengers from the North, to a destination in the South, right?"

"Yes," Cyrus said.

"The group in question supports Northern superiority," Cashe said. "They targeted you just for your destination. It's the way they think, based on our knowledge of them."

"Nothing we can do about any of that now." Lucinda stood just behind Cyrus and stared out the window as well.

Cashe cleared his throat. "Well, yes and no."

Cyrus and Lucinda watched as Cashe turned a small hand crank at the top of the stairs. A large piece of glass descended from the ceiling near the wall. It magnified everything Cyrus looked at on the ground.

"That's a powerful telescope you have there," he said.

"Thank you. Now if you'll look over here." Cashe pointed down a bit. "Can you see it?"

Cyrus squinted and tried to sort the suddenly large objects that he saw. A blue blob distinguished itself from the sky and the clouds. Another airship.

"That is *The Moon and the Stars*," Cashe said.

Cyrus recognized the name. "One of Cantolione's. Is it carrying settlers? Wouldn't be sightseers this far out."

Cashe shook his head. "It's on a private cruise. Invited guests only."

"Is Cantolione on board?" Lucinda asked.

"Don't know," Cashe said. "But we want to ask them a few questions based on what we know at this time." He moved between the telescope plate and his guests. "We have a dilemma. We need to get you *civilians* to safety—you obviously have been through a lot. If we confront Cantolione's craft, it could get messy and we can't endanger you any more than we already have. Of course, if you were to join us....We wouldn't have to abandon this opportunity," Cashe said.

"You want us to work for you?" Cyrus asked quickly.

"Didn't say work, I said join. You join the military," Cashe said. "You two know your way around a vessel—a dirigible isn't so different from a Turtle. We're a fully-sanctioned branch of the military, even if they sometimes pretend we're not or forget about us. We do what we can to make what's left of this country safe. If that means burning a den of the undead, so be it. If it means shooting down pirates, so be it." Cashe took a pause. "If Tom Preston is aboard *The Moon and the Stars*, he may be the person to ask about what happened to your Turtle."

Cyrus looked at the distant airship. It held nothing of interest for them and only served to put them in still more danger. If Preston or Cantolione were onboard, it wouldn't bring his crew or those settlers back. "No thanks. You can run your mission and catch up with whoever's on that airship, but I think you should leave us out of it," Cyrus said. "Thanks all the same."

He could feel Lucinda's eyes on him immediately. "We need to get clear of all of this," he said. "Maybe you can leave us somewhere and we'll start making our own way again." He paused and suddenly felt rude. "Not that we aren't grateful."

"Cyrus?" Lucinda asked.

"Yes?"

Her voice was barely constrained. "Maybe we should have that talk now."

The tension must have been obvious to Cashe. "I can leave the two of you alone for a spell if you'd like."

Cyrus nodded. The other man walked down the stairs and into the lower corridor.

Lucinda started immediately in a terse tone. "What are you doing? You can't make that decision for both of us."

Cyrus sat down next to her and held his hands out, pleading. He knew he only had a small window of time to get her onboard before she dug in her heels on the subject. Usually, it wasn't a problem, but this decision was potentially life-altering for both of them.

"They can leave us at some town and we'll start over," he said. "We can make our way—"

"Make our way where?" Lucinda asked. "We have no money. We have no crew. And we have no influence on anyone. No one owes us a favor."

Cyrus stood. "Look around you. You're on a military vehicle. They said it themselves—they fight people. That seems counter to keeping you safe and keeping my blood on the inside of my body."

Lucinda got calm and stared out again at the sky. "You're off the hook."

"What?"

"When I came to you, I needed a place to work and a meal, not a guardian. I don't know how you got it into your mind, but I never asked for your protection."

"I don't...."

"I asked you to help me then, now I'm asking you to stop," Lucinda said. "Cashe and his men saved us when we were in trouble, now I feel like I owe him a debt." She looked over at Cyrus. "You can go on without me."

"That's it? No more discussion?"

She turned and descended the stairs without looking back.

The gorgeous blue sky caught Cyrus's attention and he stared at it for just another second, enjoying the view before following her. Of all the times that he'd wished to be on a flying vessel, this scenario was never in his dreams.

"We've made our choices," Lucinda said to Cashe in the corridor. "You can count—"

Cyrus interrupted before she could finish. "You can count us both in."

22

The Maiden Voyage was, quite possibly, the most frightening pub down on the docks. There were frequent fights, some of which ended in fatalities. The food was awful, and upkeep was nearly a joke.

Tom Preston loved it.

It was filled with men who hated their jobs, hated the government and loved to stir up trouble. Many of them made it through the war only to be told no one won. Some were wounded, injured or forgotten. Nearly everyone there felt slighted in one way or another. It was the perfect place to recruit new members for the cause. Tom could bend his pitch to suit any grievance a body might have with authority, the government, the U.N.A. or their mortal enemies over the line into the next country.

"So you've been working the same freighter since you were discharged or have you been moving around?" Tom asked.

"Been tough," Stewart Willis said. He held a mug of ale in his good hand. "Not everyone wants to keep a man on when only one of his arms works proper."

Tom heard this story over and over again from both sides. He nodded sympathetically and leaned in to listen. He knew most of the time all any of them wanted was an ear to bend.

"Tom?" His boss's voice called from right behind him.

Cantolione stepped gingerly between the bar clientele.

"Sir, what are you doing here?" Tom asked, then to Mr. Willis, "I'm terribly sorry. Apparently my boss needs something urgently."

Willis stood and nodded politely to Cantolione and walked away as respectfully as he could.

"Tom, I'm glad I found you," Cantolione said.

"What're you doing here?" Tom asked. "Is something wrong?"

"Pack a bag, my boy—we're leaving in the morning. First light," Cantolione said. With that he turned and walked between the chairs and stools toward the door.

"What?" Tom stood and followed, nudging people aside to make room with only a cursory pardon as he went. When he was within earshot of his boss, he asked, "What are you talking about? Where are we going that I'd need to pack?"

"I hired on a ship to take us out. We're going to bring back some of those lizards for the show." Cantolione pushed open the door and stepped out onto the boardwalk.

"What? Where do you think you're going to find them?"

Cantolione huffed. "I've been pouring over the material that our friend Moose left for us. There were maps and charts and other notes in with the photos. I stared at them for hours and then I took them to the docks and had one of the seamen explain them to me. That man directed me to another sailor, who took me to a captain who claims to know the area and the lizards well."

"So we paid Moose for something that's common knowledge to the maritime community?" Tom asked.

"I didn't get that impression," Cantolione said. "It seemed like more superstition and hearsay than anything. But this captain claims to have been there. He might even be Moose's contact."

"So what is your plan?"

"I've paid the captain to take Fitzmartin, the animal trainer, a couple of wranglers and you and me out to this area to try to capture a few of these things." Cantolione smiled at Tom. "After that, my plan is to charge a little extra fee if customers want to see them, then buy some new airships, then start in on conquering the East Coast just like we've taken over the West."

Cantolione could always boil down his dreams to their simplest form, while somehow ignoring the obstacles both large and small that could crop up.

"So get your things together and meet me down by dock four at sunrise," Cantolione said.

"How long will we be gone?"

"They said it will take close to a day to get there and a day to get back. Who knows how long to catch the animals?" Cantolione looked up and did some math in his head. "Call it a minimum of three days, maybe up to five? Sounds right." He waved over his shoulder. "See you in the morning."

Tom gave a dismissive wave back, knowing very well that his boss wasn't looking anymore. He stared back at the bar and then to Cantolione as he disappeared into the night. Quickly, he did a little math in his own head and realized that he was suddenly pushed for time if he wanted to put his plan into motion.

23

"Take us in closer," Cashe said. "Let's let 'em know we're here."

Owen Corrigan put down his scope and turned with a quizzical look. "They're on an odd course. Pretty erratic."

Cashe put faith in Corrigan's assessment. The man grew up on airships, stoking boilers when he was in his teens and then working his way up to navigation and piloting. He knew when a dirigible was flying oddly.

"Trying to evade us?" Cashe asked. He wasn't sure if *The Moon and the Stars* would be able to outrun the *Polk* or not. It was smaller and lighter, but the *Polk* had been modified with enhancements not available to the general public. One of the perks of being in their little division of the military.

Corrigan shook his head. "I'm not entirely sure they've seen us yet. If anything they're crossing into our range on their own. Not moving away, but drifting."

Running was easy to deal with. Fighting was relatively easy to handle. Aimlessness concerned Cashe.

"Maybe they're tipsy? We heard they were going to celebrate." Cashe laughed. He picked up the intercom and spoke into it evenly. "Monty? Start signaling *The Moon and the Stars*. Give them the standard greeting—who we are, what we're doing. Tell them to hold a steady course and we'll be coming aboard." He heard a terse reply and hung up the intercom hose and sighed. "Here we go."

The *Polk* closed the gap easily, the other ship not attempting to run, but still not holding a steady course. Corrigan kept it in his sights. When they got close enough to see into the portals and screens, he inspected the craft in earnest. "Nothing seems to be moving over there. I can't see anyone at the windows at all," Corrigan said. "Don't really see any damage, either."

"Can you catch a glimpse of the control room?" Cashe asked. "Someone should be moving around in there. If not, that would certainly explain why they can't hold a course."

Monty's voice came across the tubes. "No response to our signals."

"Keep trying," Cashe responded. "Let's get closer if we can."

"Wait," Corrigan said. "Someone just moved past one of the aft portholes. Hold on, hold on. There they go past the next one. They're moving toward the front, passing another."

"Can you make them out?"

"Nah. The portholes are some kind of glazed glass. Can't make out a thing," Corrigan said. "Still, that's something, I guess."

Cashe didn't like the idea that there were people over there ignoring him. He could handle a lot of things, but being ignored wasn't one of them. He picked up the intercom hose again and cleared it. "Monty? Enough of the signaling. Join Bethy down at the fore cannon and put a shot across this thing's bow."

"That should get you some results," Corrigan said. "People tend to respond to firearms."

Cashe wasn't so sure.

A minute later the crack of a cannon rang out. For a brief moment Cashe could track the smoking ball as it passed the front portal of *The Moon*. He waited to see what would happen, but no official reaction was forthcoming.

"Whoever that is in the hall just stopped," Corrigan said.

"I'll bet they hit the deck and are staying down until they're sure we aren't going to shoot again," Cashe said.

Corrigan shook his head. "No. They just stopped. They're still standing there in front of the porthole."

"They can't see out, can they?" Cashe asked.

"Shouldn't be able to," Corrigan replied. "Not if we can't see in."

Cashe went over to where Lowell sat behind his controls. "How'd you like to get out from behind that cramped console and get some fresh air?"

Lowell gave Cashe an eager look and moved for the door.

"Take Zeke, Daniel and Emmett with you."

As he got up from his seat, Lowell leaned close to Cashe. "Are you sure that's a good idea? Since the dam, they haven't exactly been on the best of terms."

"Since the dam, we've been incredibly short on men, not much to be done about it," Cashe said.

"Fine, but we need Daniel on the *Polk*. He's most likely to know what to do if something goes wrong with the harpoon."

"Can the three of you do it on your own?"

Lowell nodded. "Sure, and maybe I can get one of our new recruits to help Daniel out in the cargo hold."

"Fine," Cashe said. "Just give them some time to adjust before you throw them to the wolves."

"Hey, don't worry. I'll be gentle." On the way out, Lowell stopped next to Lucinda. "Want to come have some fun with me?"

Lucinda gave him a smile. "I don't foresee us having fun together anytime soon."

Lowell acted devastated but he still managed his best smile on his way past her.

Cyrus spoke up. "I'd like to come have some fun with you. If that's okay with everyone."

Cashe laughed. "If you think you can handle it, be my guest." He hoped the man knew what he was getting into.

"Won't be a problem." Cyrus waved to the hallway for Lowell to lead the way. "Let's get to moving."

When they were gone Lucinda shook her head. "Boys and their thinly veiled dirty talk."

Cashe and Corrigan both laughed at once. Cashe was beginning to like this one.

24

At the side cargo door, Cyrus watched the men prepare. Lowell and the other three had already latched themselves into a strange tangle of straps and ropes that ended in hooks. They strung a similar apparatus around Cyrus. No one explained exactly what was about to happen, but Cyrus had a bad feeling. He should've stayed in the comfortable chair next to Lucinda in the control room.

Bethy unlatched the cargo door and leaned against it with all her might to move it aside. None of the others stopped to help her.

"This is something of our own making," she said. "Daniel was a whaler back in Maine and he designed this based on the harpoons they used on the ships. Basically, it's a big harpoon launcher. We can use it to capture ships like *The Moon*."

"Like catching big fish from high up in the sky," Zeke said.

"That too," Bethy agreed before getting back to work. She ran back with Emmett and rolled a large spool of thick wire up near the door.

Daniel loaded a harpoon and threaded the wire into the device. All of them stood back and inspected each other's handiwork.

"It doesn't look like much," Lowell said, "but believe me, we've done this before. No problems."

A bolt clanged to the floor and rolled up to Cyrus's boot.

"Oops," Lowell said. "Where did that come from?" He bent down, picked it up and examined it closely. "Nothing important." He chucked it out the open door.

Cyrus watched it fly out, but refused to get closer to the door to watch it fall any farther. He looked at Lowell and then scanned the deck for any other stray parts. About then, Bethy and Daniel burst out with laughter. They were joined by Zeke and Emmett, but Lowell remained straight-faced.

"Bethy, you've got the honors." Lowell pointed to the machine they'd assembled and moved aside.

"Will do," the short, apple-cheeked woman said as she stepped forward and gripped the handles, moving the device around some. She paused to pull her brown hair back into a ponytail.

"I've got five that says you miss it." Zeke fished a bill out of his coveralls and waved it around with glee.

Bethy scowled. "Right. I'll take that."

Lowell pulled a small telescope out of his pocket and scanned *The Moon*. The ship was very close now, only a few hundred yards separated it from the *Polk*. It was easy to make out the details of it without magnification. Nothing seemed out of place to Cyrus, no scoring from explosions, no sign of fire through the windows that he could tell. He still couldn't see anyone wandering about.

"If you can get it over the top of the door, I'd be damnably happy, my dear," Lowell said. He assembled a foot-long device with small wheels on the inside.

Cyrus watched Bethy grip the handles on either side of the harpoon gun they'd assembled on the door frame and rotate it slightly. She raised it, lowered it.

"That thing doesn't want to hold still over there," she said. "Who's driving it?"

"We think no one," Lowell said.

"Ah. That explains it." The young lady took a deep breath and gritted her teeth together. A moment later a soft thunk announced the harpoon and its trailing wire were on their way toward *The Moon and the Stars*.

Cyrus was sure she'd overshot it. The harpoon flew high—high enough he thought it would fly over the roof of the airship, maybe even puncture the airbag overhead. But, with perfect timing, it began to drop and arc back toward the side of the passenger car of *The Moon*. At the last second it seemed to wobble and waver like it was giving up, but it didn't. It struck the metal hull of the other airship with enough force to smash an outer light, whose sole purpose was to provide illumination to passengers who entered the door directly below it.

Before anyone could say a word, Bethy yanked the money from Zeke's hand. "Thanks," she said as she walked to the other side of the group.

Lowell took one of the smaller items he put together and latched it onto the cable that now stretched from one ship to the other. He motioned Cyrus over. "This is how we get from here to there," he said. "This fits over the wire, the wheels help us roll along. The hook attaches to the buckle in your suit and this..." He indicated a switch on the handle. "Is your brake. When you get about three quarters of the way there, start applying the brake so you slow down. Don't jerk yourself to a stop or you'll snap your spine."

Cyrus stared at the little device and tried to memorize the functions without making Lowell repeat himself. "Got it."

Lowell gave him a hard look. "You sure? Maybe you should sit this one out and let us show you how it goes. We've done this before. We're used to it."

"We've done this *once* before," Zeke said. "Ain't none of us experts or nothin."

"Shut up, Zeke," Lowell said. "Bethy, tell Cashe we're set and he can take us up whenever he's ready." Then to the others. "I'm first. Emmett, you're next. I'll secure the door and make sure the cable's not going anywhere."

Bethy pulled an intercom off the wall and spoke into it. A moment later, the *Polk* rose slowly until it was no longer level with *The Moon*. Lowell stepped up to the wire and clipped on his transporter.

With no fanfare or questions or even a parting word, he leapt feet first out the door and into the open air.

Cyrus stepped as close as he dared to the edge and watched as Lowell gripped the handle and kept his body stiff and pointed toward the other craft. He wavered back and forth with the line as it went taught with his weight. The cable was as tight as it could be, but some slack still let Lowell bow out away from the ships before following the line toward *The Moon*. Three-fourths of the way there, Lowell slowed. A wisp of smoke came from the transporter in his hands.

"He's braking," Emmett said. "You may have some smoke, too. Don't panic. That's just the brakes trying to grip the line. It's no problem."

Cyrus stared at Emmett for a moment and considered punching him. "Any other little details that I should know before they actually happen?"

"Nah." Emmett pointed to Lowell dangling on the wire out on the open air. "What else could go wrong?"

They watched Lowell make an unexpectedly graceful stop just before he reached the side of *The Moon*. He glided the last ten feet and grabbed a handrail next to the door. He quickly pulled out some sort of tool and began working on the lock.

"This next part should be tricky," Daniel said. "If they're lying in wait for us, they could be right behind the door, ready to kill him."

"Zeke, get ready," Emmett said. "I'm jumping the second he gets that open, and you're right after."

Zeke nodded.

Emmett stepped up and attached his own transporter to the line. He didn't look quite as calm as Lowell had.

25

Night closed in as Tom opened the door to the telegraph office. It was little more than an outhouse. The walls looked like scrap wood. The roof consisted of mostly slate and old piping. Inside, there was a small waiting area—a desk made of two old doors, a wire set up and a big wooden chair with a skinny man in a bowler waiting with a glass of water in his hand. The operator, Russell Curtis, had taken and sent many a message for Tom and managed to keep his mouth shut about it.

"Any response to the message I sent earlier?" Tom asked.

Russell pulled a paper from under the table and slid it over. "Yes, sir. Just a few minutes back."

The paper had everything he needed to direct the Sons of Grant to the last known location of Dr. Poley's device. It had coordinates to find an old Union fort called Outpost Two Thirteen, as well as a brief explanation of how to locate the device within the fortification. There were enough soldiers in the Sons that they knew people just about everywhere. It took some time to figure out the right person in the right place, but it paid off.

"Reply to the sender."

Russell got out a nub of a pencil and smoothed a piece of paper. "Go ahead."

"On our way." Tom slid several bills across the table. "I doubt you have to write that down."

"No. I don't." Russell held up the money and waved it back and forth. "Thanks again, sir."

As Tom pushed open the door, he grunted something of a reply and left. The ridiculous safari Cantolione was dragging him on seemed horribly timed at first, but the more Tom thought about it, it would work for him. It was hard to be blamed for an attack on a military installation when he was out to sea, looking for lizards and whatnot.

He smiled a little, but the hasty departure in the morning wouldn't leave much time to go over strategy with Potts. Of course Potts had been at enough battles to know how a fight worked, but that didn't always translate into the ability to lead others. Sometimes a soldier was a natural born follower and that was the best he could do. From what Tom could tell, Potts had a good head on his shoulders but they'd never been in a battle together. The business at the dam could hardly be blamed on Potts. It was impossible to predict the O.M.O. might show up at that point.

The Sons of Grant had successfully destroyed well over a dozen targets across the West, and most of those events had been led by Potts—the railroad bridge at Redwood City, the Northern munitions supply at Fort Humboldt, and the United Nations' depot in Oregon.

Potts could handle this, given the additional resources the Sons acquired recently. They had more men, more weapons, more money and access to airships now. Those were resources that could turn the tide for any force.

26

Lowell rested his head against the door of *The Moon* as he tried to unlock it. He needed both hands and, seeing as he had no other means of stabilizing himself, his head managed to do the trick. The only problem with the arrangement was it forced him to look directly down at the lock as he worked on it with his pick, which, in turn forced him to look directly down at the ground far below him. There was no way to look elsewhere and still get his job done.

They passed over a lake surrounded by a small forest and he thought it looked like a puddle surrounded by tall grass. He wondered if the water or the grass would cushion his fall if the cable gave way. This forced him to look up at the cable and make sure it was securely in place.

The lock became his sole focus as he tried to blot out the things passing below. After that his work went quicker, and in moments, he felt the door give way a little. He waited and listened for what was on the other side. He heard only the gentle rushing of the wind and the quiet thrum of the engines.

Lowell shifted and gripped a handrail next to the door with one hand and used his other to push the door inward. As it swung in, he moved away from the door, flattening himself against the side of the ship as much as his harness and cable would let him. He waited a beat. Still, he heard nothing. He hoped anyone on the other side who might want to shoot him would've had an itchy trigger finger and fired when the door opened. The silence was not helpful to him.

"Dammit," he mumbled. He pulled his pistol from its holster.

With no grace whatsoever, Lowell pulled on the handrail, using it for leverage to propel himself through the door way. His foot caught on the step and he sprawled on the floor, sliding into the wall on the other side of the small room just inside the outer door. He scrambled to his feet, gun still in hand, and got his bearings. The room measured only ten feet by ten feet. It had two doors—one opposite the outer hatch and one to the right of it. Aside from some dials, levers and cranks, the chamber was empty.

Lowell leaned back to the door he'd come through and waved to Zeke and the others. Emmett had already left the *Polk* and glided down toward *The Moon*. Lowell heard a thump coming from the door to the right. It sounded faint at first, but got louder quickly. He raised his gun and put his back to the wall, just in case someone came through the other door in an attempt to flank him. He kept the pistol trained on the door that was thumping. In another second, the door started to bow inward with each sound.

Thump. Thump.

The grip of the pistol felt sweaty and slippery as he cocked the hammer back. The door splintered inward. Two men came through. Chewers. They were covered in blood—one's face dripped with it, as though it were fresh and not his own. The other had a gaping hole in his chest that showed bits of what Lowell assumed were lungs.

Lowell fired again and again. He wasn't panicked enough to forget all his experience—he aimed for the head to bring them down.

Unfortunately, he wasn't in enough control of himself to stop firing before he ran out. He kept pulling the trigger until all he heard was the clicking of the trigger without the accompaniment of the loud crack of the live rounds. The two shambling undead at the door fell over—their heads cracked by multiple bullet holes.

Two more chewers staggered around the fallen bodies.

Lowell stepped back to the far wall and fumbled with the breach on his pistol. Empty shells fell on the metal deck and clattered to a standstill. His free hand patted his pockets before he realized his extra ammunition was pinned beneath the maze of straps around his chest. He pulled at one and it tightened another. Every time he thought he could reach his ammo pouch, he let go of a strap and it slid back into place.

In the doorway, the undead had maneuvered around the corpses and made their way toward Lowell.

One clasp unhooked, which made the straps go limp. Lowell reached in, but realized he'd never get the ammunition out and loaded before they were on him. The other door in the room looked good to him, even if he didn't know where it led. If he let in more of the dead, then he did. But if the hallway beyond was clear, he could run or shut the door on his pursuers.

He grabbed the door and tugged. It was locked. He turned the handle again and strained. It didn't open.

The monsters were nearly upon him when a loud thud and cursing drew his attention. Emmett had landed hard outside. He hadn't braked early enough and slammed against the hull.

The dead continued on, not pausing at the sound.

"Emmett!" Lowell shouted. "Gun! Throw me a gun or start shooting." He held his hands out to shove the lead ghoul away. The thing was strong and pressed forward, its jaws snapping at the open air between them. Lowell could smell the foul stench of the dead man's breath drawing nearer.

The room suddenly filled with the sound of gunfire. Lowell's second attacker was knocked down by a shot that connected with its leg. Lowell saw Emmett out of the corner of his eye. Emmett was still outside the craft, hanging on with one hand and shooting his huge pistol with the other. He was wavering—trying to steady himself to take aim at the one Lowell was keeping at arm's length. Lowell wasn't so sure which was more dangerous.

"Wait." Lowell fell to the floor to give Emmett a better chance of missing him.

Emmett dispatched the chewer with a single shot.

"Christ Almighty," he said. "Damned good thing I showed up when I did. You'd be food for the deadies right now." Emmett started working his way out of his straps.

"Yeah. Thanks." Lowell considered arguing that he'd have found a way to make it, but thought it wise to let it go, seeing as the man had just saved his life and all. He followed Emmett's lead and started shedding his own gear. Once it was done, he reloaded his pistol.

Zeke landed and pulled his way in while the others talked. "Thanks for the shittin' help, you bastards."

Both men reached out and helped him out of the maze of straps and cords twisted around him.

"Little too late now, don't you think?" Zeke brushed them aside and finished it himself. "Damn boys, you ain't been here five minutes and you've already shot, what? Four people?"

Emmett shook his head. "Look closer. Ain't people."

"Flesh chewers," Zeke said.

Lowell looked around at the things on the floor and nodded. "I guess if everyone over here's a chewer, that would explain why they're flying so erratically."

Lowell shook his head. "Let's see if we can bar that locked door with something. Make it one less front to worry about." He picked up some planks from the door that the chewers had broken and shoved them through the handle and worked it into a fixture on the wall. He looked at it and shrugged. "Don't know if that'll do it, but it could help. Make a hell of a racket if someone comes through it."

"All right, let's get ready to catch this new guy before he puts himself through the hull," Lowell said.

Emmett laughed and stepped to the edge of the hatch to watch Cyrus sail across. He completely ignored Zeke and barely heard the man's footfalls on the deck.

27

It didn't look all that fun to Cyrus. He stared at the men on *The Moon*, who stared back at him with smiles on their faces.

"We've done this before, Mr. Cyrus," Bethy said.

"Once. You've done this particular move once before." Cyrus still wasn't sure this wasn't an elaborate trick to get him to scream like a baby at several hundred feet in the air. "And it's just Cyrus. No Mr."

"That first one turned out all right." Bethy tugged on the straps that encircled Cyrus's chest and waist. "Now, let's go over it again." She held up the transporter and squeezed on the braking mechanism. "Start slowing down when you pass the halfway point. Better to stop early than late."

The transporter didn't look at all safe. It was small and seemed easily broken, but Cyrus nodded anyway as she clipped it onto the metal line for him.

"Keep your body still once you get in the open air, and keep your feet pointed toward *The Moon*. You *should* be fine."

He felt like a fool for continually nodding, but he did it again. He didn't want to wait too long—the others had leapt without a moment to consider it. If he stood there, they'd think less of him. Leading by example. That was the way he'd run his ship. That was how it was on the Turtle.

"You can go any time," Bethy said. "I'm not rushing you. Just letting you know you're free to jump. Anytime."

Cyrus swallowed and concentrated on looking good in front of Lowell, who was waiting on the other side. For whatever reason, that soldier made him feel on guard more than most. He was easy-going enough, it seemed, but there was a quality that made Cyrus uneasy. Maybe it was the way he looked at Lucinda.

He stared at Lowell and Emmett in the doorway of the ship across the airy expanse and tensed his legs to jump out. As he did, he saw the two men wobble on their feet, and fall backward.

"What the hell's going on?" Cyrus yelled.

Bethy turned to see what he meant just as it became obvious that *The Moon* was changing course.

"Hell," she said and ran for an intercom. "*The Moon's* weaving away from us," she shouted into the tube.

The Moon banked down and slowly to the east as the *Polk* maintained its steady course. Cyrus watched as the two men slid and disappeared from the doorway, the angle of the floor was quickly getting steep.

"Shit, shit shitshit," Bethy shouted.

She rushed back to Cyrus, arms outstretched. He was aware immediately that the spool of wire rapidly unwinded next to the harpoon launcher she'd used to attach the two ships.

"Unhook the transporter, unhook it!" she shouted.

Cyrus reached up to take it off and fumbled with it. The mechanism that locked in place and made the thing secure foiled him. Nothing he tried could pry the little device away from the wire.

Just as Bethy reached him to help, the wire spool stopped feeding out and the whole device began to creak. The wire was at its limit, and the two ships were pulling in opposite directions. Cyrus reached out and grabbed Bethy as the sudden jerk of the ship caught her off guard and sent her reeling toward the open cargo door, toward oblivion.

He pulled the tiny woman into a crushing hug to keep her from falling, which also forced him to let go of the wire he'd been holding. They both tilted out the doorway together.

The *Polk* shook as *The Moon* began to drag it down.

Daniel came running from a nearby doorway. A panicked yelp escaped him as he saw Cyrus and Bethy teetering at the outer door, stuck to the wire. The harpoon system roared as it began to bend on the doorframe. The last thing Cyrus saw in the cargo hold before they went over the side was Daniel opening a locker next to the door and coming at them with a wire cutter.

Cyrus gathered Bethy close and spoke softly into her ear. "Sorry."

"Bad luck," she said as they both fell out of the doorway and into the air. They immediately began flying quickly along the wire.

He admired her calm, but didn't really share it. He turned his head to see *The Moon and the Stars*. It was still at an odd angle, but the *Polk* seemed to have a stabilizing effect on it—keeping it from diving any further. He and Bethy picked up speed, as they were nearly falling straight down out of the sky. It looked like the two ships were quickly coming back to an acceptable angle. If not, Cyrus and Bethy would be going so fast when they got to *The Moon*, they'd be nothing but a mangle of bones and flesh. Through the rush of wind in his ears, Cyrus managed to make out that Bethy was saying something to him.

"Brake," she shouted. "Grab the brake!"

He reached for the device with one hand. "Hold on."

"Use both hands or we'll spin."

"Hold on to me," Cyrus said.

He felt her weight shift to the straps around his chest. He grabbed the brakes and pulled. There was a screech, but they didn't slow. Not immediately. They continued dropping out of the sky like two intertwined rocks.

Toward the end, their angle lessened and the transporter began to smoke, jerking the two of them. Cyrus tightened his grip, resisting the urge to reach down for Bethy. He concentrated on what was going to happen in a few seconds when they reached *The Moon and the Stars*. They descended away from the ships, not directly toward the door, as the others had. He hoped one of the ships shifted immediately or they might ram the hull pretty far from the door, which would make getting off the line difficult, and falling easy. And there was always the chance they'd head for *The Moon's* twin propellers that spun at the rear of the ship.

28

Lowell grabbed Emmett and helped him through the door frame which was now nearly perpendicular to where it should be. "Where the hell is Zeke?"

Both men looked back to the room they just crawled out of, but saw no sign of the other soldier.

"Hell if I know." Emmett braced himself against the wall and the floor and started to walk as best he could.

Lowell led the way down the hall. They passed two doors and continued crawling toward the wide open room at the end of the passage. As they approached, the ship began to level off and they took a moment to reorient themselves.

Before they could enter the room, the crack of a pistol startled them. They came around the corner as another shot fired. There they saw Zeke shooting at another chewer. By all appearances, he was using the ship's controls as cover, to keep them away from him. Lowell noticed several holes in the creature, but it kept coming. Emmett drew his pistol and fired one shot into its head.

"Dammit! I was just getting around to killing that thing," Zeke shouted.

Lowell pushed him aside and examined the controls, trying to figure out how to bring the airship fully under control. He'd only flown solo a couple times, and that was usually with supervision. Cashe didn't let too many people handle the controls outside of Corrigan and Bethy.

Emmett shoved Zeke aside to read the gauges. "You almost got around to killing all of *us*, you dumb bastard."

"Hey, you watch your mouth," Zeke said.

Lowell cursed under his breath as he yanked the controls to pull them back on course, but they fought him. He eased off the throttle a little, mindful of what that might do to the line stretched between the crafts. It made turning the wheel just a little easier, but not much. He knew enough to try to make the liquids in the compass and altimeter even out with the bars that floated inside them. They weren't there just yet.

Emmett reached over and pulled as well, giving the last bit needed. *The Moon* leveled off, but they were considerably lower than when they'd started. Lowell found the altitude control and eased them upward.

"You can't just wander off from your boarding party like that," Lowell said, keeping his eyes on the compass on the console instead of looking at Zeke. "That's why we come over as a group. That's why I told everyone to wait at the door. And we're lucky you didn't take us all down into the side of the mountain."

Zeke didn't respond, but Lowell could feel the soldier's eyes on him. He wondered what else lay in store for them in the rest of the ship. *The Moon* drifted closer to the *Polk* than it should so he eased it off. Cashe would have his hide if he collided with the *Polk*.

When Lowell felt comfortable with their course, he locked *The Moon*'s wheel. Emmett and Zeke checked and reloaded their guns. Lowell decided that wasn't such a bad idea.

"I'll lead," he said. "You two move up behind." He looked at Zeke intently this time. "And no stupid stunts. We're lucky no one got hurt last time."

29

Cyrus wasn't sure whether he should mention their troublesome drift toward *The Moon's* propellers to Bethy or not. There wasn't anything she could do about it, after all.

The line that had been taut enough to tug at the *Polk* became slack and bowed away as *The Moon* came back toward the *Polk* and the gap increased. This was good news, because they'd slowed, but bad news because the slack in the line had quickly begun to trail *The Moon*, drifting slightly toward the rear of the ship, where the propellers were madly churning away at the air.

"Cashe will bring us out of it," Bethy yelled. "Just you wait."

"He better."

Cyrus looked down at her and smiled the weakest smile at her optimism. His arms were getting tired from hanging on. The trip from one ship to the other, which had taken the others only a minute, was dragging on much longer for Cyrus.

At that moment it was *The Moon and the Stars* that corrected the gap. The propellers turned and the airship moved away from the *Polk*, widening the gap, bringing the line taught, and allowing them to move to the door and away from the dangerous props.

"Let me grab the door," Cyrus said. "We can let the harness keep me on the line, I'm afraid if you let go, you won't be able to keep from falling with just one hand on me."

"Don't have to tell me twice. I'm all for not falling," Bethy said.

It went well, at least to Cyrus's panicked mind. They slid down the line to the door. The wind and the loose wire conspired to smack them against the outer hull a half a dozen times. Cyrus absorbed the blows with his body, except one time when he unable to stop Bethy from getting a good knock on the head. When they reached the doorway, Cyrus stretched out with one hand to grab the rail and steady them before bracing them with his leg.

"End of the line. Everyone off," Cyrus said. He tried to keep the strain of hurting arms out of his voice.

Bethy extricated herself from the safety of Cyrus's harness. He was relieved to no longer have the responsibility for her. He stepped into a small room filled with the acrid stench of gunfire and looked at the dead things on the floor. There was a small pile of safety straps tangled in with the bodies. Cyrus figured the jostling of the ship tossed everything into odd nooks and crannies, but seeing as how none of the bodies belonged to the boarding party, he assumed they were all safe.

"You all right?" he asked.

Bethy was walking in a tight circle in the center of the room. "I'm going to be fine."

"You're pacing."

"Just need a minute."

"I'm going to have a look around." Cyrus didn't feel like taking a minute for himself. If anything, standing in a strange place with no clue what was going on around him would certainly add to his anxiety. He pulled off the straps with the hooks and let them fall to the floor. He freed his pistol and thumbed the hammer back. Oddly, he felt a smile come to his face. Having the gun in his hand was the first time he'd felt in control since he woke up. He was ready to do something he knew how to do—shoot things.

Cyrus looked out the doorway at the *Polk* and exhaled a breath he felt as though he'd been holding since he first put the transporter gear on. Across the way, he saw Daniel leaning against the mangled harpoon machine. He lifted both his hands and waved them in an odd gesture of excitement. Cyrus waved back and then snapped his pistol's chamber closed.

"Let's go see where everyone's gotten to," he said to Bethy as he started down the hall. He led the way toward the control room where he found their three missing companions standing outside double doors that led to the craft's interior. Zeke and Emmett pointed their guns at the doors, while Lowell seemed poised to open them.

Cyrus stopped at the corner and held out his hands to stop Bethy. He was worried the others were a bit too jumpy to be accepting visitors at the moment. "Lowell?" he shouted. "It's Cyrus and Bethy. Don't shoot."

"Please?" Bethy added.

They peered around the corner to see the men relax a little and lower their guns.

The room was silent. Cyrus prepared to scold them all for leaving he and Bethy to fend for themselves and dangle in the wind. Seeing the dead thing on the floor made him pause. He became aware of something breaking the silence as he chose his words. It was a light tapping and moaning coming from the other side of the doors.

"We're pretty sure there are more to come," Emmett said. "So don't get all in a bunch if you wanted to kill some of them yourself."

Zeke spit a line of tobacco onto the deck. "Yeah. Don't fret none. There should be plenty to go round."

Cyrus took his place in line and pointed his pistol at the doors as well. He hoped they'd make short work of whatever was left and get on with the process of landing this craft. Air travel was all well and good, but he'd had enough for the day. A nice little span of time on land would do him well.

"Bethy, stay back," he said.

"He's right. You need a gun?" Lowell asked.

She shook her head. "No thanks."

"Your choice." Lowell gripped the door handles and counted. "One...two...." On three he swung open the doors and moved himself out of the way.

Cyrus's trigger finger twitched but he didn't fire. The doors opened into a great salon with elegant couches in the middle and framed artwork on the walls. It was a stark contrast to the bare military metals of the *Polk's* interior. He thought how it would be a wonderful way to travel if there weren't so many bodies and so much blood. Other than that, it was grand.

The gold piping of the walls, bright against the muted reds of the carpet, contained a pattern that was echoed in the silver drink sets of the bar area. The brain matter on the walls was a negative, though. On the far side was another beautifully carved wooden door. This one had three zombies scratching and clawing at it.

The men said nothing. Lowell fired. Cyrus and the others followed his lead. Lowell probably felled them all himself, but the rest of them needed a release. The acrid smoke of gun powder quickly filled the room as the undead fell to the floor. The men stood for a moment in the aftermath.

Zeke was the first to move. "Look at this place." He got up close to a painting on the decorative walls. "This is prob'ly valuable. Look at it."

Cyrus exchanged a look with Lowell and got the impression that he didn't care for Zeke a whole lot.

Emmett stepped over a body, watching carefully to make sure it didn't get up as he passed. He walked carefully between the couches, bodies and tables toward the other door. He stopped and pointed at the various points on the floor. "Empty shells here…here…here. Someone put up a fight."

A thump came from the last door and it bulged out slightly, blocked by the lifeless bodies in front of it.

Zeke reloaded his gun quickly and used a couch for cover. "Another goddamn rotter. How many did they pack on this ship?"

The others focused their weapons on the door as well.

"Help me!" Someone shouted from the other side. The door bulged more and then opened enough for an arm to wedge its way out. "Is anyone out there?"

The arm found purchase on the bullet riddled door and managed to shove it open further. A battered and bloodied man stumbled out and stepped to the nearest couch before collapsing. "Thank God you've come."

Lowell stepped forward, gun still trained on the man. "Who are you? What the hell happened here?"

Cyrus kept his pistol pointed at the man's head as he looked him over. The blood that covered him was obviously his own, as he was still bleeding profusely from a shoulder wound.

"They call me Moose. Can someone get me a bandage, maybe a field kit? I think we can stop the bleeding," Moose said. He kept dabbing gingerly at the blood with his fingers. The tone in his voice wasn't panic or fear, but incredulity. He was fighting what he knew to be true and bargaining with the world for his salvation.

Cyrus looked over at Lowell and shook his head. There was no way the bleeding was going to stop.

"Did one of them bite you?" Emmett asked.

Moose swallowed hard and looked at his bleeding shoulder. "They were in the bedroom. All quiet. We were supposed to open the doors and get Mr. Preston and Mr. Cantolione when it was time to eat. They weren't in there."

Zeke moved from his cover and shoved his way forward. "They asked you if one of them chewers bit you, dammit. Now answer him."

"We opened the door and there they came. Not a one of us armed but the pilot. By the time he got in the room, four of these guys were bitten." Moose put his fingers close to the wound and looked at the blood he came away with. "Shit."

"So where are Cantolione and Preston?" Cyrus moved closer. There was movement out of his right eye and he saw Bethy leaning against one of the outer doors.

"Don't know. They were supposed to be in there."

Emmett slid quietly past Moose and entered the other room.

Moose started to cry, but his face still seemed fairly calm and resolute. "You're not going to leave me are you?"

The men exchanged looks before Lowell sighed and looked at his gun. "Moose, if one of them bit you, there's nothing we can do. We'll have to put you down."

Still crying, Moose shook his head adamantly. "You can't. I can help you. I know things. I know things." He reached to his back pocket and pulled out two photographs carefully folded into small squares. He started to unfold them, but moaned in pain as he did.

Emmett returned to the room in time to catch Moose's plea. "Nothing in the other room. Looks like another chewer out on the outer lounge, though." He stepped over to Moose who was still struggling. "Let me help." Emmett cautiously took the papers from the man and unfolded one of them. He stared at the image for a moment and furled his brow. "You got me. What is this thing?"

He passed the paper to Lowell, who then moved back to Zeke and Cyrus. The three men stared down at an image of a device with some tubes and dials. It was shaped like a huge bullet.

"A device that was being developed by Dr. Poley to help the Union end the war." Moose looked stiff and was going pale quickly.

"How did you get this?" Cyrus asked.

"I took it when we sent a prototype of the device through the Port of San Francisco about ten or so years back."

Emmett stepped up to look at the picture again. "That's about where and when the whole outbreak started."

"Where did this thing go from there?" Lowell asked.

"They loaded it on a big black government airship," Moose said. "Sent it to an Outpost called Two Thirteen. No idea what happened next." Moose was sweating terribly.

Cyrus looked at the others. His gaze swept over to Bethy. "Anyone here know anything about a big black government airship?"

Moose spasmed and coughed.

Zeke pushed past the others, placed his gun near Moose's head, and cocked the hammer. "Anything else important to tell us?"

Cyrus grabbed Zeke's arm. "Whoa, what are you doing?"

"Have you never dealt with what happens next?" Zeke asked. "He's darn close to being one of them right now. He's got to be taken care of, 'fore something bad happens."

"I know exactly what happens next," Cyrus said. "But for now, he's still a person."

Zeke spat tobacco on the floor, but kept his gun level. "Not for long."

Lowell shrugged his shoulders. "Better to take care of it now than later."

Moose realized what they meant to do and his eyes got bigger. "I've told you everything I told them. You can't kill me."

"Same things you told who?" Lowell asked.

"The same things I told Tom Preston, I swear. I swear. It's all I know. Preston's been asking about that thing, and I found him information on where it is. He wants to use it for the Sons of Grant for something."

The men nodded, and Cyrus knew it was time. He walked toward the control room and pulled Bethy along with him.

"I don't need protecting. I've seen this sort of thing before," Bethy said.

"Fine," Cyrus said. "Then come protect me. And maybe we can start signaling the *Polk*."

The events of the last several days came drifting back to him. He had to have a seat before his knees went weak.

"They have a signal light up here," Bethy said. "We could do code with the *Polk*." She had already picked up a match and was striking it when a shot rang out from the other room. Cyrus was startled by the noise, and Bethy snapped the match in half. She tossed the pieces away and pulled another one from a box by the signal.

Cyrus stared at the *Polk* and marveled at the gap between the two ships. He was astounded that he'd come across that distance dangling from a hook with a woman clinging desperately to him. He was floored he'd made the distance at all.

"What do you want me to tell them?" Bethy asked. She had already lit the lamp and was flipping the hinge to make sure it worked. It creaked at first, but loosened up after a few tries.

"Start by telling them we're all in decent shape. Everyone made it."

Bethy flipped the gate on the lamp a few more times and then paused. "They're signaling back, we've got their attention." She signaled a few more times as she talked. "Looks like Cashe is operating the signal over there. He says he's glad to know everyone's good. Wants to know the situation?"

There were footsteps on the deck behind them. Lowell stepped into the room. "Tell them we all need to get together to talk face-to-face," he said. "He'll never believe what we have to tell him if you signal it to him. We need to have a conversation with him."

After a few seconds of silence, Bethy turned to them. "He doesn't have a good place for both of us to set down in the mountains. We'll have to land in the morning, once we cross."

Lowell nodded.

"Wait, there's more." Bethy concentrated on the flashing light coming from the *Polk* for a minute and laughed. "He wants to know if you remember enough about flying to keep *The Moon and the Stars* in the air that long without hitting a mountain."

"Hilarious," Lowell said.

Cyrus liked a joke as much as the next guy, but wondered exactly what Lowell's competence level was with flying a ship like *The Moon*.

"Zeke and Emmett are dragging bodies out to the back sun deck and tossing them overboard," Lowell said. "If we're meant to use this vessel for a while, we wanted to have it smell slightly more pleasant." He grabbed the ankles of the zombie they shot in the control room and pulled it toward the lounge.

Cyrus looked around at the blood and carnage. He took in the destroyed furniture and bullet holes in a couple of instruments and wondered exactly how much more "home-y" tossing the dead overboard was going to make it.

30

"They'll be fine out there," Cashe said. "And you'll be safe here, I assure you." He noticed that Lucinda had been spending a lot of her time staring out the window at *The Moon*.

"Whatever's going on over there, my men can certainly handle it," he said. "And Cyrus surely seems like the type that can take care of himself."

"Oh, he can take care of himself all right," she said. "In a fair fight, on his terms. He's just not used to airships and flying and he's certainly not accustomed to swinging on a string between high-flying ships while dangling on a hook."

"I would imagine falling out of an airship is new to him as well?" Cashe asked, hoping to bring a smile to her face. He succeeded.

"I'm fairly sure he hasn't been off the Turtle in nearly two years. The rest of the crew usually went to town for supplies and to round up new clients." Her smile faded a little at the mention of the Turtle. "Cyrus usually stayed on board and worked his magic with whatever repairs were needed before the next crossing."

"How long have you been on his crew?" Cashe put his foot up on the console to make himself more comfortable.

"Nearly a year."

The information sunk in for a moment. "So, the two of you are…?"

"Cyrus is my unexpected guardian angel," she said. "He's a self-appointed shield from all the bad in the world. We stumbled across each other at a certain point when I needed help, and I've been indebted to him ever since." She looked back toward *The Moon*. "What was your question again?"

"Nothing. Never mind," Cashe said. He could tell she was being honest, that she and Cyrus were some kind of friends, but Cashe could see there was something else there. He couldn't tell if her feelings were mere fondness for the man, or something more, a longing, a desire.

"So where do you come from?" Cashe asked.

Lucinda shrugged. "No idea where I was born. My parents moved around a lot. Dad was a rifle maker, so he did work for whoever would pay the best. When the war started up, he got a job with Winchester. We lived in Norwich, Connecticut, near their factory for a bit, so I usually say that's where I'm from."

"So, you're a Northerner?"

Again, Lucinda shrugged. "I guess *you* could say that. *I* never would. But you could."

Cashe couldn't care less where she was from. His crew was made up of such a motley mix of nationalities by now that one more on either side of the issue wouldn't tip the scales one way or another. "I won't, then. How would that be?"

"Kind of you." She grew quiet then.

Cashe used the time to check his bearing and altitude. He pretended to check a number of other things, just to look busy. Just to keep from staring.

"You really want us on your crew?" she asked after a while.

Cashe looked out the window over to *The Moon and the Stars*. Most of the lights had gone out. "If your friend Cyrus is dumb enough to do what he just did, he'll fit right in with the rest of the men. Did you have some other plan in mind on what you were going to do next?"

"Hadn't really planned on the Turtle going bad, so I'm at a loss. Cyrus had an idea for later. He didn't tell me, but he said something about making things better once we got this last group of passengers across the country. He talked about family in Ireland, but I don't know if or how he planned on getting there."

Cashe busied himself with the controls. Lucinda might have agreed to join the O.M.O., but she didn't seem sure of it now. He couldn't even be sure he wanted her to be on the ship when he truly thought about it. He felt the need to suck in his gut too much. Cashe mulled over ideas in his head, but couldn't figure how Cyrus had planned on making it better for the two of them.

The hatch opened and Daniel entered the control room. "The boys detached the harpoon over there and we gathered it in to the *Polk*," he said. He held a cup in his hands and took a drink before he went on. "We're working on fixing the launcher, but it looks pretty grim."

"Thanks," Cashe said.

Lucinda reached out and touched Daniel's arm as he passed by her. "Daniel? Mr. Cashe and I were just discussing why I should join the O.M.O. Help me out. Why'd you get involved?"

It was obvious that Daniel had to force himself to keep the smile on his face. "It's a long story."

"I've got time."

"Fine, ma'am," Daniel said. He leaned back against the doorframe and sighed. "One day, a man came to my town."

Cashe chuckled.

"What?" Lucinda said. "Is something funny?"

"A lot of men ended up soldiers because a man came to town," Cashe said. He hadn't come by that experience himself, but he'd heard enough to know it was common among soldiers on both sides.

Daniel nodded. "This man started talking about pride and country. About being a man and doing what's right. He talked about how easy it was going to be to defeat the Graybacks. He made it sound so beautiful and romantic. So I lied about my age, signed the papers right there and then. I was 14 years old. Could barely tell my ass from a hole in the ground."

"Still can't," Cashe said.

Even Daniel chuckled.

"I was at the battles of Chancellorsville, Chattanooga and Cold Harbor," Daniel continued. "It wasn't beautiful. There was nothing poetic or exciting about it. It was brutal. It was ugly. And from the moment I pulled that trigger for the first time at Fort Pulaski, I wanted out. When the armistice happened, I went home to Maine and sat down on my parent's porch. My mother and father had passed away. My friends were gone. And then another man came to town, with a crowd following him. This time he was looking for volunteers to go fight the damn chewers out West. 'Cept, there weren't any young men left in town. They started rounding up the former soldiers who'd been discharged. Forced a bunch of them back into service. When they knocked on my door, I was gone. I ran. Hell, I wasn't even twenty-five yet. I wasn't going back into the trenches and fields again."

It was quiet in the room while that sunk in. Cashe was well aware of the man's past; it was one of the reasons Cashe liked him.

"One day Mr. Cashe found me running through an open field, being chased by soldiers and dogs bent on dragging me back. He offered me a job with no questions asked."

Lucinda looked at Cashe. "You just picked him up and took him on?"

"I couldn't stand to see such talents wasted in the trenches," he said with a smile. "Speaking of talents, why don't you call it a night and get some rest?"

"Well, I'd best clean up down in the hold," Daniel said. "I need some rack time, if I can get it, but I hate to leave a mess."

"Suit yourself."

Both Cashe and Lucinda returned his good night and settled into their chairs.

"You'll want to get some sleep, too," Cashe said. "Could be a busy day tomorrow." He didn't know why, but he felt the need to reassure her. Maybe it was something in her eyes—the downcast gaze. She looked like she could break down at any time. "You'll be perfectly safe in the bunk we set up for you."

Her gaze fixed on *The Moon*. "Yeah. I'm not too worried about the crew breaking in on me. I don't know them, but I trust you." She stood, patted Cashe on the shoulder and walked slowly out of the control room. "You *seem* like a good man, anyway."

As her soft footsteps got quieter, Cashe exhaled and released his gut. He looked over at the other ship, its outline defined by the moonlight. He decided he'd have to have a talk with Cyrus at some point. Cashe knew himself very well, knew his own limitations and failures, but he wasn't truly sure what he was beginning to feel for Lucinda. Regardless, it was best to meet things head on and have all the information available before running into a wall he didn't see coming.

31

Cyrus and the men found some fancy silken blankets in the bedroom area and brought them out into the control room, where they set up billets to sleep on for the night. They could also keep whoever was at the helm company if they needed it. It could be a long night.

Bethy set up a makeshift bed in the lounge, more for appearances than anything else. Cyrus was sure she wasn't the type that worried about anyone commenting on a lady sleeping in the same room with the men. She lay in the doorway and listened in on the men's conversation. She was still close enough to get in some good barbs when she felt the need. Cyrus could see her eyes fluttering from time to time, but she fought to keep awake, for the sake of being one of the guys.

It fell silent for a bit, long enough that Cyrus began to believe that everyone had gone to sleep. He looked up to a window and watched the clouds roll by with the light of the moon glancing off the glass. He wondered if Lucinda was comfortable on the *Polk*, and if Cashe was treating her well. She could take care of herself, but still he wondered.

"What do you think this Dr. Poley's machine does?" Bethy whispered.

"If the Union built it to end the war, it can't be anything good," Zeke said. "Probably some ungodly hell that goes against nature."

There was a laugh from Lowell. "You saying the South wouldn't have tried anything and everything to wipe us out? That seems a bit disingenuous."

"We'd have won at Gettysburg if it weren't for the fire you rebels rained from those airships," Emmett said. "That was a weapon that went against God if ever I saw one."

The casual comment got Zeke riled up. "That's what I'm sayin. You fellas were looking for some payback, looking to make the next weapon worse, more terrible. I was just a soldier, I didn't ask for anything of the sort. Me and my regiment coulda taken on the Union with our hands behind our backs and nothin' but bayonets."

"You were at Gettysburg?" Emmett asked.

"Sure was." Zeke cast a suspicious eye back at Emmett. "Were you?"

"Nope. I was laid up at a hospital in Washington about then, recovering from a musket ball wound."

Cyrus realized that Zeke was the only Southern soldier on *The Moon and the Stars* at the moment. He could see how the man might get defensive and lash out at the Yankees that surrounded him.

"How 'bout you Lowell? You make it there?" Zeke asked.

Propping himself up on his elbows, Lowell gave Zeke a hard look. "Yeah. I was at Gettysburg. Both times."

It got quiet again and Zeke looked away, his anger immediately subsiding.

"The fight was bad enough the first time. You Southerners were hell. But, I'll tell you what, I would've welcomed those rebel airships and the fire they spit all over the battlefield five years later when the chewer hordes came to Gettysburg. You see the way those monsters walk real slow and you think they're an easy kill, but when there are so many of them and they're coming from every direction at the same time…" Lowell trailed off. "We were all so weary from the way the war was dragging on and the relentless fighting, that we were undermanned and ill-equipped to get into that battle. It was unbelievable the things that happened that day. They didn't rest. They didn't take time to reload. They just kept coming."

The thrum of the engines filled the room as everyone let it sink in.

"I was four years old during the battle of Gettysburg," Bethy said. "So don't bother to ask me if I was there."

Everyone laughed.

"Oh and here we thought you were tough," Emmett said. "Let a little thing like childhood stop you from fighting? Shameful."

The men all chuckled at the jibe.

Cyrus laughed as well, but realized that with Bethy's joke, it left him as the only one who hadn't accounted for his military exploits. It would mean he would either have to lie and say he'd seen combat, or explain why he'd dodged service like a coward. He decided to try to avoid the question as best he could.

"So, if you all fought on opposite sides," he said, "how'd you ever get together on this ship?" It was a legitimate question, in addition to being a distraction.

"Hell, once they signed the treaty things happened pretty fast," Lowell said. "We all turned our gun sights from each other to the chewers."

"Most everyone," Emmett said.

"I'm sure you know how hard grudges die, Cyrus," Lowell said.

Cyrus was fully aware of some people who would love to do him and Lucinda in, and vice-versa.

"Yeah, well, the treaty enforcement folks quickly discovered that too," Lowell said. "They found out the hard way that they couldn't just send out a piece of paper saying we were done with the fighting and expect people to go along with it."

"They started asking for volunteers to join up with the United Nations as peace keepers and I think each one of us raised our hand," Zeke said. "Personally, I just wanted to see some fighting. I didn't really care who it was."

"That's beautiful, Zeke," Bethy said. "Your patriotism brings a tear to my eye."

Zeke rolled over with a chuckle.

"Some of us didn't join up right away, but Cashe was pretty persuasive," Lowell said. "Okay men. We'd best get some rest."

"I'm beat," Cyrus said.

"What? You get tired just hanging out of an airship and killing a few chewers? You may have joined the wrong crew." Bethy rearranged her bedding and turned toward the other room.

Later, in the silence of the cabin the ship listed gently to one side. There was the occasional blink of a light near the bow, but otherwise darkness permeated the room. Bethy took her turn at the controls.

Cyrus looked at the men all strung out on the floor, taking their own space as they slept. Emmett snored.

A sigh brought his gaze to Bethy, who was standing on a box, both hands firmly on the steering wheel. She looked ready to fall asleep on her feet and the grip on the controls was the only thing keeping her up.

"Ready to switch?" Cyrus asked.

She looked down at him with a drowsy smile. "Just started, really."

"Still."

"I'll be fine," she said.

Cyrus lifted himself up on his elbows. "I can keep you company if you like, talk a bit."

A slight smile came to Bethy's face. "Talking? Sounds more likely to put me to sleep than keep me awake."

"Saying I'm dull?"

When she didn't respond, Cyrus decided to press forward. "What do you do around here? For the O.M.O., I mean?"

The smile left Bethy's face. "I ain't the company whore, if that's what you're asking."

Cyrus felt his face grow hot. "That's not...I mean...I didn't...." The conversation stopped. He wondered what led to that reaction from her.

Across the room, Zeke snorted laughter and rolled over.

32

In a fairly expensive hotel called The Heron on the Santa Rosa waterfront, Tom looked out at the ocean and thought about the rapid onset of strange ideas like giant monsters and deadly devices. Far out on the water, a single light from a ship bobbed on the waves over and over again without advancing. Tom wondered what people would pay to see a ten- or twenty-foot lizard. And how that kind of money could fill the void of everything the Sons of Grant had recently drained from Cantolione.

Tom felt bad about what he was doing to the old man from time to time, but in general it didn't matter a whit. He was righting a wrong for the good of the country, and every good citizen should be proud to do his bit to make the nation whole again. Of course, if that were entirely true, he could just ask Cantolione for the money.

What baffled Tom the most about the whole situation was his boss's insistence on pursing the animals. The possibility that he could round up some beasts and make a pittance off them was the dumbest option he could think of in the grand scheme of things. A weapon made so much more sense. A weapon *always* made more sense.

The door opened and Cantolione stepped in rubbing his hands together for warmth. "Everything's in order. Bell managed to round up a few extra crew members for the boat and workers to help load. There's about twenty all told. Should be plenty to herd a couple of oversized salamanders into a cargo hold."

Tom nodded. "Good. That was quick. Any reason you decided to take to the water instead of using an airship?"

With a smile Cantolione said, "We're after some serious quarry here. We don't have an airship big enough."

"I see," Tom said.

"It's going to cost a bit. They were pretty reluctant to go."

"You'll make it all back, sir." Tom smiled. If there was a way to make money off the strange creatures, his boss would find it and exploit it and reinvent it and make more from it.

"I'm counting on it."

Tom stared at the man. There was something in his tone that made him wonder whether Cantolione had already checked his bank ledgers in order to pay off the captain. Was the man's wry smile there to hide what he knew? Did the bank deny him money already and expose the accountant's malfeasance? For a moment Tom feared there would be hired thugs in the hall waiting to burst in and grab him.

The two men got quiet and watched out the window. Tom became surer of the man he'd worked so closely with and started a mental countdown. He knew that Cantolione couldn't let a good silence go and would have to start talking to fill the void. It was the case for as long as they'd known each other.

"It'll take about a day," Cantolione said, "to get out to the island and the area where they say these things tend to congregate."

Tom grunted acknowledgement and waited.

It was silent for another minute.

"The captain of the ship is quite a character." Cantolione pulled a piece of paper from his pocket. "Shaggy looking gent. Terrible hygiene, but seems to know his way around. You should hear him talk about these lizards. Like he's some sort of scientist, talking about their plumes and their ridges. But he didn't want to talk about this big one that Moose character mentioned. What was it? The Dragon? Gotta be a bunch of malarkey. There's no creature that big that I don't know about."

Tom raised his eyebrows and nodded. "I'll come get you at first light, sir. We should leave as early as possible."

"Probably best." Cantolione waved and shut the door silently behind him.

Tom thought about the old man for a moment and marveled at how malleable he was. The ease at which Cantolione's bank account was drained was becoming less of a mystery. Tom felt stupid worrying about getting caught, at least by his boss. Cantolione was open to Tom's every suggestion. The only problems between them were when they were in public. It was easy to "advise" the man when there were others around, but it was hard to say no. Tom couldn't look like he was contradicting Mr. Cantolione to the world at large, so when the man gave a command, there was little recourse.

Tom was more than ready to make the break with Cantolione and head out as the leader of the Sons of Grant. But truthfully, Tom wasn't really excited about leaving the plush environs of the city for a life living in the hills and the forests in tents and under tarps. The true test would come when the Sons of Grant attacked the outpost. Their success could provide the catalyst for sweeping change in the country, but their failure would most certainly spell an untimely end for the Sons. Tom had sunk much of their resources and the money they'd pilfered into various aspects of the attack. Most of their able-bodied men were risking their lives to take the device. If they failed, were killed or captured, the recruiting efforts would take a hit, as would the organization's reputation. There was a chain of bribes that proved fruitful in getting the name of a soldier at the outpost who would help them. Then, of course, the series of messages via telegraph. Finalizing the plan had cost him dearly.

He hoped it was all worth it. They had a lot to lose over a weapon that might not even work. And if it did, he had no idea what it would do. He'd heard Dr. Poley's name in certain circles, and he hoped the legendary status imbued on the man wasn't just talk.

33

In the early hours of the morning before sunrise there was a clicking sound in *The Moon's* cabin. Cyrus awoke to see Lowell at the controls and Bethy clicking away at the signal light, messaging the *Polk*.

"Morning, sleepyhead," Bethy said without turning. "There's bacon and eggs frying up in the galley and fresh coffee's almost ready in the dining area."

Cyrus rubbed his eyes, a newfound respect for the soldiers' abilities to carry on in the direst of circumstances. "Really?"

"No." Bethy's tone remained steady.

"Shit, you just don't learn, do you, boy?" Zeke walked by Cyrus with a giggle on his way to show Lowell a map.

"Good," Lowell told Zeke. "We shouldn't have a problem with that. Hey, Bethy? Tell them there's a spot three or four miles east of the location they mentioned. The mountains'll give us some shielding from the wind and provide a decent calm."

"Right. The valley to the east. Got it," Bethy replied.

As everyone moved around in preparation, Cyrus got up and found the facilities. He splashed some water on his face and ran some through his hair to tame it. He straightened the shirt a little but it was still a mess. He'd pretty much forgotten that he was wearing an O.M.O. uniform under his coat. It wasn't something he'd ever considered—joining a team. His reflection in the mirror almost looked like someone else. A soldier for one of the armies, maybe? Didn't matter. They'd get off at the next real port of call and start scraping money together however they could. He wasn't really one for taking orders or following anyone else's lead. Besides, he saw where not being a leader got the crew of his Turtle.

He heard activity nearby and tossed a towel aside after drying his hands and face. He stretched his arms as high as he could to work out the kinks. The hard floor had seriously played havoc with his muscles and he felt sore as soon as he'd stood up. While getting his bearings, he felt the ship tilt a little and the engines rev up as they corrected their course.

In the control room, Lowell waved Cyrus over. "We're almost to the rendezvous point. When we get there, you and I are going to go down and talk to Cashe and decide our next move. I'm sure he'll want someone to stay with *The Moon*, but I've got no clue where any of us are going, though I'll be fascinated to find out what he has to say about this device."

Cyrus nodded. "Should be very interesting." If this device was anything as terrible as it sounded, he wondered exactly who would take charge of it now that the states were united, or at least friendly with each other. If one side or another took it, it could change the balance and start the hostilities all over again.

"Bethy will lower us down and bring us back up," Lowell said. "Emmett and Zeke will keep the ship steady and watch out for any unfriendlies or chewers."

"When you say 'lower' and 'bring us back up'…." Cyrus had a fleeting attack of panic at the thought of the last time he was hung from a rope with this crew.

Bethy laughed. "You are jumpy as all get out. Don't worry. It's just a winch raising and lowering a basket. Nothing to it." She patted him patronizingly on the shoulder. "In all the time I've known you, have I ever let you fall?"

"Aren't we going to land?" Cyrus asked. "I thought we talked about landing."

"We just can't find the room yet," Lowell said. "No problem, we'll just get you guys down and bring you up, if we need to. If Cashe wants us to land, we'll do it, but for now it's just a quick talk."

Their arrival did not go unnoticed. Cyrus was fairly sure that everyone that wasn't involved in making sure the *Polk* didn't crash was watching out a porthole or window of the ship as Bethy lowered he and Lowell down in the tiny bucket that barely held the two men's legs. Cashe, who was waiting on the ground already, held out his hand and personally pulled them in.

"You two look none the worse for wear," Cashe said.

Exhaustion prevented Cyrus from any nasty comments, but Lowell had no such problems. "Look closer, sir. We're worse for wear. You just can't see past my stony facade," he said. "But the worse is in there somewhere."

Cashe laughed and took the satchel Lowell shoved at him.

Cyrus spotted Lucinda waving from the ship high above. He smiled to her and she shook her head, long hair whipping about in the wind. He knew her exasperated look even at this distance. It wasn't unexpected—he was exasperated with himself. He could've avoided the last day on *The Moon and the Stars*, if he hadn't felt goaded by Lowell and become so over-protective. In trying to prove his might, he placed himself in the spot farthest away from where he could most help her. Of course, she'd been fine while he was gone, just as she'd been every time she'd been out of his sight in the last several years.

It didn't stop him from thinking he wouldn't be around the time she finally did need him.

The picture of Dr. Poley's device was already in Cashe's hand when Cyrus started paying attention again. The look on Cashe's face told Cyrus everything he needed to know.

"So, you've seen this thing before?" Lowell asked.

Cashe nodded and his face grew grave. "Yes."

"A man on *The Moon* seemed to think the device was important. Called it the North's war-ender," Cyrus said.

"That's how it was billed." Cashe handed the photo back to Lowell and took a glance at the other pictures he had of the lizards. "Those chewers ended the war, though. This thing never got a chance to see action. I took a few crates over to Two Thirteen as well. I don't see how it all fits."

"Other than the fact that all of them came into the same port, I don't think they *are* related," Cyrus said. "Just one guy we happened to come across with a wealth of odd information."

"Anything else?" Cashe asked.

"Fella mentioned Tom Preston as a Sons of Grant leader," Lowell said. "He also mentioned Cantolione, but not as a member of the Sons."

"That's no coincidence," Cashe said. "It lines up with what one of our informants is saying as well. Preston seems to be stealing money out of Cantolione's pockets to build up the Sons. We have some things to speak with that particular gentleman about. Starting with the explosion at the dam."

"Agreed," Cyrus said.

"How're the accommodations on *The Moon and the Stars*?" Cashe asked, his mood still dour.

"Shitty," Lowell said.

"They made their way up to shitty once we threw all the corpses out the window," Cyrus said. "They were horrifying before that." He wanted to spit but thought better of it.

"Think you could deal with them for another night or two? I think we should all set a course for Outpost Two Thirteen and try to find a couple of missing pieces. It would be a waste of time to shuffle crew now. If we keep everyone where they are, we can get a jump on the morning." Cashe looked to the two men.

"You look a little worried," Lowell said.

"I just want to make sure that those devices are where they're supposed to be. If they fall into the wrong hands, it could be disastrous."

Cyrus didn't want to go back on that terrible vessel again and started to open his mouth to say so.

Anticipating the argument, Lowell raised his hand to calm Cyrus. "It would take a couple of hours to move everyone around and get things moving," Lowell said. "The faster we get underway, the faster this is over."

"Are a couple of hours going to matter here?" Cyrus asked. He didn't like Lowell's gloved hand hushing him. "What's the rush?"

Lowell tilted his head and adopted a blank tone. "If you want to go back on the *Polk* with Cashe and Lucinda, that's fine. We really don't need your help here." He turned to Cashe to finish his thought. "I mean, it's not like he's one of us, or has any clue how to handle an aircraft."

The mention of Lucinda riled Cyrus. He rolled his eyes and caught a smile on Cashe's face that suggested he knew exactly what Lowell was doing. He was goading Cyrus again and Cashe knew it.

"You can do whatever you want, Cyrus. We could use you either place." Cashe started toward the large tub that served as the basket for the *Polk*.

Cyrus sighed as he felt his choices being made for him. "How many days?"

"Two, tops." Lowell laughed.

As they stood there for a moment, the bucket to *The Moon and the Stars* began to rise slowly. Both men looked up but Bethy was nowhere in sight.

"Girl's in a hurry. Must want to get underway pretty bad herself." Lowell grabbed the edge of the bucket and tried to hold it in place so they could get in.

"Long as she doesn't dump us midway up." Cyrus quickly got himself situated and helped Lowell as the bucket ascended without pause.

The Moon and the Stars was some two hundred feet above, keeping itself in the shadow of the *Polk*, whose main carriage was another one hundred feet above that.

"And don't talk shit," Cyrus said. "If you need my help, ask for it. Don't try to goad me at every turn."

The basket twisted a little in the wind as it climbed. Cyrus gripped the rope as hard as he could and watched the ground get farther away.

"There's a chance that Corrigan over on the *Polk* challenged Bethy and Zeke to a race or something and they're all trying to get moving," Lowell said.

"Fine, let's move." Cyrus gave Lowell a glance, the man so close, with his hands gripping the rope loosely. He wondered why this particular person made him so insecure when it came to Lucinda, why it even mattered.

The basket shuddered, and he hugged the rope with both arms. There were no safety harnesses or belts, no safety equipment of any kind and he knew that his arms and hands were the only things keeping him securely in place.

The Moon and the Stars grew closer, but Cyrus still couldn't see anyone guiding the ropes as they rose.

Several hundred yards away, Cashe rose with stoic efficiency and even appeared to be leaning back in his roomy little gondola as he moved closer to the *Polk*. It was at that moment that Cyrus realized he should've been riding with Cashe. He knew he was riled into staying with *The Moon and the Stars*, but it never occurred to him that he didn't belong on the vessel. He had no business with Zeke and Emmett, let alone Lowell. And he couldn't stop putting his foot in his mouth with Bethy. It was a bad situation and it took him dangling at the end of a rope for the second day in a row for him to realize that and to discover that all he wanted was Lucinda. Not in the sense of a lover or a bride, but for the familiarity. She'd been a constant fixture on the Turtle. He had checked in on her each morning and each night, eaten dinner and every other meal in her presence and now his life was full of uncertainty.

Lowell nudged him and yelled, "Here we go." He pointed up to the winch that wound them closer to the airship. "Get ready."

Cyrus was ready. "I'll grab the bar—you hang onto the rope to stay steady," he yelled. Lowell nodded.

Cyrus prepared to grab onto the wide doorframe of the cargo hold, but hoped Bethy and the others would be there to assist, considering he'd never done it and there was nothing below them but open air and solid ground. When the basket got high enough for the men to see, the hold was empty and the machinery lifted them unattended. Cyrus reached out and pulled them close enough that they could flop themselves down onto the deck and Lowell quickly got up and turned the machinery off before it pulled the bucket into the gears.

Both men stood up slowly, scanning the dark recesses of the small hold. There were just a few boxes and pieces of equipment scattered about, but not enough to obscure the men's views. With a fluid motion, Lowell reached into his jacket and pulled a small derringer.

The wide golden buttons of the dark heavy uniform jacket hampered Cyrus's own attempt to get to his weapon, but he managed to pull it—dropping the coat to the deck as he did.

Both men stood listening for a clue as to what was happening.

"Let's head up toward the deck," Lowell said.

Cyrus's foot hit the first stair and he heard the raised voices of an argument from somewhere above. He made out Zeke's deep voice easily and soon he recognized Emmett as well. Bethy's higher pitch interjected once, as far as he could tell. He glanced at Lowell and soon both were taking the stairs two at a time.

They took the short corridor that opened to the control room and stopped as soon as they made it in. Before them, on either side of the steering controls, were Zeke and Emmett, each pointing their gun in the other's face. Bethy stood a few feet away pointing at the men and yelling for them to put the guns down.

"Jesus, boys, what the hell is going on up—" Lowell's words were cut off as two shots rang out nearly simultaneously. Both of the men jerked backward and fell to the deck in a spray of blood.

"Good God," Cyrus said and ran to Emmett while Lowell dropped to Zeke's side. Bethy fell silent.

It was quickly apparent to Cyrus that Emmett would not be getting up, the bullet from Zeke's gun had torn away the upper left side of the man's head and he'd stopped breathing by the time Cyrus had gotten to him.

Across the room was a different story. Zeke writhed on the deck, a high-pitched airy sort of sound coming from him. Lowell was doing his best to keep him still, but Emmett's bullet had pierced Zeke's throat and gone out the other side. Blood seeped from him at an alarming rate. Cyrus glanced around the room for something to help stop the blood and saw a coat hanging on a hook by the door. He grabbed it and pulled at it, trying to make something small enough to be usable. He decided it would be easiest to tear the lining out. He folded it and handed it to Lowell.

"I thought they were kidding at first," Bethy said. "They *were* kidding at first. I didn't think anything of it, but then...." She swallowed and took a deep breath.

"It's all right," Lowell said absently.

"They started arguing over who was going to steer the ship." She looked down at Zeke. "That's all. It was stupid. What can I do?" Bethy said in a whispered croak.

As he pressed the cloth to Zeke's throat, Lowell looked up at Bethy with a lost expression.

"See if you can signal the *Polk*," Cyrus said. "Try to get them to stop." It was all that came to Cyrus's mind. In the midst of the chaos, he knew he didn't want to be left to fend with half the crew they started with. He wanted to go back to being a guest rather than a soldier.

Bethy backed up a step but her eyes remained fixed on Zeke.

"Go," Lowell shouted.

Bethy took one last look and began working the signal lights with trembling hands.

34

Cashe knew the question before it came.

"Where's Cyrus?" Lucinda asked. She was looking around Cashe to the hold behind him.

"They uncovered a few things on *The Moon* that I thought we should act on immediately, so he volunteered to stay behind," Cashe said. To say he was goaded into staying back sounded a bit callous. "We're setting a course for a strategic base in Nevada, not far off. We'll all meet up there and sort things out." When he saw the slightly disappointed look on her face, he added, "Don't worry. Bethy'll keep an eye on him, make sure he stays out of harm's way."

Lucinda nodded and fell into step with Cashe as he walked the hall toward the control room. "I'm sure he can watch after himself, to be honest. He rarely needs anyone's help in that regard."

The tone of her comments could've easily been sarcasm or jealousy, Cashe wasn't sure, but he decided to leave it alone. "I'm sure he can, ma'am."

After a few steps, Lucinda spoke up again. "So what's the new information that we need to get to work on so quickly that we couldn't stop and take a breath?"

"I'm about to get everyone together and talk about it. Looks like something I transported back in the war is making a reappearance and I'm curious as to why it's showing again at this particular time. Outpost Two Thirteen was a covert Union station that worked on science stuff."

"Science stuff?"

"Technical term." Cashe smiled. "They were trying to develop new weapons, transportation, gadgets and doo hickeys for the North to win the war. They came up with a few good things. That Turtle you were living on, for instance. That was one of their early innovations. The Amsterdam Cannon was another. Don't know if you're familiar with that one."

"I'm not."

They'd reached the control room stairs and Cashe gripped the railing, reminding him of another major breakthrough. "And the *Polk*, of course. There were a number of intelligent men that adapted ideas to the building of dirigibles, but the group at Two Thirteen managed to put together the salient points to get this thing off the ground. Three decks of living and cargo space - they fashioned the new metal structure that makes it light enough to lift off without a problem, added to the engine power by refining the standard steam ratio. The *Polk* is probably the largest airship you'll ever see due to the things they came up with. They helped design a few others, but the *Polk* is the best there is." Cashe patted the railing as he ascended. "She's everything we could've hoped for and more."

"Would you like me to leave you alone with her?" Lucinda said.

"Funny."

"What else have these geniuses come up with?"

"A lot of it's been hush-hush. If all goes well, we'll get a tour of their labs and warehouse when we get there. Hopefully they won't pull that classified information routine when we ask. We're all on the same side now, right?"

Lucinda smiled and started back down the corridor. "Sure we are."

35

Tom and Cantolione made their way onto the sailing vessel *Effortless* early and were whisked to their quarters. It seemed the crew didn't want them underfoot when they were making preparations to get underway. A particularly nasty sailor named Devers barked at them as though they'd been shanghaied into service somewhere in the Orient. Cantolione made some rebuttals about being in charge, but Devers just laughed.

There were calm seas most of the day and the ship rocked smoothly with the waves. In the cabin, Tom folded his hands behind his head and looked up at the steel ceiling above him. Even though the bunk they'd provided was uncomfortable and the blankets smelled of fish and sweat, he'd managed to make up for a few hours of lost sleep. Cantolione left on a mission to find out where his trunk full of food had been delivered, so he could eat a decent meal instead of what he referred to as "the God-forsaken swill" the crew had to eat. True, the food was deplorable, but Tom had gotten used to much worse in the army. The things they'd made to sustain themselves on the battlefield were horrendous, but he'd lived through it. It seemed Cantolione hadn't had a similar experience. He was used to having things his way, and that included lightly browned toast and freshly squeezed orange juice, even at sea.

As Tom snickered at the thought of the consummate showman having to eat with the commoners, he heard shouting on the decks above and the sounds of men scrambling about. He pulled out his pocket watch and found that there was no way they could be approaching the islands already. He sat up and dropped himself to the deck reluctantly. He didn't really want to be pressed into service if there was some emergency—he wasn't much for pitching in to help—but if the ship was sinking, he certainly didn't want to be the last to know.

Tom pulled on his shoes and stepped out into the corridor. It was louder out there, with shouting and clanging. He followed the sounds up one stairway and then another to the cool air of the open deck. Here, men were rushing to starboard and Cantolione was in the middle of them. He waved Tom over when he saw him.

"Tom, look. Look over there," Cantolione said, pointing. "This could be exciting."

Tom looked in the direction indicated, but could see nothing but rolling waves on the black sea. Dark clouds drifted in the pale light of morning, but otherwise, he saw nothing. "What?"

"There's a ship of some sort."

"So?"

Cantolione pointed to a man perched high above them with a spyglass. "Their lookout says the boat appears to be one called the *USS Grand Rapids*. It was a supply ship for the North."

Even squinting, Tom couldn't make it out. "Again, I have to ask—So?"

"The men claim the ship has been missing for nearly a year."

"Due back in port last October." Bell, the captain, was standing with the others and butted in on the men's conversation. "It wasn't the first to go missing out this way, just the most recent."

Tom looked over at the captain, suddenly concerned. "Wait. You said a number of ships disappeared, but I thought you meant a decade ago, when this all first started. You didn't say anything about this still happening."

"It's been ongoing," the captain said. "I mentioned it to Mr. Cantolione when he hired us."

Cantolione shrugged. "We're well-prepared for whatever comes our way. No matter."

Tom gritted his teeth. "Still would've been nice to know about the potential danger beforehand." He realized finally where the men were indicating and was surprised he didn't see the ship sooner. It was a dark shadow that stood out plainly against the sky when the waves lifted it up in the air. It drifted sideways into the oncoming sea, shaking with the force of the strongest waves. The *Grand Rapids* was a large cargo ship, its hull rusting, and its flags in tatters.

"We're sending some people to check it out," the captain said. "I'll have Devers lead a party."

"What? We don't have time for that," Cantolione said. "I hired this ship for one job and one job only. Nowhere in our discussion did we talk about stopping for anything along the way. Don't get me wrong—I understand the allure. This is a wonderfully intriguing mystery that would be exciting to explore, but we have an agreement."

Behind the captain, several crewmembers were packing equipment into two rowboats.

"We have an agreement, yes," the captain said. "I'm modifying it a bit." He walked over to the rowboats and looked through the bags, taking an inventory.

"Modifying it? Modifying it?" Cantolione was gathering wind and Tom leaned against the rail to see what came next. He wasn't getting involved. While he agreed with his boss, he found it crazy to start a fight with a man that had a crew of fifty heavily armed men on his side. It didn't seem there was any way the outcome could be pleasant. Especially when that argument was taking place on a boat in the middle of the ocean. There was no retreat and no chance of a friend showing up to help.

"All due respect, Mr. Cantolione," the captain said. "If I can recover that boat and its cargo for the government, there might be a nice little reward in it for me. Of course, if the cargo is pleasant enough, I may hang on to it for myself and add the ship to my own fleet." He smiled at Cantolione in a way that made Tom uncomfortable. "Either way, the reward would be greater than anything you're paying me. So, I'm sending some men to check it out. If they can, they'll get the boiler going and head back to port with it. We'll get back underway in a matter of hours. We won't be far behind, and we'll make the island by nightfall."

Tom watched Cantolione, waited for the uncontrolled retort that would follow. His boss turned red for a moment, but then his face softened. "Fine. Can we agree to reevaluate the situation in two hours to make sure we're focusing on my timeline?" He was quiet and calm, which surprised Tom.

"I think that's reasonable," the captain said.

"To that end, I'd like my man Tom here to go along with the boarding party. He's good with mechanical things, maybe he can help get the ship going a little more quickly," Cantolione said.

Tom looked at the derelict. "Oh, sir. I'm sure these men are better with ships than I am. I'm good with airships and the like, but...."

"He any good with a gun?" the captain asked.

Tom's jacket was pulled back quickly and Cantolione patted the pistol that rested under it. "He used to be in the army. Good shot."

"Everyone used to be in the army," the captain said. He eyed Tom cautiously. "You pull your weight over there—no one's protecting you or anything."

The sea air caught Tom's face and he shook his head. "I really don't want to go over there. We can monitor the situation just as well from here."

"You don't go with them, you can't tap their shoulders when it's time to go," Cantolione said. "I need you to move things along."

Even with his military training and numerous campaigns under his belt, Tom had no illusion about his ability to make these men follow any orders he would consider giving. He would be an intrusion to this close-knit group of men, and his survival would be an afterthought to their own.

36

"I'm not getting a reaction from the *Polk*," Bethy said. "They're not stopping or signaling back."

Even though Lowell was still applying pressure to Zeke's wound, it was obvious the life was seeping out of the man. His eyes stared off to the distance and his wheezing breaths were slowing.

"Keep trying," Lowell said.

The blood on the deck made him queasy, not because it was blood, but it was the blood of his friends. It was from someone he'd known, who'd been very much alive just moments ago. In the war, he'd lost close friends in battle, but there was scarcely time to think about it, about what it meant. Here, he couldn't get away from it. The ship was small and there was nowhere to go. And the others were looking to him for direction.

As he watched the blood move across the deck plate, he noticed something else move there as well, a black pool of oil. Lowell looked until he found a place from where the oil dripped and then followed it back up to several pipes and hoses under the controls. He slid himself across the floor and fondled each part, eliminating each as soon as he was sure it wasn't leaking.

"What?" Cyrus asked.

There was no response as Lowell continued his hunt.

"You look concerned," Cyrus said. "Which causes me to be more concerned than I was when this happened. Now what is going on?"

Lowell found the area high up toward the wheel controls. The bullet that went through Zeke also cut the pitch control down the middle, nicked the altimeter, and slashed another mechanism that he didn't recognize.

"Their gunfight ripped apart some important elements of the controls," Lowell said. "I don't know if we can keep going without fixing these first."

"How long will that take?" Bethy asked. She'd moved to keep pressure on Zeke's wound, but there was still some seeping out. She took a fresh piece of cloth from Cyrus and replaced the saturated one.

It probably wouldn't take long, but rummaging around in a ship he didn't know could be dangerous. "I think we need to set it down, if we can."

"If?" Cyrus asked.

Lowell would've enjoyed vexing Cyrus if it weren't such a dire situation, but as it stood, the damage concerned Lowell so much that he couldn't enjoy making the other man crazy.

37

The cargo ship *Grand Rapids* loomed dark ahead of the rowboat. Tattered ropes hung over the sides of the rusted metal hull. A ladder dangled off the edge of the deck, missing a half a dozen rungs. Tom squinted with one hand over his eyes, the other resting on an oar. The boat was crowded with men from the ship's crew, none of which he was excited about knowing.

"Let's go, mister. Row the damn boat," the leader of the crew, Devers, said. He sat at the front of the rowboat and watched the men row. He didn't grab the oars himself or do anything more than supervise, but he was all too happy to give direction.

Tom gripped the oars with a sigh and got to work. He did his part to get the boat up against the ship and kept his mouth shut. He had no cause to get into it with the man, as it would most likely end with him getting fed to the fish.

Two crewmen gingerly climbed the ladder up toward the deck, carefully avoiding the gaps, and Tom waited his turn to go next. The first men would climb aboard and make sure the area around the ladder was secure for the rest. Once they signaled,

Tom would be the next up. He crouched at the bow of the rowboat and tried to calm himself with the rocking of the waves.

He'd started his military career as an infantryman for the North in the days before the war. Trenches and ditches were familiar territory. He'd fought from horseback a couple of times. One spring, he found himself running across an open field with no cover at all and watched his friends fall as they charged the Rebs.

He'd never had to fight at sea. Never even set foot on a boat the whole time he was in the army. It was hard to get used to what the waves did to his stability and he had no idea what it would do to his aim. He imagined it would be somewhat like fighting on an airship, but it was still a foreign concept.

"Go." The man behind him in the boat nudged Tom with a rifle.

Tom looked up the ladder and saw the first men signaling him up. He climbed. It was about thirty feet to the top. He moved the distance quickly, managing to look down only once at the men advancing behind him and the sea below.

At the top, he swung his leg over and climbed onto the deck. One of the sailors shoved Tom aside to make room for the next man. Tom decided to take cover behind a wide crate on the deck. He pulled his pistol and cocked it. There was no one around that he could see. The deck was in complete disarray, ropes unraveled and askew, slats from broken crates strewn about with other debris and a hatch to the interior hung wide open on its hinge. The deck and various fixtures deteriorated in spots from exposure to the elements and the earthy smell of rust filled Tom's nose. The breeze brought a smell like rancid beef that suggested other things were rotting somewhere nearby.

The other seven men pulled themselves over the side one-by-one and none of them sought cover.

Devers gave Tom a chuckle. "What are you hiding from? Ain't nothing here gonna shoot at ya."

The others laughed as well.

"If there's no danger here, why are you all carrying rifles and extra ammo?" Tom asked.

Devers laughed again. "Didn't say there weren't no danger. Just that there's nothing here that's gonna shoot at you." He pulled the bolt on his rifle and nodded with his chin toward the other men. "You two head around one side of the wheelhouse. You two head the other way around and the rest will come below with me."

The four he'd indicated made their way onto the walkways on the port and starboard, and Devers stepped toward the open hatch. "Mr. Preston, you want to go first?"

Tom suddenly felt like the man was fishing and using him as the bait. It wasn't a situation he wanted to be in on an unfamiliar vessel with strangers backing him up. "Not really."

The men laughed, and a burly man in a knit cap shoved Tom aside. "Move." He peered inside the hatch and mumbled about how dark it was.

"Pass him a lantern," Devers said.

The man took it and fumbled for a moment about how to handle the rifle in one hand and the lantern in the other. It wasn't an ideal situation, but the man pressed on with a shrug. Tom attempted to go next, but was shoved back by another crewman and the next until he was last in line. He turned slightly so he could watch behind the party and still see what was happening in front of them, at least to a degree. They quickly came to two sets of stairs—one leading up, the other leading down.

"Head on up, we'll secure the wheelhouse first, then head to the engine room," Devers said.

The burly man nodded and ascended the stairs. The inside of the ship was just as chaotic as the outside. There was trash everywhere—papers, jars, scraps of clothing. The deck was rusting and the dark orange shade covered nearly everything. It wasn't to the point that it was weakened, but everyone's steps carried a crunchy sound with it. Tom heard a sound behind them, but as he turned he realized it was the groaning of the hull as the waves tossed the ship. No one else had noticed.

"Which door?" Burly Man asked.

"Straight ahead," Devers said. "Let's ignore these other rooms for now and get them on the way out. We need to make sure everything is good in the control room first. If it's wrecked, we can probably forget about taking the ship with us."

They passed two doors on each side of the corridor before coming to the sealed hatch of the wheelhouse. The men focused on the door ahead, their eyes never leaving it, as far as Tom could tell. He, however, did his best to watch behind them, in front of them, and to both sides. He didn't feel any loyalty to the sailors whatsoever, but he didn't want their inexperience to cost him his life. He stared at the doors they were passing, looking for shadows to fall across the glass, but nothing shifted in his line of sight. While the wheelhouse hatch was solid metal, the doors in the passage were wooden.

Devers stepped forward and grabbed the handles of the wheelhouse hatch. "Get ready, boys. This could be interesting."

The others tensed up and pointed their rifles at the doorway while Tom tried to watch everything else with one eye. He could see Devers mouthing a silent countdown, opening the hatch when it ended. He stepped out of the way quickly thereafter. The cabin beyond was well-lit with sunshine that streamed through broken windows of the wheelhouse. The men started forward, to get a look into the rest of the wheelhouse when Burly Man held up his hand and shushed everyone.

"What?" Devers was in a corner, waiting for the others to clear out the room.

"Shhhh," Burly Man said.

Everyone grew silent and waited.

After a moment they all heard it—the shuffle and scrape of something moving unseen within the room. It was a quiet sound on its own, but considering there were no other noises, it became deafening.

"Someone want to handle this?" Devers said.

Every one of the men scowled at him.

In a second, the source of the sound came slowly into view. It was a man wearing the tatters of a Union navy uniform.

"Chewer," Burly Man said.

"Yep," one of the other men said. Neither man sounded terribly concerned.

Taking a closer look, Tom could tell the navy man's face was a rotting mess with a good portion of his chin and lower lip missing and his gums and remaining teeth exposed.

"Are you fellas waiting for an invitation or something? We got work to do," Devers said.

The other men opened fire, shooting far more times than they needed to bring the creature down. The reports from their firearms were a roar in the confined quarters of the metal corridors. After a moment, they stopped. The chewer fell to the deck in bloody pieces.

"All right, already. Go see if there are any more of them in there and clear it out," Devers directed.

The men moved in, leaving only Devers and Tom in the corridor. As they waited, Tom kept alert to all the possible things that could attack them. As he scanned the doorways again, he saw a shadow fall across the glass of the door opposite him. There was no sound, just the bobbing of a shadow getting closer.

From the wheelhouse, a single shot rang out.

"'Nother one crawling around in here," Burly Man said.

The sound of the shot was followed by another sound in the room nearest Devers. The two men looked at each other and then at the room again. Tom fixed his pistol in the direction of the room opposite himself. "There's one over here, too."

"You boys better get out here," Devers called to the others.

As he did, the shadow on Tom's door got big and the door began to rattle. The shadow's hand began to beat on the glass.

"Shoot it, you idiot." Devers moved toward the wheelhouse.

Tom questioned the wisdom of making loud noises inside the ship. The sounds were obviously making the creatures curious and drawing them in. When the chewer's pounding cracked the glass, Tom realized he couldn't just let the beast be contained. It could get out and had to be dealt with. He pulled the trigger, his first shot cracking the glass and knocking it to the deck. His next shot pierced the thing's head, and the chewer fell out of sight. Tom waited for more movement, but after seeing none, he trained his weapon on the other room where they'd heard noise.

The other men came out of the wheelhouse and Devers watched from the doorway. They walked to the door, and after Burly Man opened it, the other opened fire inside. They then moved in and fired some more. A moment later, they emerged.

"Done," Burly Man said. "Want us to do the rest?"

"All of them," Devers said.

The two men moved to the room where Tom had just shot one through the glass. They shot the dead one again for good measure and walked around the room looking for others. Tom glanced behind him down the stairs and found nothing but waited until the men had performed the same routine on all four of the rooms on that level. They didn't find any more chewers.

Devers pointed at Tom when the men were done. "You. You know anything about wiring and steam controls?"

He didn't know anything about making a steam ship work—airships were his specialty. "I know a little."

"We're going to clear out the next level so we don't have to worry about looking over our shoulders all the time. You take a look and see what you see in there."

"Will do," Tom said. He much preferred looking over something he knew nothing about on a cleared out level then trying to dodge chewers with the sailors. He walked into the room and stepped over the bodies just beyond.

38

It hadn't been hard to gain control of *The Moon;* it was just a task keeping everyone calm and collected. None of the trio was truly intimate with the ship and it handled like a brick. Lowell had jumped to the controls at the first sign of listing. He sent Bethy to grab a handful of tools and cut the line that had been severed by one of the errant projectiles. The damaged part had controlled the direct connection to the rudder and affected *The Moon*'s ability to turn and dive with any certainty. Lowell wound down the engine and brought the vessel to a halt.

Cyrus had taken over caring for Zeke. "This is bad. He's losing too much blood. We have to find somewhere to take him." He could feel the warm life blood dripping down around his fingers. He tried to look Zeke in the eyes and tell him everything was going to be fine, but he couldn't bring himself to lie. Every time he looked down at the man, his eyes were pleading for assurance that Cyrus couldn't provide.

"We need the *Polk*," Lowell said.

"I checked," Bethy said. "Still don't see it anywhere. Maybe we should look for flares or something and try to signal them that way." She returned with what tools she could round up on short notice and handed them to Lowell.

Zeke convulsed and swung his arms wildly, like he was trying to get a grip on something, anything. His hands gripped Cyrus's sleeve and pulled hard.

"What do I do?" Cyrus asked.

The noise from Zeke's throat became wetter and he hyperventilated with each breath.

"Shit," Bethy said. "Keep the pressure on. Tighter."

Cyrus did as he was told, but Zeke's spasms became weaker quickly. "I think he's going."

"Lowell, help him," Bethy said.

There was nothing Lowell could do, and his face showed it. "I don't know what else we can possibly do on this vessel. There's no medical supplies, no doctor, no medicine. Nothing." He knelt down and took one of Zeke's hands in his own. "Zeke?"

There was no reaction—Zeke stared at the ceiling blankly.

"*Zeke?!*"

39

Other than the bodies that lay on the floor, there wasn't much for Tom to see. Everything in the control room had a fine layer of salt dust on it. The controls were rusty, and most of the dials were cracked. The wheel was snapped in two, with parts lying crushed on the deck. Sea air wafted in through the cracked windows.

He walked around the small room, picking up useless and broken objects as he went—a sextant with the eyepiece missing, a shattered lantern. He came to a small cubby with a number of holes and slots in it in a corner. He slid his finger into one of the holes and pulled out a rolled up paper. It was a map that was in rather good condition. Probably because it had been hidden from the elements. He unrolled it a bit and found it was a detail of the Seattle area's harbors and shore. Tom set it on the counter and pulled another and another. None of them were interesting to him, and few had many marks on them.

Finally, he came to one he didn't recognize. The map showed a small chain of islands several miles northwest of the islands they were aiming for in the Pacific. In fact, the bottom corner of the map showed a basic representation of where they were headed. Those islands were marked with indications of danger and lines showing that the *Grand Rapids* crew had given that particular chain a wide berth.

The destination island also had markings on it. Rings around the center of the island itself and a question mark in the middle. There was more, but Tom didn't want to waste time on the document. He reached into the slots and pulled out three books. Two of them were embossed with the words "Log Book." The small one could fit neatly into his pocket, but the large one could barely be concealed beneath his coat. He ignored them both and flipped open the manifest.

Documentation inside told how the *Grand Rapids* had carried supplies back and forth to the island for years. Unfortunately, everything was in some sort of code that Tom didn't understand. On occasion, it did indicate when the ship was empty with only ballast in the hold. Tom presumed that those were the occasions when the *Grand Rapids* was heading somewhere to make a pickup of some sort and didn't have anything to deliver. The last entry— the one specifying they were heading for the island chain—was marked only with ballast.

Somewhere below deck, there was the familiar sound of gunfire. It was followed by the equally familiar noise of men shouting chaotically. Tom did his best to conceal the books in his coat and pants and made his way out of the wheelhouse. He was descending the stairs just as Devers and his men were coming up from below. Two sailors supported Devers as he hopped up the stairs. He had his arms around their necks and his face showed his pain. A cursory glance showed that Devers' right leg was bleeding heavily.

"What the hell happened?" Tom said.

"What's it look like? One of them goddamn chewers came out of nowhere and tore into my leg," Devers said through gritted teeth.

Tom watched the men move past him, back toward where the group had come aboard. He started following, keeping an eye out for more of the living dead. He knew there was no way they could let Devers back on their ship. Once a chewer tore your skin, you were done for—it was only a matter of time. Didn't matter how it happened, there was no way to stop it.

"If you got bit, there's nothing we can do," Tom called after the doomed man. "You're going to change into one of them."

"Shut up. It only grabbed me," Devers said.

"Doesn't matter," Tom said. He stopped and checked his pistol.

The three men kept moving briskly until they could see the daylight through the portal.

"You men know I'm right," Tom said. "Do you really want him on the ship with you? Sleeping in the bunk next to you? He'll turn. And he won't remember that you were the ones kind enough to bring him aboard."

The men slowed their pace.

"Don't listen to him," Devers said. "Just get me to the boats so we can leave this place."

"You know when we meet up with the others, they're going to say the same thing," Tom said. "No way they'll let him onboard."

The men stopped walking altogether just a couple of steps short of the portal.

"Let's just do it now," Tom said. "Save the trouble of waiting."

"Shut up," Devers said. "Keep moving."

The other two looked at each other and nodded subtly. They pushed Devers to the deck back down the corridor, so he was between Tom and themselves.

"You've got to be crazy," Devers said. "This is crazy. How long have we known each other? Don't listen to him."

The light from outside was blocked by shadows and everyone turned to fill the rest of their party in on the situation, but it wasn't them. Four chewers made their way in quickly and grabbed the sailors. The lead one grabbed Burly Man and bit him on the shoulder.

Tom still had his gun pointed in their direction, but there was no way to shoot the zombies in the narrow corridor without hitting the other men. He knew one of them was already a goner, and the other wasn't having much luck getting free of his attacker.

Tom squeezed the trigger, hitting Burly Man twice and his assailant three times. He also managed to hit the other sailor in the head, knocking him to the deck. Tucking his now-empty pistol in his belt, Tom unslung his rifle and fired at the remaining chewers until they all fell to the deck with the sailors.

"Jesus God, you killed them. You killed my men," Devers said. "They weren't even bitten, you bastard."

After slinging the rifle on his back again, Tom emptied the shells out of his pistol and reloaded it with fresh ammunition from his pocket. He loaded as he walked toward Devers and the pile of dead men. "They didn't have a chance. I did them a mercy," Tom said.

"Bull. You murdered them, you—" Devers was cut short as Tom shot him in the head with the freshly loaded pistol.

"I'm doing you a mercy, as well." He stepped over the bodies and out into the sunlight of the deck. The other men were already waiting to climb down to the boats.

"Where's everyone else?" one of the sailors asked.

"Chewers," Tom answered.

"We ran into a few, too."

"How's the engine room?" Tom asked.

"Busted up pretty bad," one sailor replied. "Water supply is gone, pumps aren't working, some valves are rusted. How's the control room?"

"Devers said it was a mess," Tom said. "He didn't see how it was ever going to get going anytime soon."

Tom lied just in case anyone checked. He could blame it on Devers if everything was actually ship-shape. "Let's get off this thing in case there're more of those damnable monsters waiting to sink their teeth into us."

When they were back aboard the *Effortless Labor*, no one cared much about what happened to Devers and the rest onboard the derelict ship or why so few came back.

They asked a couple of questions and let it go at that. Captain Bell was more concerned with how much it would take to get the ship running again. He mostly asked the other men his questions. It was obvious that he didn't care much for Tom's opinions, which was fine with him.

Tom dodged Cantolione as best he could, promising to discuss things in the morning. He found an empty room and started reading the books he brought back with him. He skipped through most of the log. Weather conditions and personnel disputes didn't matter to him. He also skipped past the cargo contents—though a glance told him the ship had been pretty much empty except for some supplies for the island should they make contact.

Tom came to the morning the *Grand Rapids* arrived at the island. The captain had written:

We've finally arrived at Campbell Atoll, but there is a light emerald mist that envelops everything. It's impossible to go ashore or even see the research compound. I will send a party when visibility improves.

The fog lifted finally around midday, but we have a new problem. The island is barren. There is nothing to be found of the facility, the docks, the people. Even the foliage is gone. From the vantage point of the Grand Rapids, *not even a leaf is visible. There is only scorched earth and a giant crater in the center. We will check our maps and confirm our position before deciding how to proceed.*

The next day's entry read:

I've sent a landing party to investigate the island. Nothing so far has led us to believe we're in the wrong place. I've personally been to the island numerous times and I find it hard to believe this is the same place.

Tom closed the book after reading a few more entries and tossed it on the bunk. He had a hard time concentrating on anything for very long with the Sons preparing to put his plan into motion. He was too excited with the possibilities that would come with having a device built by the infamous Dr. Poley—destroying the Rebs, reuniting the country and taking over the White House.

Tom caught his reflection in the mirror across from the bed and noticed a spot of blood on his neck. He dabbed at it until it disappeared.

40

Cyrus held the light closer.

"I can fix this." Bethy pulled at the hole in the housing of the pitch control. Zeke's shot had pierced Emmett and continued on through the fixture, causing control to be lost almost completely. She tugged at the jagged edge of the hole with a pair of pliers. "Once I get this pulled back, I can fish out the shrapnel and get to where the control mechanism was separated. Shouldn't take more than five minutes—I swear."

"Do what you can," Lowell said.

Cyrus could hear the strain in Lowell's voice. "What're we going to do?" Cyrus asked. "If none of us knows the way to the outpost...."

"We'll figure it out," Lowell said. "We have their general direction. We're faster than they are. We should catch up easily." He didn't sound convinced. "If we can get moving soon."

Bethy took a deep breath and peeled back a metal fragment.

"Are you sure about that?" Cyrus asked. "What if they turn even the slightest? We may never know what direction they moved in. Hell, if this place is as important as it sounds, Cashe might zigzag just to make sure no one else is following him."

"Chance we'll have to take, I guess," Lowell said.

"He's not in any hurry, no reason why he shouldn't be cautious," Cyrus said.

Bethy pushed into the conversation. "If we can't get this thing moving soon, it won't matter whether we can catch up or not, wouldn't you gentlemen agree?"

Lowell looked down at her. "What do you think?"

She sighed loudly from under the console but didn't show her face. "It may take a little more than I thought. Sheered clean through half the shit down here."

"So, more than five minutes?" Cyrus said.

"What're the odds this little airship has a store of spare parts on it?" Lowell asked.

"Can we tear out something else to make this whole?" Cyrus asked. "Something nonessential from another part of the ship?"

Bethy was only visible to Cyrus from the waist down—her greasy hands occasionally made an appearance as well.

"Maybe something from the galley might make a good temporary fix," he said.

"Could be. I'm just worried about maintaining control in the meantime," Lowell said. "Let's see if we can take it down someplace relatively safe and fix it quickly without the fear of taking a sudden plunge from a thousand feet." Lowell adjusted a lever on the other side of the control room, making the engines whine.

Cyrus tensed. He hadn't been told there was a possibility of falling out of the sky. It was definitely an option he'd rather avoid. "I'm all for taking it down now. Preferably on our own terms, if that works out."

Sliding out from under the console, Bethy leaned up on her elbows and smiled. "Easy," she said. "He's messing with you. We just have dodgy pitch and yaw controls. Nothing's wrong with anything else. With this much gas up there in the bag, nothing short of a fire near the bladder or massive cannon fire is going to make us plummet."

There was a set of binoculars in Lowell's hands as he came back over to Cyrus. "Can you go aft and look for a good landing site below us? Preferably a flat area with some room for us to see anything or anyone approaching. If some chewers show up, I'd like to be able to get airborne quickly."

It wasn't hard for him to find a spot. The whole area was either forest or fields for as far as Cyrus could see. He told Lowell and Bethy what he'd found. They made a jerky descent toward the earth below.

The Moon set down in the field with a jolt and a thud.

"What do you want me to do? How can I help?" Cyrus asked, helping to get the mooring lines in place.

"Grab a rifle and stand guard," Lowell said. "We need you to keep a watch for anything approaching. You'll probably have to walk the perimeter so you can make sure to see every side. If that looks like a big problem, you shout. You see anything that looks like a small problem…shoot it."

"You sure there's nothing else I can do here? I know a bit about mechanics."

Bethy gently shoved a gun toward Cyrus. "Lowell knows airships pretty good and we'd need someone to stand guard no matter what. It's you by default. Besides, you wouldn't want me to do it, would you?" Bethy asked with a smile. "Not the little girl, right?"

Cyrus rolled his eyes and walked aft to the extended gangplank. He opted not to take a light with him. No need to make a target of himself to anyone with a rifle and a short fuse.

In two directions there was nothing but field for at least a mile, and nothing but forest beyond that. To the west was the farmhouse and barn at a quarter mile. A road ran in front of the house and wound off into the horizon in both directions. The final side was nothing but open field as far as he could tell.

He made a circle around the airship, carefully scanning as he went. No sounds, no movement. He repeated this, all the while wondering how long the repairs would take. He hadn't asked. The sweet smell of the suncups growing nearby was fairly pleasant after all the decay Cyrus had been exposed to in the last few hours.

By moonlight, Cyrus could see the area around him fairly well. The field had been plowed not that long ago. Corn stalks, husks and cobs stuck up from the ground where they'd been turned under. If the field had been worked, maybe someone was still alive in there. He looked again at the farmhouse and barn. It was probably a trick of the moonlight on the glass, but he thought he could see something in the top window. He focused, but didn't see it again.

Cyrus searched the fields, but they remained empty on all sides. He looked up at the cabin of *The Moon* and saw the faint light of where Bethy and Lowell were working.

Ten minutes. He could be to the farmhouse and back in less than ten minutes. Unless they were riding a horse or something, no one was going to make it across the field in that time.

He crossed the distance to the back porch of the house. Cyrus listened for any indication of movement or life, but nothing presented itself. After a look over his shoulder at *The Moon*, he decided to make a loop around the house, to make sure there wasn't anyone waiting on the other side. The bushes on either side of the brick foundation were long dead—dried up in the West Coast sun and parched from the summer heat. The grass crunched beneath his feet as he advanced. The heat had taken its toll on the yard surrounding the home too. Around the side of the house the scene was the same, quiet and peaceful, though dry and unkempt. Cyrus stopped when he came to the large wooden doors that led to the cellar. It was padlocked from the outside.

"What're you doing?"

Cyrus jumped as he turned and leveled his weapon at the voice behind him.

It was Bethy.

"What the hell? You're supposed to be guarding the ship," she said." I've been calling for you for the last five minutes. What're you doing way over here?"

"I thought I saw a light in the upstairs window, so I came over to see if anyone needed help." Cyrus pointed to the cellar doors. "I also thought maybe there might be some food in the cellar that we could take. They may have canned some vegetables or something."

Bethy's eyes flashed angrily. "You have a lot to learn if you're going to be a part of this team. First of all, you stay where you say you're going to. How did I know you hadn't been grabbed by chewers, or rebels or something?"

His eyes immediately focused on the uneven field below. If someone on his Turtle had wandered off, he'd've given them this speech too.

"Second, and this is something we learned the hard way," she said. "Try as you might and as much as you want to, you can't save everyone. Can't be done. If there are people up there that need help, they can ask for it. And we'll see what we can do. Otherwise we have to pick and choose our battles."

Bethy made him face her, "Understand? I want you around for a while, but I can't have you endangering everyone else. There could've been toughs lying in wait, hidden in the fields, and they could've attacked me while you were gone."

Cyrus nodded. "I understand."

"Do you? Because I need you here, thinking about what we're doing. Not off on your own, or thinking about someone else."

He nodded again.

"Good, let's go. Lowell's about done and we can get out of here."

"What about food?"

Turning on her heels, Bethy walked back to the cellar entrance. "Watch," she pointed at the doors. For a moment nothing happened but then the doors moved upward a tiny bit before falling back down.

"People trapped?" Cyrus asked.

"I'm thinking chewers. Why do you think it's locked from the outside?" Bethy replied. "You were quiet, so they didn't hear you, now that we're talking, they're attracted to the noise."

Cyrus knew how the chewers worked and how noise attracted them, but he'd been so sure there was someone who needed his help in there, it clouded his judgment. He turned and followed Bethy, who was already a quarter of the way back to the ship.

41

Tom was startled by the first one. When he was called up on deck, he'd expected a long wait for a slightly oversized lizard to show up and that would lead to quick disappointment on Cantolione's part. Truly, Tom had anticipated turning around and leaving not long after they'd arrived. His boss was stubborn, but generally had a short attention span when it came to waiting for what he wanted. He'd given up on the Carlyle Brothers when they didn't show for an audition on time. Forget that Tom had spent three months tracking down the infamous acrobatic duo, traveled to Seattle, Billings and Mexico City in pursuit of them. Money and time wasted.

But here on the island, Cantolione wouldn't have to wait long. They'd landed just after dawn when there was still a chill in the air. The crewmen, most of whom had been on the island before, went to areas that they knew had seen activity at other times, and set up traps, nets and ropes placed strategically in order to capture the creatures without harming them. They used hunks of raw meat as bait, set out in the open to calm any concerns the beasts might have as to danger.

And then they ran. They strung ropes behind them so their prey could be hoisted onto the boat without so much as any one of the men placing one toe back in the sand.

The captain nodded his head and laughed at the scrambling men. "Won't be long now. The beasts are active early. As soon as that sun starts to warm things up, they're at it." He rested his elbows on the railing and nodded more emphatically. "Just you watch."

Tom had only drummed his fingers once before the bushes began to sway and the crackling of twigs broke the morning silence. The rushes parted and one of the "little" lizards stepped out. It was exactly as Moose had described it—dark green, walking mostly upright with a long tail. Every few steps it stopped and dropped to all fours for balance and then proceeded on just the back legs. It was like some dragon from a fairy tale come to life.

Tom immediately had a vision of what was to come. There would be giant posters made up to flank the doors of Cantolione's flagship amusement show. There would be banners that hung from the airships advertising the creatures to draw everyone in to see them. They would travel with other strange beasts that the show could collect or fabricate. They'd even find a way to get the show over to the East Coast where the big money was. Tom looked over at the beaming smile on Cantolione's face and knew his vision was spot on.

"How many of these things would you say there are?" Cantolione asked the captain.

"No idea. We never hung around long enough to collect more than one or two for the Union people that came asking," Captain Bell said. He looked at the men who'd gathered on the deck to observe the traps and work the winches. "None of us really wanted to wait around anymore after we first saw the big one. No telling what that one could get up to."

"Ah yes, the giant lizard." Tom had discounted that as a flight of fancy, but the men were right about the small ones, so he had to take it into consideration that they might be right about the big one as well.

He watched the little creature stray closer and closer to the raw meat at the center of the net. It stopped once and stood as tall as it could, looking at the ship in the distance. Slowly, it let itself down and inched closer to its captivity.

"Tell me more about the biggest one," Tom said.

Two men nearby scowled at the captain and Tom.

The first gave him a grave stare that Tom found almost comical in its seriousness. "One'a the Russian fellas started calling it Drago del Vapore." He looked toward his companion. "Means steam dragon or some shit."

"First time we saw it was early morning, came out of the mists close around the island. Looked like it was made of steam the way it just rose up from the early morning fog like that," the other said. "And the man was Italian."

"He was not Italian. He was a fat Russian bastard. Or maybe Portuguese."

"You're an idiot. How are Russian and Portuguese even remotely alike?"

"Enough. How big?" Tom asked.

After some consideration, the first man pointed to the island. "See that tree?"

The island was full of trees. "Which tree?"

"Pick the tallest."

"All right." Tom scanned the island for the tallest tree he could. It felt like a card scam he'd seen many times on the boardwalk. *Pick a tree, any tree, and I'll guess which tree you're thinking of.*

"Fine," he said. "I see the tallest. What of it?"

"Now imagine a beast twice again that size," the second man said.

"Come on, boys. That tree has to be over fifty feet tall, and you're going to tell me there's a lizard out there better than one hundred feet tall? I think you're talking shit." Tom still looked at the tree, though, trying to understand what the men could be seeing. "Just talking shit."

The two men were quiet. "Let's hope you don't have to see for yourself."

"I'll say this—you'd best collect your prizes while you can," Bell said. "If we get the slightest whiff of that monstrosity, this ship is full steam back home. No questions. No stops."

Tom wondered how the priorities were set on the ship. *We'll stop for a ship full of chewers if it might make you money, but if a big lizard shows up we have to run.*

Cantolione looked gravely at the captain. "We certainly understand. Safety of the ship is the top priority."

There was something else in what Cantolione said, which only Tom Preston caught. There was a mischief in his tone, a giddiness at the possibility of seeing something truly unique. The anticipation of a world-class act to cement his reputation in the world of entertainment and showmanship. Tom could hear in that one short sentence that Cantolione was already making a plan come to life in his head. The beast lightly nibbling on the meat over on the beach was already on tour, already making money. But the concept of the giant as income was all Cantolione could think about at that moment.

With a crack, the trap on the beach sprung, closing around the strange beast and hoisting it into the air. The net swayed as the lizard struggled and made a guttural hissing sound.

The captain changed his dour expression to a smile. "They are not so smart and quite easy to catch."

Offhandedly, Cantolione responded, "Indeed."

42

"Looks like someone's beat us to it." Cashe pointed toward Outpost Two Thirteen not far in the distance. There were two airships orbiting around the compound, firing at points on the ground which Cashe assumed were men or emplacements that were giving the craft trouble. The smaller of the two was trailing a wisp of smoke and listing slightly.

"You know Cantolione better than I do, those look like his craft?" Cashe asked Lucinda. It was obvious the ships weren't built for battle—the gunfire was coming from men standing on the decks with rifles.

"He's got his hands in so many pies it's impossible to tell. But knowing what we know, I'd say it's a good bet," Lucinda said. "Look, down there. I recognize that one. It's one of Cantolione's all right. *The Sky Climber.*"

Cashe followed her finger and noticed a third airship gently coming in for a landing on the east side near what looked to be the stables. He hand cranked a control that made a siren sound throughout the airship. "Great. Three airships to two. Should be interesting."

"Could be worse than that," Corrigan said. "No one's seen *The Moon and the Stars* yet."

A groan escaped Cashe's throat when he thought about that. "Well, let's go say hello. Whoever it is, they're firing on American soldiers and that's all the cause I need." He nodded toward the few seats along the back of the control room. "You may want to sit down and strap yourself in for safety."

"Like hell," Lucinda said as she pulled her dark hair back into a tail. "You have a good long distance rifle on this overgrown balloon?"

"Down the stairs, third door on the left," Cashe replied. "I think you'll find something you like in there."

Lucinda bounded off and her boots clanged on the metal stairs.

Cashe's estimation of the girl rose just a bit more.

With a fading smile, Corrigan put down his pencil and lifted his field glasses. "Let's get our guns focused on the larger ship on the north side of the base now. It probably poses the worst threat. Seems to be heavily armed. They probably meant for it to cover the others while they landed."

It was the most powerful craft, Cashe knew, though he wasn't willing to count out the smaller, speedier craft in terms of danger. Even with fewer, less lethal armaments, they could still win the day. "All right. But let's keep an eye on the other. Get a fix on *The Moon and the Stars* and signal to have them do what they can to distract those smaller vessels."

"Even if they show up in time, *The Moon* is a pleasure craft. They don't have any fixed munitions on that thing." Corrigan scowled at Cashe. "What're they going to attack with, silverware?"

"I'm not asking them to engage, just keep the ships off us."

Corrigan shook his head slowly. "If they're this slow to catch up, there may be some problem. I think they should land and take cover. Stay safe."

"And leave us to fight them all?" Cashe knew how little use their friends would be in this situation, but if those other ships engaged the *Polk*, it would be a massacre. "We need their help in any way they can offer it."

"All right, but we still haven't seen them since we left the rendezvous. I'll see if we can spot them."

"They didn't get around us, did they?"

"Hard to say, but I doubt it."

Cashe didn't like the sound of that. "Go aft and have a look for yourself."

"You need me up here navigating," Corrigan said.

"I think I can adequately point my vessel in the general direction of danger without you." Cashe tipped his head toward the hall. "Go. But don't dally."

43

"They certainly are a noisy lot," Tom said. From the moment he'd entered the hold with the lizards, the cacophony had addled his brain. The creatures emitted high squeals and cries that got louder and more frenzied as he neared them.

"Yes. Some sort of means of communicating with each other or warning others of danger," Fitzmartin said. "Hard to tell until I study them."

"Do you know what they are?"

"Species, you mean? Not a good idea, no. They have qualities of a few different animals I know, not just lizards. They have amazingly tough skin like alligators, but so many qualities that differ. It could be a previously unknown creature or it could be...."

"Could be what?"

"With the close proximity to the old Union testing facilities, who knows?"

Tom wondered what to make of the facility and the legend that grew and grew. "I thought they just worked on weapons at that facility."

"Wouldn't a giant lizard be a solid weapon for any army?" Fitzmartin said. "They had many projects out there. Who is to say the Union didn't manipulate these animals for their own aims?"

"So what happened to this lab of Poley's?" Tom asked.

"I don't know. I've heard things, but I'm not going looking. You could take a rowboat and go see for yourself. It was supposed to be within a couple miles of this atoll."

"I don't feel much like searching around blindly for a hidden facility in a dinghy alone, thanks."

"Wise of you, I think. Very wise." Fitzmartin gathered his things about him on crates near the cages where the creatures paced. The facilities were built hastily in the hold before they left. The cages looked unstable to Tom and he said as much.

"Not to worry. These things have contained elephants and other big game. These lizards shouldn't be a problem." Fitzmartin reached out as if he would touch one of the beasts, but his hand stopped a good five feet from the bars that contained them.

"How many are there now?" Tom asked.

"We have seven so far." Fitzmartin walked around to a smaller cage and opened it. He tugged a ragged rope that pulled out a small goat. "I truly don't think we need more." He fed the goat a few scraps of lettuce, gave it a pat on the head and shooed it back into the cage.

"Me neither." Tom watched as the older man picked up an armload of equipment and began ascending the stairs.

"One of the things we were told is that these creatures don't live long once they reach the mainland," Tom said. "What makes you and Cantolione think these animals are going to live any longer for us?"

"All of the other beasts were captured by sailors and shoved in a dank hold for several days. We will make sure to keep them at a decent temperature, similar to their native lands. We're gathering plants and food from their habitat in order to help them survive with us. We're certainly more prepared than anyone before us." Fitzmartin strained to carry the load up the stairs and hold a conversation.

When they emerged back on deck, the air smelled sweet to Tom and he guessed it came from the flowers he could see on the island, blooming in the trees and in the shrubs along the beach. Their yellow and green fronds looked like diamond kites with yellow spines bobbing in the gentle breeze. He broke away from Fitzmarin and let the man do whatever it was he needed to do.

Tom gripped the rusty rails and breathed in deeply. As much as he hated to be away at such a crucial time for his people, there were worse places to be. Plus, being out in the middle of the ocean herding strange lizards gave him an alibi for what was about to happen at Outpost Two Thirteen.

He thumbed through the log book a little more as he watched the island.

Two men, Crosby and Smith, died in the infirmary this morning. They succumbed to whatever this illness is. Our people are at a loss as to how to treat them. We sent a second party out to the island with instructions to return if they started feeling ill. They didn't make it past the beach before turning around. They've been sick and covered in the same scaly sores the other crew members have.

The next entry followed later that same day.

We've noticed what appears to be movement in the first party we sent to the island. We're afraid to send more men, but we can't leave the others out there if they're alive.

Tom shuddered at the thought. Whatever happened to those men could very well be how the chewers first got started. Behind him, he heard footsteps on the deck and the sudden bleating of an animal. He turned to see Fitzmartin leading the goat by the neck.

Fitzmartin smiled as he pulled the goat along. The goat bleated.

Tom nodded to the animal. "Taking your pet goat for a little walk?"

Fitzmartin laughed. "No, no. Nothing so pleasant for little Ella." He pointed to the island. "The creatures are meat-eaters. Little Ella is going to be bait for the big ones."

The breeze hit Tom again. "Seriously? These things are all pretty big so far. What makes you think there really are bigger ones out there?"

"Our guide, for one, says he's seen one," Fitzmartin said.

"He's a drunk." Tom watched the other man chain the goat to the center of the forward deck. "Besides, don't we have enough of those in the hold? Christ, how many does he need?"

"I need all I can get, my boy." Cantolione strode up behind them, already decked out in his standard top hat and waistcoat. He looked as if he were just getting ready to step out in front of his business to draw in the rubes. "We'll build zoos at each of our airship towers, some here, and some over on the East Coast. We'll pack the houses across the civilized country. Maybe we can get the permits to take the show across the ocean and wow them in Europe." Cantolione put his hands on his hips and looked very satisfied with himself. "Plus, the word is that these things don't live too long, so it's always good to have a spare, right?"

Tom nodded.

"We'll be rich, my boy. Rich," Cantolione said.

Tom was already wealthy thanks to Cantolione. He didn't need sideshow antics and malformed dragons to do it. "You did want to be back to the business in a few days, sir. We're losing money due to a couple of ships being down."

"I haven't forgotten. We'll turn back by mid-day." Cantolione didn't seem terribly concerned.

The hatch opened again and Bell came out on deck. "We're coming around to the inlet where that big one was spotted last. The shelf drops off pretty fast and the water gets mighty deep around there."

Tom rolled his eyes and leaned against the railing. It was an annoyance to be stuck at sea with these men even for a couple of days. The worst part was knowing he couldn't walk away from them if they annoyed him. Not very far at least. He could go below to various rooms and compartments, but he and Cantolione were sharing a billet, so he couldn't be sure he'd be alone for long. The main hold was filled with cages loaded up with oversized lizards which were already starting to smell.

Tom flipped open a case and removed a cigarette. As he patted his jacket for matches, he called over his shoulder. "You bring any other animals as bait? What if one of those big ones carries Ella off?"

"We don't expect any of them to get quite that big," Fitzmartin laughed. "Though, they're welcome to try."

There was a rumbling then, and the ship shook violently; a rushing sound like a waterfall permeated the air.

Tom looked behind him at the stern of the ship in time to see the largest lizard he could have imagined rise up over the deck. Sea water poured off its scaly green and gray skin and its wide webbed limbs flailed in the air above the deck. Everything below the beast's waist remained underwater, yet the animal still towered above the boat's deck.

"Mother of Christ," Bell swore quietly. "It's here."

The men stood on the deck just a few feet from Tom, all frozen in fear and fascination. He was no different. Every part of him wanted to run to the portal and throw himself down the stairs, but he couldn't look away. They'd been accurate in their crazy rantings. The beast was immense and hideous, like the others in the hold, but magnified a thousand-fold. Its teeth—fangs really—shimmered as the salty water dripped off them.

"We're going to need a bigger goat," Fitzmartin grumbled under his breath.

More hands came racing up to the deck to see what had shaken the boat so violently. They all stopped mere steps from the stairway. Bell shoved his way past them and disappeared into the ship.

One of the crewmen unslung a rifle from his back and aimed it at the creature.

"No!" Cantolione shouted. "Don't harm it!"

The crewman with the gun shoved the old man aside easily and leveled the gun again. The crack of the shots being fired startled everyone, but they all stood where they were to see what would happen.

Nothing.

Not at first. Then the lizard reared its head up in the air and roared a gruesome and angry cry. Its elongated arms crashed down on the deck, and the talons on those webbed hands sliced into the metal with ease.

That was enough to shake Tom from his fascination and set him in motion toward the door. He shoved past Fitzmartin, who still looked slack-jawed at the lizard, then Tom dodged Cantolione and a crewman before being blocked by Bell coming back out onto the deck with a large man in a black cap. They carried a large harpoon gun.

Tom didn't stick around to see what they were going to try to do with it. He pressed in behind them and nearly fell face-first down the stairs. He stumbled but picked himself up quickly. He grabbed the nearest bulkhead and gripped it tight. For a moment, he feared the beast might reach down and pull him back up onto the deck, so he held tighter.

After a moment he heard another of the animal's terrible screams and shuddered. The men above shouted and there was a throaty cry from one of them. Tom assumed it was Fitzmartin. None of this concerned him as much as the racket that followed. The lizards that they'd collected so far began to let out cries of their own. Random whoots and whoops mixed with growls and gurgles loud enough to echo throughout the halls. He moved quickly to shut the door that led out of the room.

Tom thought better of locking it in case he needed to leave the chamber in a hurry. The other lizards were locked safely away down in the hold, but the thought of them roaming the halls in search of whatever they wanted to feed on made him tremble. He reached to his side. No pistol. Tom had grown lax in carrying his firearm. He hated himself for it presently.

He moved back to the entranceway and peered around the corner. At the top of the stairs the hatch was still open, but he couldn't see anything except open sky. The creatures in the hold were still creating a ruckus, but Tom couldn't hear anything coming from the upper deck. He stood, half-hidden by the door, waiting for some sign of activity, but the most he could make out was the rhythm of the waves.

He looked behind him and scanned the room for something he could use as a weapon—a knife, a gun, anything. In the corner of the room he found some tools, including a large wooden mallet.

Tom took the stairs slowly, mallet in hand.

44

The enemy airships were clearly unprepared for the interruption in their plan. They'd been methodically eliminating the fort's defenses and seemed to panic as a new target presented itself. The men firing on the decks switched targets from the soldiers below to the *Polk*, which was still too far out of their range.

The tube next to him buzzed. Cashe picked it up. "Yes?"

"The Little Napoleon is ready to fire on your word, sir," Monty said. The most popular gun in the war had been the Napoleon. The O.M.O. was thrilled to have a scaled down version installed on the *Polk*. It made short work of most any situation.

"All right, bring it around and target the big one. Shoot until it sinks from the sky."

"Yes, sir."

Cashe replaced the tube and leveled the ship off, keeping it as steady as he could for his men to get a good shot.

There was the slightest of vibrations in the control room as the cannon fired. The tell-tale streak of smoke showed Cashe where the projectile arched away from the *Polk*. As it approached the large airship, the cannon ball broke apart, spewing forth a number of smaller cannonballs, all of which tore into the side of the vessel. Through his field glasses, Cashe watched the munitions shatter three port windows and tear one of the gunmen in half. The *Polk* had been built with combat in mind, but the airships they engaged weren't. They had no plating to deflect even the smallest of arms. This first ship wasn't going down, but the *Polk* had his range. Cashe was amazed at the accuracy of his crew.

Cashe turned his attention to the other ships. The one was on the ground loaded and unloaded men. The other still flew erratically. Cashe guessed the pilot wasn't sure what to do with the new attackers. If Cashe had another airship to back him up, he could take better advantage of the temporary confusion. He hoped the third ship stayed on the ground. That would help them a little.

There was another rumble as the Little Napoleon let loose again. He followed the trail and watched as the latest shot tore apart one of the props and shook the opposing ship hard enough to knock two more gunmen overboard. A sputter of smoke emanated from the tail section, followed by a larger cloud.

He waited for the next shot to finish it off. Cashe started to hope this would be easier than he thought.

45

There were some shouts above on the deck and an occasional frenzied rapping on the portal that Tom had secured, but he didn't want to look back. He moved toward the interior door and found he couldn't open it with one hand, no matter how hard he tried. With a sigh, he put down the mallet and used both hands to turn the door crank. When the lock finally gave way, he grabbed the mallet again immediately in case one of the lizards charged at him.

Nothing came, but when the door opened he could hear the smaller beasts' cries more clearly. It was still a mystery whether they were loose or whether their sounds were carrying through the halls of the ship.

He walked carefully and as silently as he could. The urge to run was overwhelming, but he wanted to be sure that he didn't come around a corner and find himself face to face with something he didn't want to meet up with.

Which is what almost happened as he rounded the first corner.

He came to a T intersection—one way leading to his quarters, the other to additional cabins. As he turned to his right, one of the creatures stood in the middle of the corridor between Tom and his cabin. There was a good hundred yards between the man and the beast. It wasn't one of the largest lizards that they'd corralled, but it was still big. At nearly four feet tall and eight feet long—maybe longer with the tail. It had the same sleepy demeanor that the others had, and stood rock still once it saw Tom.

He raised the mallet high over his head and debated running the opposite way. He couldn't go back the direction he'd come from, unless he wanted to lock himself in the small room at the bottom of the stairs. That would mean he'd be stuck there, but it would be preferable to his new situation. The other direction of the intersection had another portal at the end, with a number of other doors in the twenty yards before the door. He stepped toward the new direction, but his decision was made for him, in a way.

The engines of the *Effortless* revved suddenly and the ship lurched forward. Tom, unprepared for the movement, fell into the hall where he'd come from. He crab-walked backward to get away from the intersection as fast as he could.

Immediately he heard thumping footfalls. The lizard ran past him, down the corridor and away from where Tom's cabin had been blocked. Tom ran quickly, closing the distance to his door in seconds. He looked down the hall and found that the lizard was turning around in the tight space. Tom grabbed the handle and tried to turn, but only too late remembered he'd locked it to prevent anyone from discovering the books that he'd taken off the supply ship.

The creature at the end of the hall had managed to turn itself around and was running as best it could on the metal floor. Tom fumbled in his pants pockets and then his coat before finding the shape of the key in his vest pouch. The scaly gray monster reached the T section and continued toward Tom as he fitted the key in the lock.

The ship lurched again, buffeted by some force, whether it was the Dragon or the engines, Tom had no idea, but it shook the ship sufficiently that it knocked him backward and onto his ass. Luckily, it had thrown the lizard against the wall. The monster was on its side and slightly dazed.

Tom crawled on all fours to the door, leaving his mallet somewhere on the floor, and grabbed the door handle to pull himself up. He cranked the key until he heard a click, and the door fell open inward, dragging Tom forward. He crawled the rest of the way in, slamming the door and propping himself against it. There was a thud and a scratching against the door as the beast caught up. Tom reached up and cranked the door handle shut, securing the door against the attack.

He crawled to his bunk and pulled his satchel out from under it and removed his pistol. He checked to see that it was loaded and then sat with his back against the bulkhead and the gun in his lap.

There he waited.

He wasn't sure what he was waiting for. His situation was actually worse than before. At least in the little room he had two potential exits. Here he had but one. And if the ship sank due to the creature's attack, he would have nothing to do but die.

46

Cyrus got his first look at Outpost Two Thirteen. It hadn't been as hard as they'd thought to find the *Polk*. The smoke from its cannons was visible from miles away. *The Moon* groaned as Lowell tried to pour on more speed and move toward the group of ships fighting. A fire on the smallest ship trailed a large plume of smoke as they got closer.

"Who the hell are they fighting?" Bethy asked.

"Couldn't rightly say," Lowell said, "but things look a little lopsided. Maybe we should get in on it."

The airship on fire had another explosion near its aft. It dropped like a stone toward the ground, where it exploded.

Cyrus examined Outpost Two Thirteen below.

The fort had a wall that was easily fifty feet tall that surrounded the main buildings and parade grounds. A quarter mile outside the fort itself, was a fence line that ran all the way around. The east side of the stronghold was near a deep ravine and to the west was a dry lake bed. To the north ran a set of railroad tracks that headed into the hills, and to the south, appeared to be a large area of stables.

"Things are a little more even with that one out of the way," Cyrus said. "Let's head for the one on the ground. It looks to be waiting on something. What say we land near it and see what they're up to? We surely won't be much help in the air." He squinted to try to see if there was any damage to the *Polk*.

"True," Lowell said. "This tub doesn't have much protection. We'd go down quickly. We can be the most help by going after the one on the ground. We're going to land near the stables. There should be an entrance through there, and maybe it won't be covered."

Cyrus was hopeful that at least they'd be able to push through whatever defenses these attackers might have set up and make it into the building without being shot by anyone, especially the men protecting the fort or their own people in the airships above.

In the distance, they heard gunfire and then a roar as the *Polk*'s cannon rained a barrage on the next airship. Bethy paused. Cyrus guessed by the look on her face that she wanted to be up there, firing that cannon.

He nudged her along to take her mind off it. "Let's get ready. Gather up all the ammunition you can reasonably carry and make sure everyone has what they need."

She nodded and got to work without another pause. Between the two of them, they found Zeke and Emmett's guns and pulled the ammunition out and handed Lowell what they could find that would suit him.

"Head for the door and get ready to repel any of these bastards that tries to rush us," Lowell yelled.

Cyrus and Bethy made their way to the entrance and used the doorway for cover. "This is a wonderful little organization you work for," Cyrus said.

He'd been surprised to see her not only pick up a rifle, but she had strapped a short-barreled shotgun to her back as well, which she'd brought from her cabin rather than the ship's armory. They raised their weapons together.

"I'm growing less fond of it by the day." Bethy cocked the rifle, pulling a bullet into the chamber. "The food is occasionally good, though."

From the tall grass near the other airship, a man advanced, firing his pistol. Cyrus shot him easily and waited for another target. He didn't think twice about the man as his body disappeared into the weeds.

Once *The Moon* thumped down roughly, Lowell joined them at the entrance. "Quiet so far," he said.

"So far," Bethy whispered.

The stables were built into the corner of the fortification—two rows of ten stalls with a main aisle down the middle that ended in a large open door leading inside. The trio moved forward, hunching over and using the grass as best they could for cover. Cyrus followed the other two and mimicked their movements. Having never been in the military, he had no clue what tactics they should be using, what they should be doing to reduce their profiles and their chances of getting shot. His fights had almost exclusively been with chewers. All of those had been real fights—close quarters inside a building or vehicles. He knew how to take cover and protect himself, but moving out in the open scared him more than a little. The enemy could be anywhere and you'd never see the one that shot you.

When they reached the stables Cyrus looked at the empty stalls and haphazardly strewn bridles and saddles and hay-covered floors. It was quiet inside compared to the mayhem in the courtyard and the air above it. The smell of manure was strong.

With a nod of his head, Lowell encouraged Cyrus and Bethy to follow him silently into the stables. With his first step, two men appeared near the door and began firing at them. All three dove for cover in the first set of stalls, Lowell on one side, Cyrus and Bethy on the other.

"Christ," Bethy yelled over to Lowell. "I thought you said it was clear."

Lowell shrugged in response.

Cyrus lay on his stomach and pointed his rifle out in front. He took a deep breath and leaned into the aisle, firing as soon as he was clear of cover. He watched both men duck back to their hiding places as he also moved back again. He looked across to Lowell and watched as the man did the same thing, firing off three shots before finding his own hiding place again. After that, there came a return volley from the opposite end.

"This is going to either get us killed or draw more of them in here to kill us," Cyrus said. He couldn't risk looking back outside to make sure no one was coming up behind them, the gap was too large and would open him up to an easy shot from the enemies that he already knew about. "We need to get ourselves into that building or we're in trouble."

Lowell fired a few more shots, and then hid. It drew the expected response from the others. The post at the corner of the stall exploded with splinters. "They're with the Sons of Grant," he said. "Look at the bands on their arms."

"I'll take your word for it." Cyrus considered charging forward while Lowell covered him. There was a possibility they could work their way up while they still had an advantage. Out of the corner of his eye, it registered that Bethy was pulling the shotgun from its holder on her back. She breached it and checked the shell inside. Her hand went to her jacket and pulled it off, then she snatched several more shells from the pocket of the coat and cupped them in her hand.

"Cover fire, please." She smiled and nodded at Cyrus in a way he was sure meant to convey that she'd be fine but it only amplified his fear for her.

His arm reached out to stop her. "Wait."

But she was already climbing over the top of the stall. Cyrus turned to get back into firing position, but Lowell had already started firing and when he stopped, Cyrus started. Over the gunfire, he heard Bethy land in the straw of the next stall. Both men leaned back and started reloading as the return fire started.

When the gunfire died down, Cyrus and Lowell began again and the sequence repeated again and then again as Bethy cautiously made her way over stall after stall.

Finally, when it came time for the enemy troops to reload there was a yelp of surprise from both men as Bethy landed near them. A loud report rang out as the girl let loose with the shotgun. There was a shuffling in the hay and Cyrus broke cover to go help her before another blast like the first filled the room. After a stray rifle shot rang out there was silence.

Cyrus dropped his rifle and drew the pistol. He didn't know whether to yell to her to see if she was ok, or rush to her side or start shooting randomly to scare everyone from their hiding places. He decided to run to her, but Lowell held his arm out and stopped him, forcing him to approach slowly.

The stable area was filled with the thick blue smoke from the gunfight.

"It's fine," Bethy said. She sounded out of breath. "I'm fine. Come ahead."

Lowell moved to the open doors to the outpost and scanned inside while Cyrus moved to Bethy. He looked her up and down for any signs of trauma. "You sure you're all right?"

"You gonna be this prissy after every time I get in a fight?"

Cyrus tried to look nonplussed but couldn't answer. He probably would feel the same way every time she was in danger, in fact. It was transference of a sort from the last several years watching Lucinda.

"Then you're gonna be like that for the rest of your life, so you'd best get over it."

"If you two are done checking each other for Blue Ticks, I'd like to continue before more men with guns show up to kill us," Lowell said.

Cyrus shook off the embarrassment at his sentimentality as best he could, but he could see that Bethy got some joy out of seeing him squirm. The two of them checked their weapons and moved to the door. There was a chunk of it missing, splintered, he assumed, by the Sons of Grant as they made their way into the fort.

"The hall is empty, but it goes in two directions," Lowell said. "I have no ideas on what lies ahead. I don't want to go one way and leave our rear open for some of them bastards to sneak up on us, but I can't see splitting up since there are so few of us." He looked at Bethy and Cyrus. "I'm open to suggestions."

"There's nothing for it. I say we pick a direction and go," Bethy said. "We just watch our asses so they don't get shot off."

"Well put," Cyrus agreed. "Right seems as good a direction as any, unless there's some objection?"

"Fair enough," Lowell said. "I'll take the lead. Bethy, you follow with the shotgun, in case there's a surprise around the next corner."

Bethy fell in behind Lowell and they both looked to Cyrus. "You have the rear," Lowell said, "and the job of keeping said asses in good condition."

Cyrus nodded and raised his rifle to the left. They moved together, as quietly as possible toward the bend in the hall to the right. At the end of the hall they could see a man lying on the stone floor just before the bend. They moved up and put their backs to the wall, Cyrus again mimicking the things he saw in the others.

As they approached the corner, they could see the man on the floor was shabbily dressed and dead, with a good portion of his head removed. Lowell motioned for them all to stop and wait.

He peeked his head around the corner and was immediately greeted by a volley of gunfire that splintered the wood in the walls.

"There's a number of men barricaded behind barrels and other makeshift cover pretty close by," Lowell said, his lips pressed hard together. "I think they're soldiers with the outpost."

"You think?" Bethy asked.

"We can always ask," Lowell said.

When he turned his attention back to the hall behind them, Cyrus saw a number of men advancing from the far end. "We'd better find out quick, there are more men coming up behind us."

Lowell turned his head to check for himself. "Shit."

Bethy chimed in with her own "Shit."

Making sure he could be heard by the men around the corner, Lowell cupped his hands and shouted. "We are with the O.M.O. ship *Leonidas Polk*, currently fighting above this encampment. We're here to help if we can."

At that, the men coming up behind them opened fire. The trio dropped to the ground and Cyrus fired back.

"I think we can be sure who isn't on our side," Bethy said.

The group around the corner remained quiet.

"We're receiving fire from another group behind us," Lowell said. "We're coming around." He turned and whispered to the others before getting up to a crouch. "I'll go first. I'm wearing a proper uniform."

"That's great, unless they're not on our side." Bethy gripped her shotgun and waited.

Lowell stood and dashed around the corner. After a moment he reappeared and pointed his gun down the hall. "Come on, they're with us, apparently." Then he shot at the men advancing quickly down the hall.

Cyrus grabbed Bethy and practically threw her to cover. He hadn't meant to be so rough, but he told himself he'd have done the same to anyone in harm's way.

The men in the hall stopped at the stable entrance and used the door for cover. There were four men in the front, followed by four more that were busy carrying a crate. Two more men followed with rifles pointed at Cyrus and the others. The men took turns firing and reloading as they advanced. They were using older muskets, which allowed them only one shot before reloading, but the group was well organized and gave each other time to move.

"I'll be damned. That looks like one of the crates in the pictures we saw," Lowell said.

There was a rumbling behind them as the soldiers rolled their barrels up to the turn. They set them up and took cover behind. Each of them also had the muskets that seemed primitive next to the repeating rifles that Cyrus's party was using. They opened up on the attackers by the stables, but the crate had already disappeared through the door. A man lingered, firing off a shot and then vanished as well.

The soldiers from the outpost kept their cover, but Lowell ran toward the stable door and Cyrus got up to follow. He could hear Bethy behind them.

They reached the door just as a man appeared and Bethy leveled him with the shotgun. They paused in the hall to let her reload. As she did, Lowell stuck his head around to check the situation.

"They left at least one man to cover their retreat," Lowell said.

"I'm not climbing over those stalls again," Bethy said.

They heard a shot outside. There was a pause and then another shot after a good minute or two. Lowell peered around the corner again and motioned the others forward as he advanced.

When they stepped into the stables, one man lay dead just outside. They advanced cautiously and found another man dead against the last fence. Cyrus couldn't see what had ended the men's lives, but he was grateful. They could see the other soldiers loading the crate on their waiting airship. Some of their men fired at Cyrus's group again, but as they did, yet another of their numbers fell from an unknown shooter.

The gunfire became more staccato and quick as someone began firing a Gatling gun from the dirigible. The corner of the stalls disintegrated under the barrage and everyone was forced to lay flat behind cover.

There was a roar as the airship's propellers shoved it aloft, but the Gatling fire continued. It was more sporadic as the gunner tried to keep a bead on Cyrus and the others, even though the ship was changing its orientation. It lifted quickly, peeling away from the fort with haste.

Cyrus stood up and fired his rifle, once and again.

A hand grasped his barrel and Bethy said, "Save it. There's nothing more you can do."

Cyrus reluctantly lowered his gun.

A voice from behind them startled the trio back into the moment. "You three better be who you say you are." The soldiers from the hall were pointing their weapons at them.

"I'm really getting tired of working for you guys," Cyrus told the other two.

"Being your friend hasn't been a Sunday picnic for us either," Bethy said.

Cyrus looked over at the soldiers and pointed to the dead men from the Sons of Grant. "See these men? Our sharpshooter brought 'em down and now he's drawing a bead on you. Less you want to end up dead as this lot, you'd best point those things somewhere else." Cyrus hoped he was right, maybe the *Polk* dropped off some men to help out, but maybe not.

A cannon report brought their attention skyward. The smoke of the Napoleon enveloped the front of the *Polk*. The airship it was chasing seemed to hiccup and then it twisted onto its side before descending from the sky. It didn't arc toward the ground, rather it fell like it had boulders tied to it. Immediately it crashed into the nearby hills where it burst into flames.

"All right," Cyrus said. "You don't believe our sharpshooter's out there?" He pointed up. "That's our ship, so I suggest you get those guns pointed elsewhere before it comes over and rains down some of that on your sorry heads." He couldn't help himself—he'd had far too much gunplay in the last several days for his own taste.

Bethy laughed, presumably at his big talk.

The soldiers seemed a little confused, but they tentatively lowered their guns.

After a moment, the tall grass in the distance began to rustle. Lucinda stood up with a rifle. She slung it over her back and joined the others.

"Jesus, girl," Lowell said. "Where'd you learn to shoot like that?"

"A girl picks up things from time to time."

47

The *Effortless*'s engines worked steady and the seafaring vessel sailed smooth for nearly an hour before Tom fell asleep. In the meantime, he thought of little but the lizards and the beast that they called Drago del Vapore. He took his mind off the beasts in his hallway by counting how many rifles the Sons of Grant had stolen from various storehouses, some abandoned to the chewers, others they had taken by force. He closed his eyes and saw them one by one, like sheep jumping over a fence.

The handle on his cabin twisted a little back and forth, waking him. He panicked in the moment of disorientation that followed as he struggled to remember exactly where he was and what was happening. He wondered if the lizards could operate door handles. The door was locked again, but he supposed that wouldn't keep the captain out if he had a key—or anyone else for that matter if they had it.

"Tom? It's Cantolione." The voice was grave. "You'd do well to come out and eat. Big day ahead." There was no mention of beasts or chaos or even that anything out of the ordinary had transpired—just a dull, emotionless string of words. It was unlike his boss not to have an optimistic lilt to his speech.

When Tom got up, the gun on his lap clanked to the floor and rattled. He bent to pick it up and looked at it for a moment. He'd gotten rid of all the people in his plot that could possibly lay blame on him in *The Moon and the Stars*, save one—Cantolione himself. There might be a time, he supposed, when he'd have to rectify that, but for now the man was important, though Tom's patience for looking like Cantolione's stooge was wearing thin.

He decided it would be wise to tuck the gun into his belt and keep it on his person at all times. Yes, that would be his new policy.

48

Inside Two Thirteen, the crew of the Polk were given a warm welcome as they followed Cashe through the corridors.

"We're thrilled that you're here, Mr. Cashe." The man who'd introduced himself as Captain Hersh said. "We've been hoping to get some word from the provisional government for the last several months." He paused. "What took so long?"

Cashe looked around to see who was paying attention and found his own crew was distracted taking in the sights. "Things have been a little confused out East. Nothing happens fast with this dual government. The Yankees want one thing, our people want something else. The U.N. wants a whole other thing. You can't get them to agree on lunch, let alone how to allocate their meager allotment of troops."

"Well, we're glad you're here now," Hersh said.

"What happened to your telegraph? Why didn't you just ask for help?" Cashe asked.

"Went out in a storm. We sent a team to fix it. They didn't come back."

"Neither did the next team we sent," a second man, Anders, said. He'd fallen in step at some point as they were walking.

Cashe looked at them sharply. "Chewers?"

"Suppose so," Hersh replied. "We had a lot happening at once. Storm, flooding, chewers and a lack of food."

"Sounds like a rough spring," Cashe said.

Hersh stopped at a set of sturdy wooden doors and tugged on the handles. "Spring? That was just the month of April."

"Tell you what," Cashe said. "I'll have my people help you with that. We can use the *Polk* to find the problem in the line, and then use the ship to cover the men as they set to repairs. In fact, that'll be the first thing we do."

The doors opened and Cashe got a look at the interior of the room and the flurry of activity within. Men in white coats crossed paths with soldiers hurrying from one side to the other. Several of the white-coated men, who Cashe assumed were doctors, huddled over bleeding bodies in the center of the room. Everyone in the procession got still and quiet at the sight. There weren't many men getting operated on—a half dozen, maybe—but they were in bad shape. The smells of antiseptic and seared flesh made Cashe turn away. He watched as Bethy went back into the hallway and Cyrus followed.

On the far side of the room, a grey-haired doctor peeled his gloves off and looked up. Hersh lifted his hand in a half-hearted wave, which the doctor acknowledged with a nod.

"Come on," a soldier said. "Captain Hersh will join up when he can." The man led the remaining people down the hall to the bench where Bethy and Cyrus sat.

"Are you—" Cashe started.

"I'm fine," Bethy cut him off. "Just wasn't any cause to stand there staring at those boys, that's all."

Cashe didn't say a word. He felt like turning away from that ugly scene himself, so he couldn't imagine what it was like for a young thing like Bethy. He did a quick count of the party. A few were missing. "Where are Emmett and Zeke?"

Lowell stepped up before anyone else could say anything. "They're gone. They got into it just after we talked about coming here and…."

"What?" Cashe said. "They're dead?"

"They shot each other before we could get them calmed down," Lowell said.

Bethy stared at the wall, rather than meeting Cashe's gaze. "I was there when it broke out. I had no inclination that they'd go so far. You know how they got into it."

Cashe knew very well, but, as Bethy had said, he never saw it coming to something like that. Zeke had a temper, but Emmett knew better than to bait him. They knew their jobs and had been able to keep their feelings out of it for so long. Lowell had suggested they were coming to an impasse, but Cashe was sure even Lowell hadn't seen this outcome.

"Jesus." Cashe thought about the way the two of them had started out together during the war, delivering packages on horseback and wondered how it had come to this and wondered how they ever thought it would come out differently.

He turned at the sound of footfalls in the hall and watched the doctor from the other room approach. He was tall and gaunt, with longer hair than Cashe had thought—it was just matted to the man's head with sweat. His white coat was smeared with blood.

"I think it would've been much worse in there had you and your friends not happened along," the doctor said. "Thanks for that." He extended his hand to Cashe and shook it. "I'm Dr. Hastings. I'm the head of the research department hear at Two Thirteen. And head surgeon by default."

Cashe shot his hand out in return. "I'm Lyle Cashe. I'm the leader of this O.M.O. squad. Nice to make your acquaintance." Cashe wasn't used to so many people being happy to see him in such a short span of time. It made him uneasy to think they might ask him to fix all their problems when he knew he couldn't.

"Let's get away from here to someplace we can talk," Hastings said. "You can catch me up on the civilized world and then let me know what this was all about."

Hastings led them through the halls, around the western side of the fortification, then into an area with a number of doors. Lyle noticed as they walked that there weren't many people along the way. It seemed to be a huge base with very few forces occupying it. It explained a lot, in Cashe's mind, about how such a diminutive attacking party was able to do so much damage. The small, disorganized defending units didn't stand a chance without leadership.

"Where is everyone? I thought this place was at garrison strength the last time I was here," Cashe said.

"From what I understand, that was a few years back, sir."

Cashe guessed it was three years. Maybe four. "Still, levels shouldn't be this low."

"We were hoping you were bringing fresh troops," Hastings said. "We've lost men to chewers, starvation, weather, sickness, accidents, skirmishes with bandits and thieves, not to mention animal attacks, and a few men that took their own lives. All the while, we've been holding out hope for relief from the government." He looked sharply at Cashe. "And here you are. Finally." He sighed and looked at the half dozen people behind Cashe. "Did someone notice us missing, or did they suddenly wonder what happened to all the wonderful weapons they'd dreamt up?"

Cashe spoke quickly, to keep the last comment from sinking in with the rest of his crew. "Actually, we haven't had contact with command in several weeks ourselves. That's not unusual, though. We're pretty autonomous."

"You don't have orders to relieve us?"

"No."

"You just wandered in here at the right time to save us from an all-out coordinated attack?"

"Yes," Cashe corrected himself quickly. "Sort of. We're here in pursuit of one of those weapons you mentioned."

Hastings stood there for a few seconds. "You just showed up to ask about something lying around in the warehouse on the same day our warehouse is ransacked?

What a coincidence. Let me guess—you're looking for something from Dr. Poley's archive? It's very popular."

Cashe turned and looked at Cyrus and Lowell. "Why would the Sons of Grant want that weapon?"

"They could easily sell it to the highest bidder," Lowell said.

Cyrus nodded. "Or they could quickly become the most powerful men in the country, if they threatened to use it on the right people."

"What're you talking about?" Hastings asked.

Cashe pulled out the photos. "Our people found these on an airship we captured, but the owner is an over-ambitious entrepreneur. I recognized the device as something I delivered here, so we thought we'd come check up on it."

Hastings sorted through the photos that showed the device with men standing around it. "Huh. I've never seen these pictures. Any idea where the pictures came from?"

"Not really," Cashe said. "Some seedy informer that the Sons used. You recognize them?"

Poking his finger at each of the men in turn, Hastings spoke offhandedly. "Sure. One in the middle is Poley, of course. That's Hink, Frasier, Lindy. All scientists. One in the back is an assistant, Gerard. Probably isn't much more than a teenager here."

"That piece they're standing around look familiar?"

Hastings handed the picture back. "You don't forget something that comes in with a warning about hair loss and vomiting."

"What?"

"Yeah. Most of the things Poley sent us were crated up with vague instructions on how to operate them. This." Hastings pointed to the photos. "This came with a tome on what *not* to do with it. Seriously, the notes went on and on about what to do if the crate broke open, how to treat wounds if anyone developed lesions, where to store it properly. Went on and on."

"So, what does it do, exactly?" Bethy asked. "This dread device of Dr. Poley's? What is it?"

Hastings looked at Bethy as if he'd just noticed she was there. "What does it do?" He shrugged. "No idea."

"No idea?" Cyrus asked.

"We never opened it. The instructions were quite clear. And terrifying."

"And none of the communications ever alluded to what it did?" Cashe asked.

Hastings shook his head and pointed the way around the next corner.

"How is that possible?" Lowell asked. "You've had this thing for what? A decade? That's slow, even for government work."

Hastings smiled but turned silent. He led them a few more paces to several sets of dark oversized doors that rose all the way to the ceiling with rusting metal hinges. Gripping one of the handles tightly, the doctor turned and put his weight into pushing the door open.

Cashe and the rest moved forward to find their view blocked by tall stacks of crates and boxes, bags and papers. The stacks went on for the length of the storehouse, maybe a quarter of a mile, stacked three crates deep. The crates were marked with all manner of numbers and letters, some with the Union flag on them, others with the Confederate, and at least one had a Union Jack on the side. Cashe couldn't even begin to fashion a guess as to how many packages and crates there were. It had to be hundreds he thought, could even be a thousand.

"Only a few of us here aren't soldiers, and this is what we have to work our way through," Hastings said. "Each of these crates has something that was sent to us by Dr. Poley or one of his cronies or was confiscated at some military depot from one side or another. Once we came under the U.N.A.'s auspices, we got inundated with all the shit that both the North and the South were tinkering with, and a few things the U.N. itself wanted developed and examined. We used to develop devices and weapons ourselves here, but we haven't had time to do anything original in years. We just work our way through a crate, try to make the objects inside work, and then move on."

"What do you do once you make these things work?" Cashe asked.

"We move them to the room next door," Hastings said.

"So none of these advances have made it to the field?" Lowell asked.

Hastings shook his head no. "We've been waiting for someone to deliver them."

Nearby, Alek shoved his way to the front of the O.M.O. group. "Did you say all of the working experiments were next door?" He cracked his knuckles and grinned. "Any chance we could get a look at those and maybe 'field test' them?"

49

Tom shoved his way down the gangplank, happy to be back in Santa Rosa. He knocked aside a crewman carrying a canvas bag over his shoulder and continued to the dock and the glow of the lights. He looked up and down the line of ships, through the crowds of sailors and dockworkers who choked the area even so late at night. A growing group of people gathered at the stern of the ship to gawk at the torn metal there. The beast had left some astounding damage. Claw marks, shredded iron and splintered wood made up what was left of the rear of the boat, and it made a puzzle of how the boat stayed afloat so far out to sea. Tom wasn't interested in dwelling on it and kept moving.

Farther on, standing near the light of a warehouse, Tom spied Potts smoking a cigarette and trying to blend with the background. Tom pulled his bowler a little lower and stepped toward his fellow conspirator.

"Tom? It's a bit late to unload the animals tonight," Cantolione's voice bellowed. "We'll wait 'til morning."

Tom kept walking.

"Tom? Tom Preston!"

Tom stopped and shuddered just a bit at how badly he needed to get away from his boss. The annoyance was immense, but he still needed to keep up appearances. He turned and scanned for Cantolione, finally finding the man leaning on the rail of the deck and waving wildly.

"I'll meet you here in the morning." Cantolione cupped his hands as he talked, as if that helped Tom hear any better. "Make sure they're prepared back at the animal cages, okay?"

Tom tipped his hat, waved, then left.

As he approached Potts, he nodded his head toward a nearby alley, hoping his friend would get the idea. After they exchanged quizzical looks for a moment, Potts turned and moved into the darkness.

"What's going on?" Potts asked as Tom entered the shadow of the alley.

"What's going on?" Tom mocked. "I've been at sea with a ridiculous crew of madmen, a ringmaster and a lizard bigger than life itself." He kept his voice low, but grabbed Potts by the shirt. "But the best reason for hiding out in an alley to talk is that we're still supposed to be keeping things a secret. Tough to be secretive when you're having your conversations in a crowd, wouldn't you say?"

"Jesus, Tom, what's gotten into you? I bring you good news and you snap my head off?"

"It's been a trying few days, Ian. If you have good news for me, you'd best give it to me now." Tom turned his head to watch the alley's entrance for interlopers while he listened.

"We got it," Potts said.

"That's what I wanted to hear," Tom said. "That's exactly what I needed right now."

Potts nodded. "I thought you'd like that. It was exactly where you said it would be. We were in and out in record time."

"Where is it now?"

The response was slow and considered. "We have the ship in the hills just outside of town, but we dropped the device off here in the warehouse. Thought you'd like to have a look." He thought for a second, and then added, "No problems."

It almost got by Tom, but he caught the wording of Potts's answer. "*The* ship? What ship? Where are the others?"

"The base had some airships of its own protecting it. They came out of nowhere after we were already attacking."

"We have a man on the inside of that base," Tom said. "He never mentioned airships."

"What can I say?" Potts said. "There they were." As if it would help, he added, "One of them was the biggest damn thing I'd ever seen. Knocked Rollie's ship out of the air with two shots."

It was distressing to say the least. Losing two thirds of their armada in one battle was a definite blow to the Sons of Grant. "How many men did we lose?"

"We left with somewhere around thirty-five, forty, and came back with…" It wasn't evident whether Potts was counting in his head or pausing before telling Tom bad news. "We came back with fourteen."

"Less than half? We lost that many on this one simple attack?"

"Simple? We attacked a secret military base. We were lucky to get away at all," Potts said. "And we hadn't suffered any casualties as far as I know, until those ships showed up."

"I had information on the base's strength and armaments. They were languishing out there in the middle of nowhere. It should've been easy."

"You weren't there," Potts said.

A good thing, too, Tom thought. He probably would've been on one of those ships that went down. Of course, it was a stretch to say he'd been safely somewhere else when all this happened. He'd been on a boat with cutthroats and killers, stalking large lizards with sharp teeth and watching sailors get devoured.

All in all, he found the losses at Outpost Two Thirteen to be acceptable. Twenty-five men and two airships in exchange for a device of almost mythical proportions?

"You're right," Tom said. "I'm sorry. You and the men have done an amazing thing, and your names will be remembered when the history of our new America is written. You'll be remembered alongside such patriots as Washington and Revere, Grant and Adams." He patted Potts on the arm. "In fact, there will be a position for you in the new government when Lincoln and his band of bumbling peacemakers are swept out with the tide."

If not pleased, at the very least, Potts looked mollified. "Thank you, sir, you know we just love this country."

"I know," Tom said. "Now, here's what we have to do, right now, to get this country back on the straight and narrow. You return to that encampment and bring the ship here in the afternoon, with the men and whatever else you have there. Come at first light and I'll have the boys here start loading up our equipment from the warehouse, including Poley's device. From there we make our way to Atlanta."

"In the afternoon?" Potts asked. "Didn't you just get angry at me for not being sneaky enough? Everyone and their kin will see us."

"Yes. But we're using one of Cantolione's ships, which shouldn't draw much attention. Besides, by that time, there will be nothing anyone can do. Anyone gets in our way, we'll handle them. Once we're airborne, no one can touch us."

"What's the rush?"

"If an O.M.O. ship engaged you at Two Thirteen, then they may have followed you here," Tom said. "With only one ship on our team, that is one conflict I'd like to avoid."

"I understand." Potts turned and walked down the alley briskly.

"Ian?" Tom said, just above a whisper. He waited for the man to turn. "The North *shall* rise again."

"Yes, it shall," Potts answered.

For good measure, Tom waited a few minutes before leaving the alley himself. He headed north and walked the five blocks to the warehouse he'd rented to fill with supplies for the Sons. He wasn't challenged by any of the men guarding the place, and he didn't dally in giving the orders to load the crates of rifles and ammunition onto wagons. No one questioned his orders to start taking the material to the airship tower at noon and he left with no pleasantries or grandiose speeches.

In the lamplight, he made his way to their warehouse and passed the various sentries that were posted with a tip of his hat. They let him pass without a word and then slunk back into the shadows. He walked back through the rows of equipment and provisions, back to where two single lamps shone. A woman on her knees poured over the gray device in silence.

"Well?" Tom made his presence known.

Geraldine Yardley looked up at him. "Well, what?"

"What does it do?"

"Damned if I know, Mr. Preston." She stood and wiped her hands. "Ain't no instructions for it or nothing."

Tom sighed. "What do you know about it?"

"Well, bear in mind that I'm used to working on trains, but here's all I've found." Yardley pointed to a small lever. "You pull this down and that sets the device to working." She pulled it and a low hum started to emanate from it. "Seems to be an engine of some type, I'd suppose steam powered." She pointed to one of the three hoses protruding from the side that disappeared into the engine. It began to shake. "There's something going through these things. I'm assuming water. After a bit, that sound gets higher."

"What happens then?"

"Well…." Yardley pointed to another piece on the machine. "After a minute, this switch pops up from the pressure of the steam."

"What happens when you press that?"

Yardley gave him an amused look. "I have no idea. I'd imagine it sets off the weapon, or starts a timer, but I certainly haven't tried it."

Tom saw her logic, but didn't admit it. "So how would we possibly test it?" With a tick, the little switch popped up and both looked at it.

"Be my guest, sir. But let me get a fair distance away before you try it."

Tom stared long and hard at it, before deciding not to chance it. "No idea what it does?"

"Best guess would be that the bottom part is an explosive of some type. *Best guess*. But the top part is a mystery. I'd imagine that the explosive activates or distributes whatever is on the top, but I don't know."

"Distributes what?"

"Just said I don't know. It could be full of metal shavings, it could have some gas of some sort. Hell, it could be filled with hot apple pie."

Tom didn't know what it was either, but from the log entries he'd read, he was sure it was more dangerous than anything Yardley suggested. "Fine. Keep looking. We're leaving tomorrow afternoon, and I'd like a better idea of what it does."

Yardley nodded. "I'll certainly try."

Tom took a room back at the nice hotel he and Cantolione stayed at the night before they left. He sat down on the bed for a moment before running a bath and taking off all his clothes.

He soaked in the water for a good half hour, letting it wash off the smell of the sea, the lizards, the blood, the stench of the chewers and everything else. He read from the log:

The men on the island have begun crawling and I've decided we have to mount a rescue. I've called for volunteers and received three brave souls willing to risk their lives for their fellows.

They were all idiots, Tom thought. If he'd been in charge, the ship would've weighed anchor long before anyone got off. A scorched island? No thanks. After a description of the preparations, the captain continued later in the afternoon:

As our rescue party made its way closer to the fallen men on the island, they were attacked. The men, who had laid still for over a day, leapt up at their comrades and tore at them, rending their flesh. Those of us still aboard the Grand Rapids *were astonished to see our men being devoured by their friends. Then, the blood-covered fiends began making their way slowly toward the shore. The* Grand Rapids *is anchored a half-mile out.*

Tom fell asleep in his bathrobe—his last thought was how tomorrow would be a new day, for himself, for the Sons of Grant and for America. In that order.

50

The satchel hit the bed with a *thunk*. Bethy pulled off her coat and dropped it to the floor. "Good to be home," she said. "No way I could've slept in that shambles of a fort." She grabbed a small tin toy off the floor and began winding it.

Cyrus watched from the doorway as she set it on a shelf. It spun slowly, throwing pinpoint dots of light on the walls and ceiling. It made patterns like the stars all around the room.

Bethy sighed. "It used to play music, too. One day we hit rough weather and it fell off the shelf, smashed on the floor. Haven't been able to get it to play right since."

Cyrus nodded his head. "Still, it's…nice. Pretty." The spinning points of light were soothing and Cyrus needed calming after the events of the last couple of days.

"You making fun of me?"

"No. I like it. It's too bad the music doesn't work, but I can see why it's special to you." Cyrus took a step into her room, and then stopped himself. "I should get to my bunk. I'm barely standing, I'm so tired."

Bethy's voice was quiet. "Oh. Yeah. I suppose you'd better. They set you up in one of the better bunks."

"I spent the night in it when we first got here. It was good," Cyrus lingered another moment. "So, I'll see you in the morning."

"Or you could stay," Bethy sounded like she'd held her breath. "I mean, nothing… Nothing funny. I just mean you could stay here tonight."

His boot squeaked on the metal deck as he stopped. Cyrus had already moved to go and let himself turn slowly as he thought about what she was saying. "I…."

"Never mind. It was a mistake," she said.

Cyrus stepped in and closed the hatch behind him. He stood staring at Bethy and she stared back. The toy stopped spinning and the room grew dark.

"Wind that up again," Cyrus said. He could hear Bethy stumble in the darkness a bit before he heard the sound of the key being wound again. He took off his coat and tossed it on a nearby chair. He awkwardly hopped as he took one boot off and then the other.

He dropped himself wearily onto her bunk and slid himself against the wall to give Bethy as much room as he could. She stepped over and took her satchel and dropped it on the floor.

She looked him in the eye briefly before looking away and lowering herself onto the bed with her back to him. In a few seconds, Cyrus heard her breathing grow deeper and he assumed she'd already fallen asleep. His ability to investigate that was hampered by the fact that he was out soon after.

51

Tom woke with a start when the hotel shook. The pages he had been reading slid off the bed and onto the floor. He looked around to see if it was a dream. Nothing else happened immediately and he started to fade back to sleep. Then he heard the boom of a cannon off in the distance. Then more reports followed.

Another shot originated close to the hotel, and his bed rumbled again.

Tom stood and pulled his robe close about him. Without an ounce of caution, he approached the shaded window.

It had grown silent again.

He pulled the curtain aside and looked out onto the ocean. The clouds shaded the moon, allowing only a little light through. Some lights on the shore weren't much help in discerning what was happening.

Further out to sea, a half mile maybe, a ship opened up with its cannon, illuminating the night. Tom caught sight of another ship, and it fired as well. The flashes were all too brief to be of any help, but it appeared that they were both aiming in the same direction.

The window was stubborn, and it took some muscle for Tom to open it. Once he lifted it all the way up he could hear shouting and general confusion from the people on the dock and the street nearby.

As he considered shoving the window shut again and going downstairs to investigate, an ungodly roar erupted from out to sea. It was a terrifying sound that he recognized—the beast they called Drago del Vapore. Tom scoured the skyline and water, until a sudden simultaneous burst of cannon fire from the two ships illuminated the beast. It was between them, its head barely above water. In another moment it disappeared beneath the waves.

His first thought was to curse Cantolione. If he hadn't been so all-fire excited about the sickly little lizards, the thing wouldn't be in the harbor.

Tom's next thought was for his own safety. The beast had obviously come to kill him specifically.

Before he could process the best way to avoid his own demise, one of the two ships, which he recognized as the *Oregon*, bobbed up violently on the ocean then fell back with a displacement of water that created a number of great waves. Tom could see nothing of the men on the ship, but the ensuing wave crashed all the way up onto the decks and he could only assume that a number of sailors had to have been swept away.

Due to the creature moving so close to the ships, the firing from the big guns had ceased, replaced by smaller arms fire, presumably men trying to hit the beast with rifle shot.

Tom turned and ran, the mesmerizing scene broken by the dragon's disappearance from view. He grabbed his pants and slid them on, threw his shirt and coat over his shoulder, propped his hat on his head and ran out into the street bare chested. The boulevard was crowded with people running with no real direction, other than to get to the streets that led east and inland. The roads that led away from the fight in the harbor. Tom was nearly knocked down by a man watching the attack while he ran. It was hard to pull himself up as more and more people ran by without trying to avoid Tom. He grabbed a woman's dress and pulled himself up, using her momentum.

The woman tugged against him. "Let go, dammit," she said.

"Thank you, ma'am." Tom walked away, pushing his way toward the edge of the docks. Something had changed—he could make out the other ship, but the *Oregon* wasn't in sight.

The other ship released a new volley of fire and the ensuing light showed where the *Oregon* had gone—it was listing to the side so severely that Tom had at first taken it for waves.

The beast had taken it down and none of the cannon fire seemed to have done the Dragon any harm.

"Shame we couldn't have captured that one."

Tom turned to see Cantolione standing directly behind him, dressed in his usual dapper coat and top hat.

"Think we still can?"

The bow of the *Oregon* lifted out of the water as the stern sunk lower. "No. I really don't think so, sir," Tom said.

52

Cashe walked the wall of Outpost Two Thirteen, stopping to watch the *Polk* high above, slowly patrolling in its long circuitous route. It would be nice to be back onboard, in familiar territory in his own cruddy little bed. The fort's hospitality was fine enough, but everyone looked at him expectantly, no matter where he went and what he was doing. He figured it would wear off after a few hours, but it didn't. And the wall was the best he could do to get away.

This side of the Outpost was built onto an embankment, at the base of it, a long fence of rock, wood and other debris surrounded the perimeter. Beyond it, a wide open field stretched for half a mile, making it easy to see anything that approached from that direction, and it would give anyone in the fort plenty of warning. Cashe took in the sight, enjoying the view of the surrounding mountains and the flat desert that stretched out before him.

"It's a pretty area, isn't it?" Dr. Hastings approached, and Cashe couldn't help but notice the man carried a long barreled rifle and a pouch for ammunition.

"It is," Cashe said. "Seems like a strange place for a military base."

The doctor nodded. "That's part of the charm of it. No one would think to look for it here. You know?"

"I suppose there is a logic to it."

"Plus, between the mountains and the desert, not many people really feel like venturing out here." Hastings paused and packed the rifle with powder. "Well, except for fools like the men who came here earlier. Those men were on a mission."

"Yeah. I'm surprised they found you so easily," Cashe said.

Hastings continued to load the gun, stuffing the rod down the barrel to pack the ammunition. "I'm not. We were a secret facility at one time, but the end of the war brought an end to a lot of that. People got real loose with things they swore to keep quiet when they were soldiers. We became a curiosity, everyone wondering what we did out here. Hell, I'd lay good money there are some idiots over there in the mountains staring at you and me right now through a telescope."

Cashe was a little unnerved by the idea that someone had eyes on them. "Is that what the rifle's for, scaring off the curious?"

"Nah. Sometimes I like to come up here to blow off steam. You look down at that skirmish line we built and you're bound to see some chewers wander up and get stuck there. We have to weed those out from time to time, just so's they don't climb over each other and then over that barrier." Hastings flipped up an oversized sight on the rifle's barrel and then got down on his knees to use the wall to steady himself. He twisted the barrel of the sights back and forth. "Ah, yes. We have a few struggling in the rocks." He reached into his pocket and pulled out a pair of field glasses. "You want to take a look?"

With a nod, Cashe took the glasses and looked down to the makeshift fence line. He couldn't make anything out at first but rocks and debris, but when he focused and moved a little more slowly, he could see movement in the mass.

Hastings took a deep breath and fired when he released it. On the barrier, one of the chewers fell backward from the impact of the hit. The doctor lowered the gun and picked up the next set of materials to load the weapon. "It took me a bit, but I finally remembered you." He poured the powder down the barrel. "You'd been here before, sure. But you weren't in charge then, were you?" Hastings packed the powder good with the rod and looked up at Cashe.

He had the option here to tell the true story. Cashe could explain to the man exactly how it happened and where they done good and how it had helped so many people, but the lie was too ingrained in Cashe to let him speak. "Why are you using an old-fashioned musket to do this? There's a whole store of weapons down there that could do this job more efficiently and easier than this."

"Sometimes it feels good to do something yourself, you know what I mean? Most of my job is going through those crates, picking up doo-dads that other men built and seeing how they work." Hastings put the finishing touches on the charge and steadied the barrel on the wall again. "But, another part of that job is when I have to sew up some soldier that got himself hurt or shot or something. There's a lot less of them getting shot lately, but it happens. I like to keep my hands active, and my thoughts busy. I like to think about what I'm doing just to stay sharp in my mind and this certainly helps."

"You keep your medical skills honed by killing things?" Cashe asked. "Seems incongruous."

"But there you have it," Hastings said. He focused the sights and pointed the gun back at the barrier.

"You really don't know what Poley's device does?" Cashe asked.

Hastings didn't blink at the question. "I think it blows up and leaves a big hole in the ground."

"A bomb? We figured that."

"Yep," Hastings said. "But it seems to do more than just blow things up. It leaves some residue that turns men into these ungodly things. That's my guess. From the tests they were doing and the timing of it all. I think they tested one of these out there and that's where our chewers came from."

Cashe wanted to pursue that further but Hastings changed his line of discussion too quick.

"The last time you were here...." Hastings paused for a second as he tracked something below. "You were basically a postman. You delivered some of these crates, some mail and packages from the O.M.O. and the like. What? You were a quartermaster or something?"

"Yes."

"You certainly weren't on that massive ship you're flying now."

"I had a small cargo airship," Cashe said. "*The Messenger.*"

The musket roared again and another chewer fell off the line below. Dr. Hastings chuckled. "Don't kill the messenger."

"So what now?"

"It has been only a few years since you were last here, so if you rose through the ranks from quartermaster to captain or admiral or whatever you are now, I'd be quite impressed with your abilities. But that's not the case, is it?" Hastings sat with the gun across his lap. He patted his pocket and came up with a gnarled cigar and offered it to Cashe.

"No thanks, I have my own." Cashe pulled a carefully-rolled, thin cigar from his breast pocket, produced a match and struck it against the wall. As the flame erupted, he immersed the end of the cigar in it until smoke poured out of his mouth and then leaned down to let Hastings light his off it as well.

The two of them smoked in silence for a few minutes—Hastings facing the parade grounds inside the fort, Cashe staring off into the desert beyond the barriers.

"We just used the *Polk* to get out of a bad situation one time," Cashe said. "Never meant to keep on with it. When we landed to turn it over to someone, we were mobbed with people with problems, wrongs that needed righting, and even soldiers that wanted to join the government's efforts. It was disheartening, to say the least, to see how things were going out there."

Cashe tapped the ashes off his cigar and sat down next to Hastings. "The first few civilians that approached me and Emmett...we told them straight that we weren't the people they were looking for. But as the day wore on, we found that the O.M.O. hadn't been around. Ever. I don't know how the conversation went, but Emmett and I decided to take on the roles of authority. By the end of that very same day, we were recruiting soldiers to join the cause."

Hastings looked up and exhaled a cloud of blue smoke. "How long ago was this?"

"Hell if I know anymore. Five, six years now?"

"And nobody's questioned you?"

"No. Not really. In all that time, I've gotten a couple of sideways glances from O.M.O. officers, but the lines of communications are almost nonexistent. Even if someone wanted to challenge me, I'm not real sure they could get a definite confirmation one way or another without getting ahold of headquarters out East. That's something I've tried to do myself, with no luck."

Cashe paused and thought about the half-assed attempts he and Emmett had made over the years to end the charade, but decided not to go into them. "To be honest, after you and I met, I thought that was all that was going to happen. You give me a funny look, jog your memory and then forget about it."

Hastings laughed and started loading the gun again after he stabbed his cigar out. "See? That's what happens when you exercise your mind and keep it active—you remember things better." He got back on his knees and aimed the rifle out toward the barrier again.

Cashe waited until the shot rang out before he spoke. "So what do we do now?"

"What do we do now?"

"About this situation?"

"Look, Mr. Cashe, if you want to turn that ship over to the O.M.O. right here and now, you can cut your act with no consequences from me or the senior staff here. Otherwise, as you said, none of us have any means of verifying your credentials and you can continue on."

"I really think the crew I've assembled and the new people I pick up do some real good from time to time."

"I think you probably do too, or else I'd have blown the whistle and you'd be in irons right now."

Cashe nodded and saw his point. He looked through the field glasses at the land below them and waited for the man to pick a new target. "You really think there are people out there staring at us at this very moment?"

Hastings pulled the trigger and another chewer's body jumped down on the barrier, catapulting parts of the creature's head all over the rocks. "Yeah. It's kind of creepy."

53

The only light in Bethy's room came from the moon as it peeked through the clouds. Cyrus had been careful as he removed himself from her bed, so as not to awaken her. It wasn't easy, as every muscle in his body ached with each movement, but he managed to stand and quietly walk over to look out the portal.

The moon was visible in bits and pieces as the clouds rolled by. They were big and puffy clouds that went blue in the light, with little halos around them. It was nothing like the noisy, gear-grinding Turtle. Just the thrum of the *Polk's* engine indicated they were moving at all.

"You like the view?" Bethy leaned on her elbow with the blankets all around her.

"It has its charm," Cyrus said.

Bethy gathered her blanket tight and stood, slowly walking over to him. "I'd never flown before I joined up with Cashe."

"You mean when you joined up with the O.M.O., don't you?"

"No. It was Cashe that convinced me I had a place here. I was really putting my faith in him, or at least I was flattered by his faith in me." She got close to Cyrus, nearly leaning on the portal. She was considerably shorter than him, to the point where he wondered whether they were seeing the same section of sky.

"What is it about him that seems to instill such a following?"

She shook her head and smiled. "Don't know."

It wasn't an answer that Cyrus would've expected from her. She seemed free with her opinions.

"Follow me." She walked to the door and opened it, still gripping the dark green blanket with one hand. She looked out into the corridor and then waved to him to follow.

Cyrus crossed the room and stopped at the door. Corrigan had walked into the hall and noticed Bethy.

"Lovely sleeping gown," Corrigan said.

Cyrus walked into the hall behind her and Corrigan went red in the face. "Oh, sorry. I…." He stepped through the nearest doorway, nearly bumping his head on the frame.

Bethy giggled and grabbed Cyrus's hand to pull him along. They stopped at a stairwell that wound down in a spiral to the deck below. The pair carefully moved down it, Bethy minding her blanket so as not to trip. At the bottom, she lit a lamp and turned it low. Cyrus stepped off the stair and immediately noticed another dim glow coming from the floor ahead.

"Go ahead. Take a look." She leaned against the wall and waited.

More than a little perplexed, Cyrus did as she said. When he got to the center of the room he realized that a large portion of it was glass. He stepped closer and was greeted by the beauty of the open land below. He could see trees and fields passing languidly as the *Polk* floated on. They were high enough that thin wisps of clouds drifted on occasionally. "My God, it's amazing."

"Yeah. I think we all take it for granted, we get so busy."

"What's this room for?"

She pointed to some mechanisms in the rear of the room. "We can drop explosives from here if we need to. The glass area helps in aiming and navigating."

He nodded and knelt down by the edge of the area and stared.

"Tell me about the Turtle," she said.

Cyrus was taken aback by her straightforward question. "What?"

"You've been handed a lot in the last few days. You haven't had time to grieve for those people," she said. "I wouldn't consider it a burden if you want to tell me what you're thinking."

Cyrus stood and felt himself close up. He didn't want to go over it with anyone, let alone this girl he hardly knew. "I don't think…."

"You aren't ready."

He looked at her and had no idea why he suddenly felt ready in that moment, when he wasn't in the previous moment.

"All those people," he said. "The crew. I was talking to the crew just minutes before. They should have made it out with Lucy and me." His own mention of Lucinda stopped him from continuing. Something made him close his mouth firmly.

"It's ok," she said. "Go on."

"No. That's enough. I don't want to talk anymore."

"You don't have to," she said.

But he couldn't stop himself once he'd started. "Those people counted on me. I was in charge of two hundred sixteen lives and I let them all down." Tears began to fall down his cheeks, but he turned away and forced himself not to make a sound.

"Cyrus?"

He didn't turn. "Yeah?"

"Turn around."

"I don't think—"

"Just turn around."

He took a deep breath and composed himself by wiping his eyes with his sleeve. "Look, I just…." He turned to find Bethy lying naked on the edge of the glass, the blanket beneath her. "How did you? You were fully clothed when we went to bed."

"You're a heavy sleeper."

He took in the sight of her—her short brown hair falling around her apple cheeks, the roundness of her breasts.

"If you're still trying to figure out how I got out of my clothes," she said. "You're thinking too hard on the wrong subject."

He agreed and walked toward her, fumbling with his shirt buttons as quickly as he could. As he approached, she leaned back, and he could see the thin clouds moving behind her head.

54

Cashe, Daniel and Lucinda sat around a table with the doctor and some of his men in the main mess hall of the fort. They looked at maps and discussed the nearby towns, what was left of them and delved into the state of the roads, the rails and the easiest path through the mountains on foot and by air. Cashe knew the ground to the south pretty well, but hadn't ventured up this way. His general route when taking passengers went well to the south.

A number of the post's men were milling around, meeting the *Polk*'s crew and trying to wind down from the day. It was well into the night, but no one seemed ready to leave.

"Hey Lucinda," Daniel waved a deck of cards around. "We're trying to get a friendly game of Spanish Monte together. You interested?"

"Spanish Monte? I'm afraid I'm not familiar with that one." She took the deck from Daniel and examined them.

Alek laughed and sat down with them. "We'd be more than happy to teach you."

"How kind." Lucinda suddenly shuffled the cards from one hand to the other and quickly fanned them out in a circle on the table face down. She then flipped them all over at once so the numbers were visible and then flipped them back over. She shuffled them again and tapped the tight deck on the bottom, making the ace of spades jump out. She put it back, cut the deck and then shuffled them with one hand until the same card fell out again. She fluttered her eyes at Alek and Daniel as she made all of the cards zip from one hand to the other. Finally she set the deck in front of Daniel again.

"That's very…nice," Daniel said.

"Flip the top card," she said.

He did and found it to be the ace of spades.

Cashe laughed. "Well done."

Lucinda shuffled the cards slowly. "I lost everything I had recently, so if I'm going to get involved in a game, we'll need someone to stake us."

"I'm not sure I want you playing with the men around here. It could be bad for morale," Hastings said.

A soldier pushed his way past everyone in the room to get to the doctor. "Sir, just got a message off the telegraph from Santa Rosa. I think you should read it."

Cashe looked up. He'd been following the prelude to the card game half-heartedly.

"Why?" Hastings was scrubbing his hands vigorously with soap and water.

"It's a bit unusual," the soldier said.

Cashe watched as the doctor read it and then lowered the paper. "This is obviously a mistake of some sort."

"I thought so too," the soldier said. "So I asked them to repeat it. Twice."

"What is it?" Cashe took the paper and read it.

"The message claims a dragon is attacking Santa Rosa," Hastings said, "and has already destroyed a number of the Navy's ships stationed there."

Some of the men in the room chuckled, Cashe among them. He couldn't help himself.

"Those photos you showed me included some big lizards," Cashe said. "Maybe this is just some exaggeration of those things."

"How big of lizards are we talking about?" Hastings asked.

"Big," Lowell said. "Maybe ten to twelve feet. Maybe bigger."

"This says the dragon destroyed a number of ships in the harbor," Hastings said. "I don't think one of your twelve foot lizards could do that."

Cashe had seen the pictures himself and had to concede. Even at the largest possible interpretation of those creatures' measurements, they weren't in a league to break a battleship. "So, what do we do to figure this out?"

"We send back another message to clarify what they said, and we pack up the *Polk* to head for Santa Rosa while we wait, I guess." Cashe was already moving toward the hall with the others following.

Daniel looked at Hastings and smiled. "What're we going to do if this lizard is a chameleon? We might never find it." It was a lame joke and the sour look on the doctor's face told everyone it was just as bad as he thought it was.

"We'll be on the airship if you get any more information," Cashe said, and he quietly backed out of the room.

Lowell followed him. "Look, we've still got *The Moon and the Stars*, why don't I take a couple of men and check it out? We can get there pretty fast."

"I'll go," Daniel said.

Cashe thought about it. "You'll just scout ahead and report back. That's all."

"That sounds agreeable," Lowell said.

Daniel nodded and smiled. "I'm a little tired of being cooped up on the *Polk*. I can help out with the navigation."

"You think that ship will handle it?" Cashe was thinking of the trouble they'd had along the way.

"I fixed it," Lowell said. "It's fine."

Daniel and Cashe both gave him a sideways glance.

"Please. You know I took care of it." Lowell was met with more skepticism. "If I said I fixed it, I fixed it. It's fixed."

Cashe realized it would be advantageous to have an advance force to give them a true assessment of the situation. "All right. You go. You see. You report. Get with any local military and send us a wire."

Lowell nodded.

"Well, what are you waiting for?" Cashe asked. "Go. And see if you can find a couple of soldiers from the fort to go with you, just in case you need help."

"Yes, sir." Lowell waved over his shoulder and he and Daniel ran off.

"He's a little too excited for his own good, don't you think?" the doctor said.

Cashe thought the same thing from time to time, but knew Lowell was a good man at heart. "Sometimes, but he knows what he's doing," Cashe said. "Most of the time."

55

Sometime after four in the morning, the other ship sank. Tom had heard from the gathered crowd that it was a Confederate gunship called the *Harper's Ferry*. After that, the dragon disappeared beneath the waves in a flurry of bubbles. Everyone gathered on the docks was relieved to see the beast go, until someone pointed out that there was nothing in the harbor to occupy the thing's time, leaving it free to come ashore and wreak havoc on the harbor town, including everyone gathered to watch the fight.

Tom got close to a light post and stayed there, letting it become a natural barricade to keep from being swept away in the panic that came next. Cantolione had wandered off hours ago, disinterested in the battle, though still intrigued by the big beast.

When the crowds cleared, Tom was virtually alone, except for the occasional straggler or brave soul.

A detachment from the nearby Benicia Arsenal had arrived to help quell the panic, see people safely evacuated and to engage the beast. They arrived in the early evening and set up camp in the northeast part of the city. They were almost immediately ineffective. They'd given up quickly when their muskets were useless against the animal. They fell back to their camp and set to the task of mismanaging the evacuation. Once the monster disappeared, people wanted to go home. Instead of making them wait it out to be sure it was safe, they allowed anyone to return when they wanted.

Tom watched people with all their worldly possessions wander the streets, headed back to their homes, and he shook his head, knowing they'd be running away again if the beast came back. And that was almost assured.

He pulled out the log book from his pocket and turned to the where he'd left off. The fires and the lamp gave him ample light to read the last few passages.

We have decided we cannot risk any more lives and are prepared to leave the island to warn others to stay away. I don't know what is causing all of this, but I'm sure other ships that came before us suffered our fate as well.

About goddamn time, Tom thought. He would've started swimming long before this. What sort of idiot was this captain anyway? By the time he'd gotten underway, surely the walking dead were well understood and yet he'd drifted right into it.

We are underway and should be home in a couple of days. The California coastline will be a welcome sight. I'm not sure what to make of these events, but my recommendation to the government will most certainly be to stay clear of Campbell Atoll. There is some commotion in the infirmary and I've been asked to go down and settle it. I'll continue my report upon my return.

Tom laughed at that. "Not likely you'll be continuing this log anytime soon," he whispered. He thought about whether he or anyone else had killed the good captain when they went aboard the *Grand Rapids* and considered it a strong possibility.

Tom walked toward the circus. When he came to a pile of burning rubble, he chucked the log book into it, and stopped to watch it burn for a minute.

56

The morning was awkward for Cyrus. He and Bethy had made their way back to her quarters and fell asleep on her bunk.

Neither of them had much to say when they awoke. For Cyrus's part it was because of the conflicted feelings that Bethy brought up in him. His first thought on waking had been *Where is Lucy?* Even on a ship that was populated with people that seemed entirely devoted to the protection of each other as well as the general populace, he worried about what she might have gotten into and who was targeting her.

On Bethy's part, he had no idea what her silence meant. She was pretty quiet around him even before this happened—other than when she was making him look like a fool.

"We ought to get around, before someone thinks poorly of us," Bethy said.

"Why would they do that?"

"I'm the only woman on a ship full of soldiers. They get protective of me," she said. "You don't think they might hold a grudge against you?"

Cyrus didn't correct her about the number of women on board. "Don't they already?"

Bethy leaned down and kissed him. "Aww. Are the other boys teasing you?"

"Lowell in particular doesn't seem fond of me."

"You didn't seem real fond of him either."

It was true, and Cyrus knew it. He'd been so suspicious of the man's motives that he didn't give him much of a chance. The preoccupation had clouded Cyrus's judgment since he arrived and tainted the way he'd seen all the crew. "Yeah. You might not be wrong there."

"Lowell is a good man to have around," Bethy said. "He's handy with a gun and he's got some smarts to him. You could do well to learn from him."

Cyrus came close to admitting that he could, but Bethy kept talking.

"Come on, grab you trousers and get out. I'll see you at the breakfast table."

"You don't think they'll have us go down to the fort and have chow with everyone else?" Cyrus asked.

"They'll switch out crews so the *Polk* can keep patrolling the air. We probably need to take on water and coal anyway."

Cyrus quickly pulled on his clothes and put his hand on the door. "Maybe later, we can…?"

"That would be the perfect Sunday afternoon, wouldn't you think?" She laughed at Cyrus's grimace.

"You don't know what I was going to suggest."

"Doesn't matter," Bethy said.

She was an odd bird, but Cyrus was beginning to find her hard to do without.

His next thought was as to whether it was actually Sunday or not. The hours and days were a fleeting thing in his mind lately.

57

The Moon and the Stars strained to move faster as Lowell pushed it harder.

"We just need to get there and make sure this is real," Daniel said. "Maybe we should take it back a bit before this thing shakes apart."

"This isn't the *Polk*," Lowell said. "This ship is designed for speed."

Daniel shook his head. "No. This ship was made to take little old ladies and children on whale-watching tours up the coast."

"I've been running this rig for the last several days. I know what she can do," Lowell said. "Trust me. We can make it after first light."

"Fine, but don't come crying to me if we both die."

"I'll keep it to myself."

There was silence for a good portion of the trip, but eventually, they conferred on the status of their new cohorts onboard the *Polk*.

"What do you think of them?" Daniel asked. "They seem wicked crazy if you ask me. Anyone wants to live in one of those Turtles has to have something wrong with their mind."

"Still. Ain't a reason to be unsociable." Lowell felt maybe Cyrus's ability to prioritize the dangers in his life were a bit misaligned. "True. A man has to be friendly when among friends."

58

"I will tear your goddamn arm off and feed it to you," Tom said to the telegraph operator. His usual contact, Curtis, was replaced by a military man. He was from the army that had marched in to contain the threat in the town and help evacuate the townspeople. Their first priority was to set up communications.

"I'm sorry sir," the soldier said. "No civilian communications out or in until this crisis is solved. And I'll thank you to keep a civil tongue."

"What crisis? The thing went back into the sea and hasn't returned. I'd say we call that a solved problem."

"Thank you, sir. I'll pass that along to the general in charge," the soldier said.

Tom leaned in close enough that he could tell the man had eaten beans fairly recently. "You don't know who you're dealing with here. I am Thomas Preston, the right hand man to Mr. Umberto Cantolione, and he's asked me to send an urgent message on his behalf."

The soldier stood up behind the counter and smiled. "The circus guy? You work for him? And he has some all-fire important message to send? 'Bout what? Low on peanuts for the elephants? Shit." The man started around the counter and pointed to the door. "Get the hell out of here before I have a soldier or two escort you out back and knock the stupid out of you."

There was an ache in Tom's hand that made him want to pull his gun and shoot the man that stood in his way. Or at the very least Tom considered pulling it and beating the soldier with it. But the thought that anyone could walk in at any time dissuaded him, not to mention that fact that there were nearly a thousand soldiers with guns just outside the door.

Tom backed up and raised his hands in surrender. He turned and stepped out of the little wooden telegraph shack and onto the rickety steps and off into the mud. He needed information. He needed to know what was going on back at the outpost and whether the O.M.O. was on their way. The Sons of Grant had a camp not far outside of town, but there was no way of contacting them without access to a telegraph.

The muddy ground was so bad that Tom nearly fell.

"Hey," the telegraph operator said. "Mr. Tom Preston. You tell Mr. Cantolione not to bother coming down here himself to try and send anything. He'll get the same answer." The soldier started back into his station. "Unless there's some sort of terrible clown accident or something. That might constitute an emergency." The door slammed behind him and the whole shack shook.

Tom was developing a course of action to make the soldier's life a misery when he noticed something in the tent city that served as the military's headquarters.

An airship was landing in their midst. And not just any airship—*The Moon and the Stars.*

Tom nearly fell again. That ship should have crashed into the mountains days ago. Everyone on that craft should be dead, a chewer, or twisted into a pile of wreckage. He could feel a bit of sweat forming on his brow. If anyone survived, they could be here to ruin everything. They might just have a chance at doing it if they got to Cantolione with what they knew. They probably wouldn't have proof, but it could still upset everything.

When he saw two men from the O.M.O. disembark, it formed in his head that his situation could be more dire than he thought. If someone had survived and went to the military, they were surely closing in fast.

Tom had tried his best to maintain a low profile but things had begun to pile up. Even though he'd eliminated the people that could connect him to the worst of the offenses, there were others. Their ship was in front of him, and he had no reason to believe every one of them wasn't telling tales on him to the authorities right now.

59

Lowell stopped at the command post that the military had set up, but they had no plan and no order to what they were doing. They had been reduced to directing the traffic of the evacuees. Daniel stayed behind to see what he could do and to be ready with *The Moon* if it was needed.

Lowell came into the waterfront district of Santa Rosa with the ground pounders—some infantry from the Benecia Arsenal—and truly wished he'd stayed on the airship. Everyone in the city was running in the opposite direction of the soldiers, making it impossible for them to take up defensible positions. The mad rush of civilians, the screaming, the sudden bursts of gunfire were all too disorienting. Better to float high above the melee and watch the terrified population scatter like ants.

"Which way?" he shouted at the nearest person he thought might help, but the man kept running without a pause.

Lowell moved up to the corner of the next building and peered around it. More people ran in his direction. Up the next block, he could see a small group of soldiers huddled against the side of a row house.

"What's going on? Where is this thing?" he shouted as he approached the group.

One of them grinned a buck-toothed smile at Lowell. "You haven't seen it yet? What're you, blind?"

"Just got here." Lowell didn't like the implication in the other man's words.

One of the other men turned and stuck out his hand. "I'm Clayton Jennings, who're you?"

Lowell shook his hand. "Lowell Sanderson. Lyle Cashe of the O.M.O. sent me."

Lowell could feel Jennings sizing him up. "What exactly did the good Mr. Cashe send you to do?"

Somewhere nearby a cannon roared to life and the evening sky lit up. Lowell watched the glow fade as he thought about his answer. Truth was, Cashe told him to stay away.

Lowell shrugged. "Help restore order, I guess."

"That's Riley," Jennings indicated the smiling man. "And that's Dex. Stick with us. We can always use more chum."

The men laughed.

Jennings moved quickly up the block, staying close to the building to avoid the people fleeing the scene.

"I'm sure he meant chums," Riley said and ran after Jennings.

Lowell took a deep breath and followed. He should probably wait and find someone in charge of the assault, but he remembered the chaos of the staging area. Better to hook up with three men that had some sort of plan than a company of soldiers with no direction.

The small group turned down an alley that nearly blotted out what little light was still around this late in the day. It was littered with filth and smelled of waste. Lowell's eyes watered, making it that much harder to follow his guides in the dark grey uniforms.

"Christ, slow up," he called to the others.

"The faster we get through this alley," Jennings yelled, "the faster you get your look at the freak show."

A fresh barrage of cannon fire erupted on one of the streets behind them.

"What the hell are they firing at?" Lowell asked. "Surely they can't get a good shot at that thing from way back here. All the buildings are in the way."

Ahead the others came to a halt where the alley emptied out into the street. They all cautiously looked to their right, barely allowing their heads to penetrate the light that was shining in from some streetlamps.

"You want to see what they're shooting at? Have a look for yourself." Riley tipped his head toward the street and stepped aside, giving Lowell room to squeeze in with the others.

He moved up between Dex and Jennings, both of whom stood silently with their mouths agape just a bit. Lowell leaned cautiously out of the alley. It was dark down most of the thoroughfare, with only the occasional lamp lit to help identify things. The street sloped slightly downhill for a half mile or so before taking a serious dip toward the waterfront. Lowell could make out a light down by the docks reflecting off the waves. It was a good mile and a half, maybe two, down to the water. Aside from the occasional pile of trash or abandoned vehicle, he couldn't make anything out except the tall buildings that made up the city of Campbell.

"What's going on? What am I supposed to be seeing?" Lowell asked.

Jennings held up his hand. "Watch and wait."

Lowell stared in the same general direction as the others, scanning the streets and storefronts for some sign. He saw nothing overhead, nothing in the water, and nothing in the buildings. He sighed and started to make another comment until he finally noticed something unusual—one of the buildings moved.

"What in hell?"

Riley giggled. "He sees it."

Lowell watched as a large dark shadow that he had assumed was another downtown structure shifted toward the street they were on. It was in the water and moving south. Even from their fair distance away, they could clearly hear the water sloshing with the beast's every step. Lowell watched as the white cap of a great wave broke over onto land and flooded the shipping areas before the water retreated.

"I was told it was big, but...."

"I know," Jennings said. "The last report we looked at said the beastie was about twenty-five feet tall. I'd say they were wrong by at least half, wouldn't you?"

Lowell nodded. Fifty feet was a decent estimate, but he guessed it was even bigger. The fact that he couldn't see the whole thing made it worse in his imagining. As the form disappeared once again behind buildings, its tail slapped the mast off a trawler in the water, snapping it like a match stick.

"What're we doing back here?" Lowell asked. "Why are we hiding and ducking from a thing that's all the way down in the harbor?"

Riley, who was still behind him, had broken out a cigarette and was cupping his hand around to light it. As he got it going, he passed it to Dex. "Well." Riley exhaled a cloud of smoke. "We were closer. A lot closer. It came ashore over on the other side of town. We were right up against its slimy little fun bags when it came up Main Street and proceeded to chew on The Hotel Marigold."

Jennings waved off the cigarette and Dex passed it back to Riley.

Riley took another drag and held it. "So, we were closer. We were also a full battalion." He let the smoke slip out his nose. "Now we're light by about six hundred or so men. You'll have to forgive us for not wanting to head right back into its flapping jaws again so soon. And who knows if it can hear us clear out here. Not taking any chances on attracting its attention."

Lowell took a good look at the men for the first time, finally noticing their torn uniforms and the bloodstains on Dex's sleeves. "The cannons we've been hearing—"

"Haven't been doing a damn thing to it." Jennings interrupted. "Rifle fire, pistol shots, cannons—nothing. The 21st infantry had a Gatling gun and gave it their best shot, but nothing happened. I'm thinking of digging up a bow and some arrows just to be able to say we've tried everything."

An animal that can't be affected by bullets and bombs?

"You're with the O.M.O.," Jennings said. "Are there airships on the way? Maybe they can rain down some damage." He didn't look hopeful.

Not wanting to let on about the state of the airship the last time he saw it, Lowell nodded. "Should be."

"The *Amber Fire* didn't help much," Dex said. "That thing tore through it like stale bread." The *Amber Fire* was one of the largest warships the Confederate States had in their arsenal, with twin five inch cannons on her bow and a front-loading mortar off her stern.

Riley pointed down toward the docks. "That's her, burning down by the garment district."

"What about the crew?" Lowell asked.

"Most of them lost. Hard to say how many made it. There wasn't much time." Jennings waved the others on to follow him and started cautiously sprinting down the sidewalk toward the bay.

It took a minute for Lowell to follow, and as he looked around he realized that the people who'd been fleeing on the other streets were not fleeing here. When he listened, he couldn't hear the chaotic screams or the steady footfalls that accompanied the people as he went. The cannons had also fallen silent and the gunfire was only sporadic. He discovered that, except for these three men he didn't know, he was alone in the battle ravaged city. No Cyrus, no Cashe, no Lucinda. Worse, the only people he knew here were running toward a giant lizard. He thought he understood why Riley was smiling so much—there really wasn't any other way to handle it, not without running away.

Lowell took a deep breath and tried to catch up with the others.

60

Lowell climbed the last stair behind the men, and they motioned for him to keep low. He moved in a crouch over to the windows. The last of the evening light filtered through the half-drawn shades. Gunfire outside had all but died out completely.

"The navy and the army got batted away like gnats," Lowell said. "What do you think we're going to do here?" The question was directed at the soldiers, but he felt himself trying to answer it as well.

Jennings parted the shades using the tip of his rifle. "Well, we could wait for the air corps to show up and see how they do."

Riley snickered and pulled the weapon off his back. He flicked the safety and breached the gun, basically folding it in half. He took a fist-sized bullet from his pocket and dropped it in before snapping the gun shut with a flick of his arm. "Least the airships can keep out of that thing's reach," he said.

The building began to shake with intermittent rumbles. Lowell and the soldiers were in an office of some sort, and with every shock, books and pens and paper jumped from their perches and fell back into place, slightly more disheveled than the last time. A lamp hit the floor and shattered, but none of the men were startled, they were too intent on seeing what was causing the ruckus.

"It's still coming up Angola. It's going to pass right by us." Jennings said it with confidence, like it was a good thing.

"And we'll do what? What's the plan here?" Lowell asked. "I've got a revolver, a carbine, and pocket knife. Should I throw them at this beast and run away, or is there something better on offer?" He'd followed these three blindly, hoping they'd lead somewhere where they could do some good. This was not that place.

"This thing's been eating its way up the boardwalk, so Riley here is going to give him a little after-dinner mint." Jennings patted Riley on the back. Riley patted his recently loaded gun.

A shelf gave way on the other side of the room, sending tomes sprawling onto the floor.

"He's going to shoot into the monster's mouth?" Lowell looked from one man to the other as he thought about it. He'd known some crack shots in his time, but to get that big ordinance into the admittedly large, but not gigantic, mouth of the creature would be a feat of some note.

Dex tensed up and moved away from the window. "I see it. It's coming."

He didn't sound excited or frightened, but when Lowell turned to look, he saw the man was pale, and his wide eyes stared across the room blankly.

Lowell reached up and pulled the shade aside on the next window over.

He realized that his earlier glimpse of the creature was misleading. Riley should have no trouble putting his explosives in the beast's mouth. It was massive. It was massive and lined with teeth that were possibly taller than Riley himself.

The men were on the fourth and top floor of the building and when the monster passed by, it would be at eye level with them. Or possibly mouth level.

"Christ almighty," Lowell said.

"You said that right," Dex agreed. "You said that damn right."

61

The *Leonidas Polk* made its way down the coast as fast as the engines could move it. On the bridge, Lucinda and Cyrus stared at the book of notes and tried to make sense of it all while Cashe leaned against the controls and stared out the front portal.

"Any ideas?" Cashe asked.

Dr. Hastings took his reading glasses off his nose and dropped them on the table. "Not a one. This thing is full of formulas and figures that I have no clue how to understand or read."

"If it's got you beat," Lucinda said. "I daresay no one on this craft is going to have a clue how to handle it."

Cashe winced. "Is it some kind of bomb, for certain?"

"Yes," Hastings said. "A weapon of some kind, anyway."

"It either is, or it isn't," Cashe said. He couldn't believe that the man could be so unsure of something that had sat in his storehouse for years.

"We haven't started any sort of testing on it. It has a lever. It has buttons. I don't know what any of it does." The doctor pointed to a diagram in the notes. "This bottom part easily mirrors something designed to explode. That much is certain." He flipped a few pages over. "This top part. That's a mystery. I don't know what is in that part."

The engines groaned with the effort of carrying the extra weight they'd picked up.

"Maybe Alek and the boys have better news on the other pretties we acquired." Cashe leaned gingerly toward the intercom tube and pulled it to his mouth. "Alek? How're we doing there? Good things, I hope."

A muffled voice came back through the tube. "We can't exactly take it out for a test right now, but we think we got the gist of it, boss."

In the distance, Cashe could see an orange glow that he knew would be Santa Rosa. "You've only got another ten minutes at best, so stop talking to me and concentrate."

He replaced the intercom and took a deep breath. He checked the compass and his watch again. Something was off. The lights were so bright for so early in the evening. "Something's burning," he said to the others.

They all turned and looked toward the city as smoke trails from various sections of the town began to become more distinct.

Cyrus grabbed a telescope and snapped it open. "Bunch of buildings burning… looks like the harbor house, too." He turned a bit. "There's a ship moored at the tower that looks familiar."

"I noticed too," Lucinda said. "*The Sky Climber*, one of the ships the Sons of Grant used to attack the outpost."

"The one that got away." Cashe continued to scan the city. "If the Sons are at the tower, Tom Preston may be there as well."

"So which problem do we tackle first?" Lucinda asked.

Cashe took a moment to answer. "We stick with the lizard. Cyrus, what else can you see down there?"

"There are a few large ships, sunk or sinking," Cyrus said. "Looks like a warship or two plus some civilian boats. And we're soon going to pass the city's outer fence, which keeps those chewers from wandering into the streets and bothering the nice people of Santa Rosa."

The fences should hold. Cashe focused on the harbor and wondered how many ships had met their end. If the navy was already done for, there wasn't much hope for the air corps to do better. He picked up the intercom again. "Alek? You may have less time than we thought. We're looking for a place to set you down now."

"Uh, ok," Alek said. "We don't...ok."

"Start looking for someplace we can get low enough to release that monstrosity from the hold. The buildings aren't quite as tall on the outskirts," Cashe said.

Hastings pointed toward the city, which really didn't help Cashe at all. "What about Delancy Street? It's got low buildings and a pretty wide avenue."

"Too soon, with all the extra weight. I can't turn us that fast."

"The rail yard," Lucinda said. "Plenty of room, not a lot of people and it's not far from the waterfront."

Cashe nodded. The yards were coming up quickly.

"Hold on to something." He slapped the engine controls off, waited a second and then reversed them for three beats. The *Leonidas Polk* slowed with a sudden lurch, jostling everyone. Cashe let off the air control and the dirigible began to drop suddenly—faster than it should, weighted down by Alek's new toy. After a moment Cashe pulled the ship out of the dive and made the descent less steep. The rail yards already filled the forward portal's view.

Cashe looked away from the controls to see the terrified faces of Lucinda and Hastings staring back at him.

"Are you going to do that again anytime soon?" Hastings asked.

Cashe smiled and shook his head.

62

Potts grabbed Tom's arm and pulled him close. "The men report seeing a dirigible headed this way. It sounds to me like the same one that showed up at the outpost when we were stealing the device."

"You idiot. I told you they would follow you." Tom was disgusted with Potts. The man had fought in some of the toughest battles of the war against overwhelming odds. He knew what to do in battle, and yet he'd allowed himself to make such an easy mistake.

"They could be here to help fight that monster in the harbor, Tom."

"They could be," Tom said. "But they might just as well be here to look for us, isn't that right, you dumb bastard?"

Before Potts could defend himself, verbally or otherwise, Tom grabbed him by the shirt. "I want you…you personally…to take a Bulldog and find some high ground. First chance you get, I want you to fill that ship full of holes. Aim for the control room, if you can, but shoot the hell out of it. And don't stop until you run out of ammunition."

The Bulldog was a smaller, tripod-mounted and slightly less powerful version of the Gatling gun, but it would do the trick as far as handling the O.M.O. was concerned.

"High ground?" Potts asked. "Where in hell am I going to find high ground here?"

Tom looked around at all the buildings in the town. "Are you blind, man? Go to the tallest damn structure you can find and climb it." He glanced around again. "There." He pointed. "Get in the tower near the rail station and rain hell on them from there."

Potts looked around and pointed to the airship tower. "Cantolione's launch tower is higher."

"Think. Goddamn it. Think," Tom said. "That's where the rest of us will be, so we can load it up with the rest of our supplies. If you were there, it would draw added attention to us."

"All right," Potts said and drifted off slowly, still looking at Tom.

"Go, for shit's sake." Tom watched him grab one of the other men and they both picked up a Bulldog and several boxes of ammunition.

Tom looked toward the harbor and hoped they still had time to get out before everything came to a head.

63

Cashe eased the *Polk* toward the rail yard and prepared for the descent.

"We're going in with Alek to see if we can find any of the others, maybe meet up with the army and see what their plan is," Cyrus said. "Maybe they have a handle on this."

Cashe rolled his eyes. He was never a fan of military intelligence. He'd been privy to some of the dumbest moves imaginable in the war. "I find that hard to believe. Take some flares to signal me if you need to be evacuated."

He listened for the sounds of their boots clanking on the deck to fade. "Okay, Corrigan, let's take this monstrosity for a nice, gentle set-down."

Corrigan gripped the tube and shouted through it. "Brace yourselves everyone, we're descending toward the landing area."

Cashe looked over at his crew mate. "Was that really necessary? I said it would be gentle."

The other man braced himself on the control panel in front of him.

64

Alek was smiling when Cyrus dropped himself down into the strange vehicle and pulled the hatch shut behind him. It wasn't a happy smile. More nervous than anything.

"We ready to move?" Cyrus asked. "This thing does move, right?" His hands felt the rough, thick wall nearest him and he patted it with a light touch.

"How do you think we got it in the hold?" Alek said.

Monty slid into the tank and sidled past the men to sit next to Alek. "'Scuse me, gentlemen. Where's the least dangerous seat in this thing?"

"We have no idea." Cyrus looked around the strange interior of the box-like vehicle, staring at the gauges, dials and pipes that twisted and turned along the walls.

"Think of it as a very small Turtle without the legs." Alek barely looked up from the controls.

"Or a huge metal coffin," Monty added.

"Here we go," Alek shouted.

It was quiet at first, as the interior began to rattle and vibrate. The sounds built quickly and Cyrus looked around to make sure things weren't coming apart. After another minute he was sure all the armor plating on the outside of the tank had been knocked off by the shaking engines. A couple of men from Two Thirteen were strapped in with thick buckles hard-welded to the vehicle's frame. The soldiers manned Gatling guns that poked to the outside. Cyrus found an empty spot on the port side and began hastily pulling at his own straps.

"Is everyone that worried about Cashe's ability to land?" Cyrus shouted to the nearest soldier with a smile.

"Land? Didn't anyone explain this to you?" Monty shouted back. "We don't have time to land. We're afraid the airship's going to attract the monster's attention, so we don't want it to stay in one place for very long. We're going to slow down, get close to the ground and drive this thing out while the *Polk* is still moving. Backward of course, we're facing the rear of the craft."

Cyrus unbuckled his straps and fought his way forward. He looked up at the hatch he entered the vehicle by and found it closed. "Let me out," he said to Alek.

The engines began to rev. "You better sit down and strap in. It's too late to go now." Alek waved Cyrus back.

"It's not too late." Cyrus reached up and started to unlock the hatch when he heard a clack-clack-clacking sound that made him pause. The cabin of the vehicle was illuminated with the light suddenly streaming in through the front windows. Cyrus ducked to look out and took a deep breath at what he saw.

The back cargo door was open and the tank was right at the edge of it. Beyond the hold, rooftops and trees flashed away from them off into the distance. By Cyrus's estimation, they hadn't really slowed at all.

Alek pointed to the interior of the cargo hold. "See that set of flags over there? When the last of the three fall, that's our signal. We're going."

Cyrus looked at the three flags just as the first fell. He felt himself being pulled backward. One of the other soldiers had grabbed his arm and quickly shoved him into a seat and started strapping him in.

"Let's get you somewhere safe," he said.

"Thank you," Alek yelled back. "Two flags."

"I got it." Cyrus took over and finished with the buckles while the soldier deftly took care of his own.

There was a loud scraping noise from the bottom of the craft and a sudden jostle that knocked Cyrus's head against the frame. He could still see the flags and watched as the third one fell. A warning bell chimed just as it did.

"Here we go," Alek shouted.

The engines revved once, twice and then again. The whole tank shuddered and then lurched forward. The *Polk* scraped on the ground and then there was nothing for a moment. Everything was smooth and peaceful. Cyrus looked out the front window and realized he had a perfect view of the sky above as the tank went airborne leaving the cargo hold.

The peace ended with an abrupt crunch as the ass end of the tank landed first, then the front. The rear lifted a little as the momentum brought it forward. Everyone grabbed the straps and handholds near their seat to try to stabilize themselves, but their bodies whipped back and forth within the restraints anyway.

"Christ," Cyrus shouted. His neck ached.

He watched Alek and the man next to him recover their faculties enough to get control of the vehicle, which was poised to move forward at what seemed like its greatest speed. He saw the nearby soldier hug his straps as tight as he could, but otherwise seemed unharmed.

Even as the initial bounce subsided, the tank jostled everyone about as one of its treads settled into the gap between the rails of one of the lines.

Cyrus looked ahead and shouted to the drivers. "There's the train tunnel ahead."

The tank slowed to a halt near the long covered entrance to the rail yard.

"We saw it, but thanks," Alek said. He checked the gauges and dials before him. "Let's see what kind of damage our wonderful landing did to this thing."

Cyrus sat still, waiting for an all-clear. He wanted desperately to get up and out of the belly of the beast, but couldn't make himself unbuckle the straps before someone said it was ok. Even stationary, the machine shook and rumbled back and forth, with a terrible noise that seemed to grow worse as they sat. Cyrus was used to the great racket the Turtle made, but most of the engine and boiler noise was generated far below the main quarters and control room of the main deck, so it wasn't nearly as bad as the tank.

He thought it was odd, though, the way that the noise got worse and louder as the vehicle rested. He sighed and tried to relax. He looked at the buildings of the rail yard and all the tracks that criss-crossed it. He was impressed that they had managed to keep the yard so clear and clean and wondered at the lack of actual engines. Maybe the yard masters had heard of the danger and moved all their valuable machinery to somewhere safe. He looked at the uniformed soldiers in the tank and had another thought—maybe the military had them do it. A lot of the army's firepower was linked to the rails, transported or attached to flatbeds.

The rumbling increased and Cyrus looked up at the tunnel before them. A light seemed to be growing larger by the second.

"Alek…" Cyrus said. The driver was arguing with his co-pilot over some gauge reading or another. "Alek. Move out." He took the four steps closer to the men so they could hear him. He grabbed Alek's collar and pointed out the viewport. "I think there's a goddamn train coming."

Everyone, not just the pilots, strained their necks to look into the tunnel to see what Cyrus was waving and yelling about. To their credit, none of them screamed when they saw it.

Alek shifted gears and slammed his foot down on a pedal in the floor. He stood up on it in what looked like a hope that the extra pressure would make things happen faster. Cyrus watched as his copilot leaned hard on one direction of the steering levers. The tank jolted backward with a roar and turned sharply to the left as it did. The machine jumped the tracks that it had been stuck on and then its rear crunched itself up onto the next set as an engine hurtled out of the darkness of the tunnel.

The cowcatcher on the front of the train connected with a corner of the tank and knocked it clear, sending it half-spinning onto another line. Cyrus caught himself on the center pole of the turret and hung on till the tank stopped. Everyone else was still strapped safely in their seats.

Out of the viewport, he could see the train continue on, unfazed, toward the edge of the massive train yard. The black engine was sleek, covered with armor plates and add-ons that the military deemed useful for a combat train. It had added panels with slits for soldiers to fire their weapons from, which allowed them cover from enemy attack. The trailing cars were similarly decked out. One was a modified coach that the army used as a troop carrier. The windows all had steel panels welded over them, with slits cut in them like the engine panels. Cyrus couldn't see inside to discover if it actually carried soldiers or if they had been left off somewhere along the route.

The next car was a flatbed with two smaller cannons strapped on it. They were excellent weapons, but Cyrus noticed there weren't any vehicles to pull them into place, and without that, those men were never going to get them into a position to be effective, or even off the flatbed for that matter.

The third car dwarfed the others. It was twice as long and carried a cannon that was nearly as long as the rest of the cars. Cyrus's best estimate placed it at forty feet tall and he wondered, outside of a giant lizard, what targets had previously felt its wrath.

His admiration was cut short as the tank began rumbling forward again.

"Shouldn't we get out and check for damage?" Cyrus yelled.

Alek's copilot shook his head. "Nah. The train seems fine." He pushed two levers in front of him forward and the tank jumped back up onto the track. Without hesitation, the tank moved toward the main street into town, toward some mythic beast and its gaping jaw.

65

Cashe leaned hard on the ascension control, tugged hard to reverse the thrust. The train yard was fairly wide open with ample space between the buildings, but the *Polk* didn't turn as fast as some of the smaller airships. Ahead lay what looked like a fitter's yard and had at least three stories on it, with a tall spire on the roof.

Though his muscles ached, Cashe put all his weight on the controls to bring the ship up.

"Let me get that," Corrigan said from behind him. A new set of hands wrapped around the stick and pulled it back even more.

"What're you doing? Stay at your station, and get us ready to move into position."

Corrigan moved back, balancing in the rapidly rising craft. "Nothing to navigate at the moment," Corrigan said.

"Just do your job, I have this under control," Cashe said and pointed to the other panels.

The *Polk* began to give way a little faster.

As he looked back out the viewport, Cashe was relieved to see that they would easily get over the building, but the tower on top would be a problem. As he considered this, he noticed two shapes on the metal structure of the rail yard's tower. Two men.

A second later, the windows of the *Polk's* control room shattered, and he felt his body wracked with pain. He let go of the controls and fell backward. His hands immediately gripped his side where something burned like a brand.

"Cashe!" Corrigan shouted. He was beside Cashe immediately.

The sounds of gunfire continued from outside and more rounds clattered against the *Polk's* interior until the whole ship shuddered in collision with the rail tower. After the initial impact, the impediment was removed and the ship moved on, though it was no longer rising and listed to the port side.

"Take the controls before we crash," Cashe managed to croak out.

Corrigan turned reluctantly and tried to level the ship off.

Cashe used the time to look at his wounds. He'd been hit in the chest and waist, but those were the only wounds he could discern for sure. Blood poured onto the deck below him.

"Somebody help us up in the control room. Anyone." Corrigan threw the tube down when he was done. "Shit." He steadied the wheel and adjusted the trim to gain control.

Cashe deliberately avoided looking at Corrigan. With some effort, he managed to push himself up on his elbows.

"Let me take over." He reached out to take the station from Corrigan. "I'm fine," he snapped. He was hurting, but they needed every last man elsewhere to keep the *Polk* aloft and battle ready.

"Just rest for a moment for God's sake. You're bleeding like a stuck pig," Corrigan said.

"I said I'm fine. Go back to your station." Cashe pulled himself up using the control panel for leverage. "I'll take us up toward the harbor. That seems to be where the action is."

"No."

"I can do this."

Corrigan backed away from the controls and stared. "No. If you're fine, you can navigate and I'll handle this. All we would need is for you to pass out and we all crash."

Cashe gave him a cross look.

Corrigan stopped him before he could say anything. "You say you're fine, but we'd all be up a creek, wouldn't we? I'm staying here, thanks."

Cashe saw some wisdom in that thought, even if he didn't admit it. He said nothing and hung on to the panel. "To the harbor then."

As the ship came flush with the fires burning along the waterline, the men got their first look at the monster they'd come to destroy. They were scanning the skyline for a look when the top floor of one of the larger downtown buildings came partially down, caving in suddenly as an explosion rocked the area. After a moment the monster lifted itself from the rubble, pushing off with its massive arms. It stood eye to eye with the windows of the highest floor and tossed the building's debris off with ease.

"Am I seeing what I think I'm seeing?" Cashe asked. "Or have I really lost that much blood that I'm hallucinating?"

The dusk could be playing tricks of the light, he thought. He feared his injuries were playing havoc with his mind and he was imagining things.

"Do you see a four story lizard tearing the top off a very big building?" Corrigan asked.

"No," Cashe answered. "But let's shoot at it just to be sure."

"That's reasonable. Just to be sure." Corrigan grabbed an intercom tube and shouted into it. "All gunners to the fore weapons racks immediately. Aim well and give yourself a moment to adjust to what you're seeing. We'll pass it on our starboard side." He looked over at Cashe. "Does the cannon control up here work?"

Cashe shook his head. "It was rendered useless at Two Thirteen." Having said that, he fell back down on the deck as his arms gave out and his legs couldn't support him.

66

Lowell aimed his rifle at the massive creature passing by the window and gasped. It was unlike anything he'd ever seen and anything he'd prepared himself for. It looked like a gigantic lizard walking upright. But it was deformed just as much as it was anything else. Its skin had patchy coloring of dark greens and gray. One side of the face hung slack, gum line exposed. A series of plates ran down the creature's spine all the way to the tail where it ended with spikes. Its eyes scanned the streets and buildings. Its mouth opened and closed in a series of repetitive motions.

Dex patted Riley on the shoulder and then quietly backed away.

Riley nodded and shouldered the gun, squinting down the sights at the beast in the street. He waited and took a deep breath.

Lowell looked from the creature to Riley and back. He tried not to be mesmerized by the strange thing that seemed close enough to touch, but it was nearly impossible. It was an abomination to everything Lowell knew about what nature was capable of creating. With every movement the muscles on the animal's hide flexed, causing the scales to ripple like a wave on the ocean.

When he finally tore himself away from the beast again, he noticed Riley was moving his lips, almost like he was reading a book and mouthing the words. Lowell watched and tried to figure out what he was saying. When he couldn't, he looked back to the monster and noticed the way it was moving its mouth. When he looked back at Riley he understood the man was trying to get a sense of the rhythm of when it opened its maw the widest.

Riley tensed up and went rigid, holding his stance as still as possible. A split-second later, the room echoed with the thump of Riley's gun firing. Lowell watched the round zip toward the monster's head, a thin trail of smoke behind it.

The beast's mouth opened, closed, and then opened wider.

The fat bullet wavered in its trajectory, but corrected its course.

Near the moment of impact, shots rang out from another building down the street. Someone with a repeating rifle opened up on the creature with a report that echoed off the buildings. The monster turned to find the source.

Riley's shot bounced off the monster's palsied cheek and exploded in the air five feet away.

The monster looked over to where Lowell and the others were watching. One eye narrowed and it stepped toward them.

"Move," Jennings said. "Out. Move."

"God in Heaven," Dex whispered.

Jennings grabbed Dex's arm and dragged him toward the door. Riley ran past them, his gun breached again, another huge bullet in his free hand. After a few steps, Dex began running on his own. Lowell fired his carbine at the advancing creature in an attempt to cover their escape. The bullets didn't slow the thing down. Firing as he went, Lowell retreated for the door. The creature opened its mouth and lurched forward. Lowell watched as the thin orange tongue snaked back and forth.

Lowell ran and didn't look back. In the hall, he took the stairs two at a time. He could hear the others already nearing the base of the stairwell. Behind him, he heard a massive explosion and the crush of the walls caving in.

67

Cyrus stood ready with one of the metal powder kegs held tight between his hands.

"Yes, sir!" Alek's co-pilot shouted. "That got 'im!"

"Keep it up," Alek said. He shouted to the others as loud as he could. "Concentrate everything you can on it now."

Cyrus stuck his head up into the turret and shouted at the man in turret named Mulgrave. "He said to hit that big bastard again."

Mulgrave looked down and gave Cyrus a nod.

The quiet of the engines at rest was broken by the roar of the heavy guns at the front of the vehicle opening fire on the monster. The revolver barrel spun and loaded another cannon shell into the turret. After another minute the entire tank jumped as the thunder of the cannon let loose.

Cyrus grabbed the center pillar for balance and thought about climbing out the hatch. He'd been in fights in the Turtle before, but at least there he had some control—he could command people, he could do something tangible. At the very least, he could see what was coming. Here, he couldn't see out unless he ducked down and looked through the tiny rectangular viewport in front of the drivers. Helping to load a gun for someone else to fire wasn't his idea of productivity.

He envied the gunner for getting to pull the trigger in one of the turrets with twin machine guns. That was a task that allowed for immediate verification of results. He imagined the gunner relished the opportunity as well.

Two soldiers sat near the back, still strapped in. "You want to switch places with me? You guys hear how this job works?" Cyrus asked.

Both men shook their heads no. Cyrus assumed they meant no to both questions. He scratched his head and looked up at the hatch again. He wasn't sure if he wanted out because he was feeling trapped or because he was the only one who wasn't getting to shoot something.

The barrel turned again, loading another shell. Cyrus braced himself for a fresh jolt from the cannon.

68

Lowell bounded into the alley and ran to a doorway to brace himself in case the whole block of buildings came down. As soon as he got situated, he stared at the opening he'd run from, waiting for someone else to come out. Nothing happened. The others had run in front of him, but they were nowhere in the alley that he could see. He wondered if they'd been stupid enough to run deeper into the building. Maybe they reached the bottom and ran to the front parlor of the hotel and ran out the front. It was a possibility, but that would've put them directly on the sidewalk by the beast on the street. Surely they didn't want that.

The high-pitched roar of the beast shook the windows nearby and it was immediately joined by the rhythmic thudding of a Gatling gun. In another moment, a new sound erupted. It sounded like a train chuffing up to speed in the street. It was a roar all its own, though it wasn't from anything living, that much Lowell knew. Soon, there was shouting on the street as well.

After another loud report from a cannon, the lizard screeched.

Lowell rested his head on the doorframe and took a deep breath. He'd come for reconnaissance, but he was sure he'd make a difference in the fight. Reports are always exaggerated, so the odds were good he wouldn't have to fight the thing that everyone had claimed was running rampant. Who knew it would've been bigger and ghastlier than everyone had made out? He peered down the alley for any sign of activity at either end, but especially the direction of the fight. He saw nothing.

It occurred to him for the first time that day that he could turn in the other direction, that no one would say anything if he turned back and met up with the troops that had been retreating when he first landed. No one would know, no one would care. And if they did, he could make his own story with no one to dispute it.

He looked at the quiet end of the alley that led from the fight. What possible effect could a man with a bolt-action rifle have on the fight at hand?

"Lowell? Lowell!" Jennings yelled from across the alley.

Lowell focused on Jennings and the other men who came out the door.

"Christ man, you ran right by us," Dex said. "Didn't you hear us shouting? We got under the stairway in case the building collapsed."

Lowell laughed. "Sorry. I just had to get out. There wasn't anything stopping me, I guess."

Jennings nodded. "I understand. Anything happening out here?" He looked up and down the narrow passage.

Lowell took a good look at the end of the alley that led to relative safety. "Not a thing."

69

Cyrus stared at the hatch that led out of the vehicle and into the crazy fray that had erupted outside. The stench of smoke, sulfur and close bodies made it hard to breathe. People bumped into him as they tried to make their way past. He rubbed his forehead with his sleeve to wipe off the sweat that accumulated. He bent down to try to look out the small portholes that the drivers used to see where they were going, but he couldn't see what was happening outside.

"Hit it again, before it recovers!" Alek shouted over the roar of the engines and the shouts of the men inside. The riflemen in the front corners of the machine fired almost constantly, stopping only to allow their Gatlings to cool and to allow their feeders to string up more ammo.

"I've got to go," Cyrus heard himself mumble. He was used to small spaces—the Turtle wasn't the roomiest of berths—but at least he was in charge there, and he could look out the windows whenever he damn well pleased. At least there and on the *Polk*, he could see what was coming. Here, anything could happen.

"I have to get out," he said to one of the feeders as they passed him on their way to grab more ammunition in the back.

The soldier kept shuffling past.

Cyrus looked to another. "Can you take over for me? Excuse me? Can someone take over for me? Anyone?"

Everyone kept doing their jobs and he wondered whether they were ignoring him or couldn't hear. The dirty metal walls were beginning to feel like they were closing in on him even more.

There was a shout from the turret and everyone grabbed on to something to brace themselves. The vehicle leapt off the ground as the huge cannon fired. The roar covered Cyrus's attempts to get anyone's attention. He reached to grab the nearest soldier and make them hear him but he stopped when his stomach suddenly rumbled violently. He put his hands to his midsection and groaned. He knew what was coming.

"Excuse me," Cyrus said as he pushed to the ladder and started to climb.

Another scream came from the turret. "Load! Someone load the goddamn cannon." Cyrus wasn't there to do it.

Behind him, someone finally noticed. "Hey, where're you going? Someone stop him."

Cyrus couldn't tell whose voice it was, but he didn't care. He had to get out. The metal handle was warm in his hand as he cranked it hard. It turned easier than he expected and he hoisted it away. Fresh, cool air flooded in and he took a deep breath as he dragged himself out of the boiling interior of the tank. He kicked the hatch closed behind him, stifling the shouts from the crew.

He could feel the contents of his stomach coming up and he grabbed the edge of the tank in anticipation.

70

When he finally felt well enough to look up, Cyrus got his first real glimpse of the dragon.

It was just as tall as they'd suggested—forty feet maybe and wide as a riverboat. One side of its face hung down oddly, like it had too much skin sagging from its eyes and jaw. This only served to expose the beast's teeth and make it all the more fearsome. Cyrus couldn't look away from the monster. He misstepped and fell over the side of tank, landing on his back in the muddy street. When he could open his eyes again, he looked directly to the beast to make sure it hadn't advanced, but it still seemed to be recovering from the hit the tank had delivered.

"What in the name a God are you doing out there?" Someone shouted from inside the tank.

Cyrus assumed it was Alek, but couldn't be sure.

"I'm fine," he said weakly. His breath wasn't coming back as quickly as he'd hoped. "Dandy."

"Get back in here. It's not safe out there,"

"Not safe in there either," Cyrus replied. At least lying in the middle of the street on his back, Cyrus could see the sky and breathe the open air. It didn't feel like a fist was closing around his chest.

"Get out of the street, you dumb bastard," another voice chided. This one came from outside the tank. "You're going to get eaten if you're not careful."

Lowell. It had to be.

A coughing fit erupted from Cyrus's throat and when it stopped, he took a deep breath. "Don't talk shit, boy. What self-respecting animal would lower itself to chewing on me for sustenance?"

"All the same, it may decide to step on you," Lowell yelled.

Cyrus started to laugh, but was interrupted by the sudden thundering of the tank as it fired again. The whole vehicle jumped to within an inch of Cyrus's leg and he immediately decided to move to a more defensible position of cover. He put his hands to his ears and gracelessly hoofed it to a nearby alley where Lowell and several others were waving their arms madly.

Behind him, the tank's engine rolled over and roared to a crescendo. The beast roared back, though Cyrus couldn't bring himself to see if the thing was screaming in pain or as an angry challenge to the tank. He kept focused on the alley and the men standing at its edge.

"Christ Almighty, what are you doing out there?" Lowell said. He reached out an arm and Cyrus took it.

Allowing himself to be dragged into the alley, Cyrus was aware of his aching back. He'd injured more than his pride falling off the tank, but hadn't noticed the full extent until he'd begun running.

"Hell if I know, but I was mostly useless in that metal contraption," he said.

"Well, get used to that feeling 'cuz we ain't done a damnsite much more out here," one of the others said.

"Cyrus?" Lowell pointed to the others one by one. "That's Riley, Dex and Jennings. They've been dragging me closer and closer to your pointy-toothed friend there since I arrived."

Jennings extended his hand, but continued to watch the entrance to the alley. "Good to meet you," he said. "That your ship?" He pointed up in the sky.

Cyrus looked up and caught a bit of the *Polk* as it disappeared behind a building. "Lowell and I are on their crew, yeah. It's an O.M.O. vessel. That's where the mobile cannon came from."

"Looks like a giant bathtub with a Napoleon on it," Dex said.

"When's your airship going to open up on this thing and put it down? We could use it's firepower about now." Jennings leaned back against the wall and looked Cyrus straight in the eyes. "We could've used its firepower earlier this morning, truly."

"Not my ship and I'm not the captain." Cyrus tried not to sound defensive. He wanted to blurt out that he was nobody's captain and never would be, but he stopped where he was. "We ran into some trouble with some rebel group back at the outpost. The *Polk* took some damage, pretty bad stuff. They've got everything working as best they can."

There was a another barrage of Gatling fire from the street and more heavy fire from the tank's forward guns as the machine's engines revved again.

High above, the *Polk* came along broadside, and two of the cannons mounted on the port railing opened up on the creature. Both shots went wide and splintered a storefront just to the east of the monster.

Cyrus heard the roar of airship engines and looked to the *Polk* to see what it was doing, but the ship floated on slowly without the use of its engines. He leaned out of the alley and looked up and down the street. Several blocks down, he could see *The Sky Climber* still docked at the tower. He could hear the revving of the engines clearly.

"Hey." Cyrus tapped Lowell and pointed. "That ship look familiar at all to you?"

"Can't tell," Lowell said.

"It's the ship those Sons of Grant bastards used to attack the outpost."

Lowell's expression quickly changed to recognition. "Maybe we go say hello? If the device is there, I'll bet Preston is too."

Cyrus was already edging into the street—the thought of confronting Preston rising in his mind right along with the possibility of getting farther from the seemingly impervious beast that was bedeviling downtown Santa Rosa.

"And we can take their ship," he said. "It could be useful to have a second craft to fight this monster, right?"

Riley stuffed another huge piece of ammunition into his gun and snapped the weapon shut. "By the time we get there, this'll all be over. It'll be useless."

"Really? What part of this battle so far would indicate it'll be over quickly?" Cyrus asked.

"I don't know," Jennings said. "We should stick by to support the others."

"By doing what?" Cyrus asked. "Getting the thing to eat us, while they shoot at it?"

Jennings and Lowell looked at each other for a beat before reluctantly nodding.

"Worth a shot. At least we'd be in the air away from it," Jennings said. "Maybe Riley can get a good shot with that weapon of his."

"Give me a good angle and I'll drop one right down his gullet," Riley said.

"Fine. Let's go," Cyrus said as he began running down the street, staying as close to the buildings as possible, in the hopes that the awnings would hide them from the beast.

71

"Let's go! Move faster everyone," Tom said. "I want these boxes loaded in the hold of the airship before the others get back with the last of the weapons from the storehouse."

The dozen or so men scurried to lift the boxes of weapons and ammunition that the Sons of Grant had managed to steal, save, buy or otherwise acquire. They'd already stacked the foodstuffs, tents and supplies onboard *The Sky Climber*. Tom was already thinking of a more fitting name to paint on the side once they were away and able to set up a base. For now, it would make for a good cover. Who would expect the salvation of the United States to come from such an innocuous source?

The prize of the collection, Dr. Poley's device, was the first item to be loaded. It got its own spot nearest the cargo doors, so it could be loaded and unloaded quickly. It had been covered with a tarp and then hidden by blankets and other boxes on top. None of the soldiers of the cause had been told what exactly it was or what it did. They only knew that the Sons of Grant had the means to make the North the dominant power again and end all of the United Nations of America nonsense. None of them knew it was right there for them to touch except Geraldine Yardley, who walked next to Tom with a sheet of paper and a worn-down pencil lead.

Tom had seen what happened to the rail station tower and had to assume the worst had happened to Potts. He grabbed Geraldine to fill his position.

"When can we leave?" Tom asked.

"We've got one wagonload of arms coming." Geraldine walked quickly to keep up with him.

"How long?"

"Another five minutes. I have Marquet watching for them in the street. He'll blow the whistle when they're approaching."

"What else?" Tom asked.

Geraldine looked at the paper with the scribbled notes. "Three men are handling water detail. We should be filled by the time the hold is full. Eric is leading five men in restocking the wood. They should finish right on time as well."

"Good," Tom said. "Any other problems in the foreseeable future?"

The woman turned around and looked out the large picture window that overlooked the rest of the city. The landscape was dominated by the large lizard thing in the distance, the demolished buildings around it, and the burning ships in the harbor. "Well, *that* could be a problem at some point."

"It's slow, and the U.N. troops are making it slower," Tom said. "Besides, if I'm right, it's making its way toward the other smaller beasts that we captured. That would lead that thing to Cantolione, not us." It was a theory, but he didn't feel the need to flesh it out—he'd be gone before the beast was a problem he needed to deal with.

"It still might have to go past us and who knows what kind of damage it might do to the airship," Geraldine said.

"Then we better hurry up, wouldn't you think?"

"I'll let you know when Marquet signals."

"Thank you," Tom said.

He stepped to the window and watched the dragon on the edge of the city. Its tail flailed wildly, knocking out windows and crushing unlucky obstacles. Suddenly, everything rumbled and a bright plume of fire erupted from the street. The lizard took a step back and steadied itself with its hand on a rooftop. Tom moved until he could see the source of the volley. The metal vehicle had been hidden from his view by other buildings.

"Now, that would be a weapon to steal," he said out loud.

72

Onboard the *Polk*, Lucinda had joined the crew on the deck and was ministering to Cashe's wounds. "Just lie still."

"Look." Cashe took a stuttering breath. "I need to tell you something. Just so somebody else knows."

Lucinda shook her head. "You're going to be fine, don't worry about it. Whatever it is, you can tell me later."

He could feel a trickle of blood run down his lower back, and Cashe wondered whether she was right. It wasn't nearly as painful as he'd expected, but he was beginning to feel cold and numb. "No, it's better if you know, so you can tell the others if something happens."

He could see the indecision in Lucinda's eyes. She was looking around, hoping someone else would come in to take her place.

"It's all right." He clutched her hand tighter as a wave of pain seized his spine. "I...I have to know that someone else knows what's going on. Emmett knew. He was the last one that was in on it."

"In on what?"

"I delivered the device and other things to Outpost Two Thirteen frequently."

"I know, you told us that," she said.

Cashe swallowed. "I didn't deliver these things as an officer of the O.M.O. or anything. Not really. I was a glorified delivery boy. I took inventory and moved things from one place to another. I only learned to fly an airship because they needed real pilots elsewhere."

Cashe quickly told her the story of how he'd come to take over the *Polk*, and how he found himself where he was now. It was the shortest version he could tell.

"It had a good effect. People seemed to be reassured that there was someone in charge of something."

"Why not just tell them the truth?" she asked.

"Emmett and I thought if we told them what was really happening, they'd choose to stay holed up in the woods surrounded by chewers before they joined us."

"And nobody caught on?"

"Nobody wanted to, I guess," Cashe said.

Lucinda shook her head at Cashe. He felt foolish spilling out his feelings to her. Whether he lived or died, he had no right burdening her with his past sins. For a second, he hoped he would, indeed, die right there on the floor rather than face the consequences. The weight that was lifted from his shoulders didn't match the burden he'd placed on hers.

"I just should have been honest from the start," Cashe said.

He looked up to scan Lucinda's eyes for some idea of what she was thinking. She conveyed a confusion that he attributed to her wondering whether he was delirious from the blood loss.

At that moment Bethy tromped back onto the bridge with cloths and bandages. She quickly knelt beside Cashe and started doing what she could for his wound.

"Can you help hold this in place, while I wrap some gauze around him?"

When Lucinda didn't react, Bethy looked back up at her. "I need your help, now."

It was loud enough that Corrigan looked over. "Do we need to get him to the hospital back at the outpost?" he asked. "Where is Dr. Hastings? Get him back up here."

Cashe suspected that the tall dark-haired woman who had suddenly dropped into their lives was dropping out just as quickly.

"We can't turn back," Lucinda said. "We have to help them down there."

Bethy pressed on Cashe's wound a little harder than she should have and he couldn't help but cry out. "Lord, girl."

"Sorry," Bethy said. She turned slightly so she could look at Cashe and still be heard by Lucinda. "How are you going to help? We need you here."

Lucinda grabbed a pistol from a nearby table and quickly strapped it to her side. Then she was gone.

73

Lowell and the others ducked into a doorway when they heard the latest shot from the tank. "Is it still standing?" Lowell asked.

Dex stuck his head out and looked behind them. "Oh, yeah. That shot barely tickled it."

"Dammit," Lowell said.

They started advancing again before Lowell noticed something. He motioned for the others to stop and get down. When they did, he pointed to the man standing outside of the airship tower. He had a rifle across his chest and a white cloth on his arm.

"The Sons of Grant must've left a lookout so no one sneaks up on them."

"Dex?" Jennings asked.

"I'll just be a moment." Dex pulled out a knife and moved off quickly, ducking behind boxes and other cover until he faded into the mid-day shadows and Lowell lost sight of him.

Dex emerged a few seconds later and grabbed the sentry from behind. They both disappeared from sight, with Dex emerging alone to wave the others on.

"I don't see anyone else down here, so we should be safe to go up," Dex said.

Jennings patted Dex on the shoulder. "Good work. Let's get going, gentlemen."

"Wait." Lowell looked around. "Where the hell did Cyrus go?"

"He was behind me when Dex took care of the sentry," Riley said.

"Do we look for him or move on?" Jennings asked.

Lowell opted to move on. Cyrus could take care of himself, and they had a small window of action. "Keep going."

They entered to find the lobby of the airbase empty, much like the rest of the town.

"Up the stairs," Jennings said.

"There's an elevator." Lowell pointed to the far side of the room. He was tired of walking, sick of running and climbing stairs was not a pleasant thought.

"Stairs," Jennings repeated and waved everyone on. "Dex, you're on point. Riley's got the rear."

They all filed up as quietly as possible. Noise filtered down the stairs from above. Men were shouting, though the words were unintelligible.

The soldiers made their way up, guns drawn. Jennings motioned for Riley and Lowell to stick to the right side of the curved stairwell, while he and Dex stayed left. Lowell tried to count the voices—three, seven, a dozen maybe? There were only four of them without Cyrus, not that one more gun on their team would make that much of a difference.

74

Cyrus nearly tripped on the cobblestones of the street. In his haste, he didn't pay much attention to his path. He wanted to make sure he wasn't imagining things. As he'd stood with Lowell and the other men, Cyrus swore he saw a dark shape pass over the street and disappear from view behind the buildings. He was pretty sure it was the Goose from the *Polk*. And what's more, he thought he saw a familiar flip of dark hair trailing the pilot. There hadn't been time to tell Lowell and the others he planned to intercept the pedal-powered flying machine.

Cyrus searched the sky. There! The object passed over him. It was most definitely a Goose. He followed its jerky descent. It turned hard, at times nearly clipping higher buildings. The pilot pedaled hard, straining to keep the craft in the air. For a moment, Cyrus stopped and stood in the street, waiting for the thing to circle and find its way. It finally came down quickly over the last two dozen feet, disappearing behind the building next to him.

Running down an alley and then around the corner, he found the Goose on its side against a red brick building. It rested on one snapped wing, with the others sticking straight up into the air.

"Hello?" Cyrus asked. "You all right? Lucy, is that you?"

A voice came from inside what was left of the craft. "Of course it's me." One of the wings parted and Lucinda climbed out of the wreckage.

"Let me give you a hand." Cyrus ran forward and helped her navigate her way out of what was left of the Goose. "What the hell are you doing in that contraption?"

"I came to help." Lucinda rolled her head back and forth a couple times, working out some injury she'd sustained in the landing. "Besides, these O.M.O. men seem lost without me."

"Oh, we're doing fine on our own," Cyrus said.

"I'm well aware of what your version of fine looks like. It's not much different than terrible, wouldn't you say?"

"You've known me too long," Cyrus said. He hitched his thumb toward the main street. "The monster is that way, if you'd like to follow me."

"I can find a four-story lizard on my own, thanks."

Cyrus shook his head and pointed to the tower, which was just visible over the top of the buildings a few blocks away. "We're pretty sure Tom Preston is loading up that airship and running away. I just slipped away from our friends to come get you. They could probably use our help about now."

"You're probably right about *The Sky Climber*," Lucinda said, "but I want to talk to Cantolione. If Preston has taken advantage of him the way Cashe and his men seem to think, I want to inform him."

"You sure you want to be the one to do that?"

"Someone should. Let's go. His office is just down the block."

"And how do you know that?" Cyrus asked.

"I used to live here, remember? Everyone knows the Hall of Amazement."

Cyrus stared as she ran down the alley toward the next crossroad, away from the monster in the main street. While he didn't like the idea of leaving their new teammates, he was warming to the notion of moving farther from the beast that had so far shrugged off everything that had been thrown at it. An empty zoo would be a much better option.

75

Cyrus and Lucinda made their way down the winding deserted streets of Santa Rosa, following the outhouse stench of animals until they arrived at Cantolione's menagerie. They passed the barker's stands and the refreshment carts, then walked up the stairs through the front doors.

The interior was dark, with only the glow of daylight filtering in from outside to light their way. Cyrus squinted at the posters that lined the walls of old exhibits and shows Cantolione had taken on the road. Everything was new to Cyrus, though he knew Lucinda had been here numerous times in the past.

"Are you sure you want to be here?" Cyrus asked.

Lucinda nodded. "I just want to settle this."

"Fine. Where do we go next?" Cyrus pulled his pistol and let its weight settle into his palm.

"Hard to say. If he's here, he's probably in his office."

"I'll follow you," Cyrus said.

Lucinda led the way to the office area, which was just as deserted as the rest of the building. There was a roar from a nearby animal, followed by a commotion from a number of others.

"Let's check out the cages," she said. "Sounds like something's got them spooked."

"Spooked? Do you think maybe it's that four story lizard that's lumbering this way? That could have something to do with it. I mean, it's got me a little riled up, I can only imagine what it's doing to them."

"Maybe." She motioned for him to follow as she made her way toward a patch of light down the hall. A sign pointed that the exhibits were ahead, but Lucinda turned instead and pushed open a door marked *No Admittance*. This led to another dark hall, and here, Cyrus could hear voices and the occasional crack of a whip. He motioned for Lucinda to pull her gun, but she shook her head and continued on.

It was lighter at the end of this hall. She paused to look around the corner. Cyrus caught up and took a look for himself, finding they'd come to the areas behind the cages, where animals were loaded and unloaded or moved for other reasons. There were buckets and sacks of feed stacked in one corner and Cyrus presumed this was how the trainers and other caretakers gained access to tend to the animals.

A door to the largest cage was open and inside was a large lizard, which was easily taller than the man guiding it to its spot. He held a long baton that he struck the animal with when it didn't turn quickly enough. The beast seemed groggy and moved at a sickly pace. It moved when the man beat it, but it would turn and flash its teeth in a display of useless defiance. Cyrus watched as the yellowed rows of sharp teeth snapped shut and he wondered what would happen if the beast let loose on the man.

There were more voices and exclamations as two more men lead another beast through the far doors, moving it toward the same cage as the first. This creature was just as large as the first, over six feet tall and nearly twenty feet long or so. As the last of its tail entered the room, Cyrus and Lucinda saw Cantolione following with another man.

"Make sure these two get in there and get comfortable," Cantolione told the other man. "Take the rest to the ranch with the extra animals. Should be plenty of cages. We'll pick a couple out to travel in the show, but I think these two are the best of 'em."

Before Cyrus could formulate any sort of opinion of the situation, Lucinda stepped out of the shadows and broke cover. "Umberto," she said.

Everyone stopped, and turned to look at Lucinda. The room fell silent except for the sounds of the lizards stepping on the straw strewn about the floor of the cage. After a moment the animal tenders turned to Cantolione for a reaction.

"Lucinda Garrison?" Cantolione asked. "Am I hallucinating? I was fairly sure I'd never see you again. Last I heard you were working on one of those pilgrim transports with some low-life scum. I had good odds that you'd stay out east on the next trip and never come back." He scowled at her. "Looks like I owe people some money on that bet." Cantolione contemplated the girl. "Who'd you bring with you?"

Cyrus knew he'd been seen and stepped from the shadows with his gun prominently displayed. "One of the low-life scum she's been associating with."

Cantolione nodded.

The gunfire that seemed so far away edged closer. The rumble of the tank and the stomp of the beast were beginning to make the floor tremble and the animals in Cantolione's menagerie ran in their cages, frightened and looking for a way out. The Hyenas howled and the elephants trumpeted in long bursts. In another wing of the complex, a canine bayed nervously.

Lucinda spoke low. "I know you had nothing to do with all this. I just wanted to say I'm sorry for running. I loved your son, Ardell. He was the—"

Cantolione interrupted her. "Stop. Stop right there. You ran away the day after he died and we've never seen your face since."

"I was devastated and I blamed myself for what happened," Lucinda said. "I thought you blamed me as well and might want to see me paid back."

"Why would you think that? I've never hurt a body in my life. It was an accident."

"Sure, you never hurt anyone," Cyrus said. "But maybe you had those thugs from the Sons of Grant do your bloody work for you."

Cantolione snorted. "The Sons of Grant? Those buffoons couldn't find their ass cheeks with both hands. Why would I ever get involved with those zealots? I'm a legitimate businessman."

"We've fought with them at least twice in the past couple of weeks and they've led us here to you. If you have nothing to do with them, how did they suddenly have so much to do with you?" Cyrus asked.

"I have no idea what you're talking about. If our paths have crossed, it wasn't my doing."

There was a voice behind them, and another man emerged from the darkness. He wore baggy pants and clown makeup. His mouth was painted in a smile. "I think I can help with that," he said.

Everyone shifted nervously, and went for their guns and suddenly the room was filled with people pointing weapons at each other. Cantolione was the only exception.

"Whoa," Cyrus said. "What happened to the man who wouldn't hurt anyone?"

Cantolione ignored him and peered at the new addition to the group. "Cappy? Cappy Marks? Is that you? Excellent. We have them surrounded. Now maybe we can get to the bottom of this nonsense."

"Sorry," the barker said. "I'm actually with them. The O.M.O. asked me to help them out long ago. They planted me here to keep an eye on someone we suspected of working with the Sons of Grant from out of your organization."

"We just joined up with Cashe and O.M.O. too," Cyrus said, hoping the man wouldn't mistake him and Lucinda for the enemy. He hadn't been informed of Cappy's presence by Cashe or anyone else, but he wanted the man on their side in the situation.

The clown nodded. "My few weeks here have been very informative." He looked at Lucinda. "We thought Cantolione was the man behind it all, maybe knowingly supplying the Sons and their efforts. As far as I'm able to tell, he's only guilty of being a poor judge of character and having questionable taste in clothes."

Cappy seemed incredibly serious for a man in full smiling clown make-up. He turned to Cantolione. "You want to know why they're accusing you of associating with the Sons of Grant?"

Everyone in the room eyed him suspiciously.

"Two words…Thomas Preston."

"My right hand man? What about him?" Cantolione asked.

"He's the new leader of the Sons of Grant," Cappy said. "He recruited your accountant, Liddy, into the organization, had him steal a lot of your money, then had Liddy killed. Your money is now funding those idiots. And, I don't know how much is left, but you are pretty broke, Mr. Cantolione."

Cyrus listened, but his focus was more on the mobilizing lizards. They were slowly positioning themselves to a better advantage. The men next to the beasts were oblivious as they focused on the weapons throughout the room.

"What? That's ridiculous," Cantolione said. "Tom would never do such a thing."

"I heard a similar story from a man named Moose." Cyrus tried to keep from staring at the large beasts.

"You can verify it with your bank at your convenience," Cappy said.

Cantolione was shaking his head. "No. That's ridiculous."

"Right now he's boarding one of your airships—" Cappy said.

"No," Cantolione said.

"—with a number of his men—"

"No."

"—and leaving to join the rest of the Sons of Grant—"

"No."

"So they can continue their plan to wreck havoc on this country—"

"No."

"All using your money," Cappy said somberly.

"No. That is a lie. A couple of our ships were damaged in a storm, and they're not supposed to be fixed until the end of the week. There's no way anyone is going anywhere with them," Cantolione said.

"Who told you that?" Cyrus asked.

"Tom, but he has no reason to lie to me. I pay him very well. He wouldn't steal from me."

"You don't pay him well enough for him to outfit his own army," Cappy said. "I can't believe there was no way you knew."

There was a loud explosion nearby, the sound of the tank firing another round at the advancing beast outside. It was followed by a roar that set the lizards in the room into motion. One of them lashed out and bit the nearest trainer, gripping the man's arm in its jaw. The man screamed and tried to tug himself free, dropping his pistol in the process. The noise excited the second lizard and it snapped at another of Cantolione's men.

There were two more lizards standing between Cyrus and Cantolione.

Cyrus turned to Lucinda, "Well, do we fight our way past them to get him, or work our way around another direction?"

"I don't know," Lucinda said.

Cyrus nodded, but before he could react Cappy was beside them and spoke up. "Are either of you aware of the large creatures loose in the room, or the larger one loose in the city, all of which seem to be making their way here?"

"I'd like to believe I can tell what you're thinking," Cyrus said. "We should save him if we can. We'll feel bad about it later if we don't."

"Only if we hurry up. I'm all for helping a moron, but not if it puts me in danger," Cappy said. "Then I'm wholeheartedly against it."

76

"So what do you think we should do here?" Lowell asked.

Jennings shook his head. "Don't look at me. I'm just an army sergeant that showed up to fight a giant lizard. I don't even know who these people are."

"Yeah. You're the O.M.O. guy," Riley said. "What do you think we should do?"

They all looked at each other before Lowell had an idea. "You guys want to work for the O.M.O.?"

The three soldiers looked at each other without blinking.

"It could be as temporary or as permanent as you'd like the arrangement to be," Lowell said. "I just want to deputize you so you can help me arrest these men."

In a whisper, Jennings asked, "And these men are?"

"Ever hear of the Sons of Grant?"

"Bastards," Dex said. "'Course we know them, besmirching the good name of the Union army with their acts."

"This is them," Lowell said.

"Fine, lead the way," Jennings said. "Hopefully you know what you're doing."

In the years before the war, Lowell had been a deputy in Chagrin Falls. Even with the minimal training he'd received there, he'd learned a lot of official-sounding language. Still, what came next was purely off the top of his head and had never been suggested in any official capacity. He looked to each of the other men to see if they were ready and then turned his head toward the landing.

"Attention inside," he shouted. "Stop what you are doing and put your hands in the air. This is the United Nations task force and you are in violation of Article 34-A, regarding unlawful assembly, and Article 60-B, regarding unlawful stockpiling of weapons." He paused to think briefly. "You are also violating Section 11 of the Treaty of Cleveland, regarding plots to overthrow the government."

Every man in the waiting room stopped, but none did much beyond stare. Most had boxes in their hands or were in the process of putting things down or picking them up. Each had the white handkerchief tied around their right upper arm, marking him as loyal to the Sons of Grant.

Crates were piled in front of the elevator door and in various places around the room. At the far end, the bay door stood open—the loading plank extended to the airship. Beyond the plank, more boxes and supplies waited. Lowell could see at least two men inside the ship in addition to the five in the anteroom. Those were just the people in his sightline. None of them had weapons in their hands, and only a couple seemed to be wearing holsters.

"You heard the man," Riley said. "Throw down your shooting irons and lay on the ground or some shit." He advanced into the room alone, waving his Colt.

Lowell was happy to see the man had a pistol in his hand rather than the little explosive launcher that he'd used against the beast in the street. That weapon was strapped safely to his back.

"You people are wanted for questioning in the destruction of the Denver line of the B & O Railroad," Lowell said, "the explosion of the River Gorge Bridge, the bombing of the French River Dam and subsequent deaths of several U.N. agents."

Lowell and Jennings both stayed in their positions, allowing the stairwell to give them some cover, but both pointed their guns into the room. Dex quickly moved into the room with his rifle against his shoulder and positioned himself behind some crates. The other men in the room stayed still.

"Let's go. Does anyone speak English in this place?" Riley shouted as he moved to the closest man. "Down on the ground." He shoved the barrel in the man's face. "Now."

"By the authority given me by the provisional government of the United Nations of America, I order you to surrender, immediately," Lowell said.

"You idiots think we're playing here?" Riley shoved the gun hard against his opponent's cheek.

"Riley," Jennings warned.

Slowly, the man Riley was menacing lowered himself to the ground and covered his head with his hands, but he was the only one in the room. Everyone else remained still as statues.

There was a rustling on *The Sky Climber*, followed by the footsteps of several people moving about unseen in the hold.

"Hey," Riley shouted. "Get your asses out here."

His shout was met with gunfire from the direction of the airship's hold. It was easy for Lowell to identify it as the crack of carbines, though he didn't know how many.

Lowell shouted, "Get down," hoping to get Riley out of the line of fire. He also ducked his head behind the corner to keep from getting hit himself.

"I don't know who you men are, but I suggest you leave immediately." A deep voice came from the ship's hold. "We don't have time for this nonsense. We'll kill you and move on. It's that simple."

Lowell didn't recognize the voice, but he assumed it belonged to the man leading the Sons of Grant at the moment. Lowell turned to Jennings. "I'm actually all for it. Leaving sounds intelligent. I'd love to take these men in, but we are quite outnumbered here, from what I can tell."

"Running away seems pretty sensible at this point, but I can't leave Riley out there," Jennings said.

"True enough. We probably could consider the fact that we'll be returning fire toward a Hydrogen-filled vehicle that's loaded with ammunition and explosives." Lowell looked at the other two men to make sure they understood the danger.

"That's only a problem if we miss who we're aiming for, which has never been a problem for me." Dex smiled. "You boys may want to watch what you're doing, though." He raised his gun, fired and charged forward.

Lowell watched the man Dex shot at fall to the ground.

He also saw Riley grapple with the man closest to him. The Union sympathizer had pulled a knife, and the two men were locked together in combat.

77

Onboard *The Sky Climber*, Tom reached for a tube and spoke to the control room. "Get this thing ready to leave. I want to be underway as quickly as possible." He didn't wait for an answer.

He walked through the hold until he reached the men with rifles he'd stationed by the cargo hold door. "Save your bullets. Whoever these yokels are, I think they're smart enough to know the possible consequences of shooting into a craft like ours."

One of the men turned around. "Consequences?"

Tom scowled at him. "Boom." He pointed up to where the airship's gas bags would be. "On military craft, the risks are pretty low. They're insulated and prepared for explosions and such. This is an old civilian craft. They had a low expectation of gunfights on these things. It could go up like a frog fart in a guppy pond."

The man's eyes widened.

"Think about that when you're pulling that trigger indiscriminately."

There was a shot from the stairway and one of the Sons of Grant went down with a hole in his chest.

"I stand corrected, maybe they aren't that smart." The ship shook as the engines grew louder. Tom steadied himself on a stack of crates.

78

The lizard bit through the keeper's arm just below the elbow. The man's screams slowed down Cyrus's rush forward to help Cantolione. The cries riled up the second creature, causing it to thrash its head and tail wildly. The tip of the tail cracked against Cyrus's leg, deflecting him sideways. He stumbled, but kept his momentum as best he could.

"Umberto, go out that hall with Cyrus, I'll go with the clown and we'll meet in the lobby," Lucinda said.

The other attendants were trapped with the lizards between them and the exits. When they heard the plan and how it didn't involve them, they yelled over their friend's cries of pain.

Lucinda obviously heard them, and Cyrus watched as she fired several shots at the nearest lizard's head. The beast flinched, then advanced toward her. Its claws scraped the hard floor as it ran. The two handlers, no longer trapped by the animal, rushed past their injured friend to get out. Cyrus and Cantolione were only a few steps ahead of them, hastening down the corridor and into the hallways of the inner building. Cantolione turned and dragged the heavy doors shut, cranking the latch closed then fumbling with a padlock before clicking it in place.

"Let's go." Cyrus grabbed at Cantolione's arm. "We're meeting in the lobby."

"Nothing to worry about now that we've locked this. Even if the beasts got this far, they'd never make it through the door," Cantolione said. "This barrier has held back elephants and hippos. There's no rush now."

"Except for that giant lizard making its way in this direction. That might be of some urgency." Cyrus didn't feel like saving the old man no matter whose side he was on. He wanted to grab Lucinda and get back to the business of quietly surviving and making sure she survived. "Let's just move."

"I need to check things in my office first, and then we can go."

"No."

Cantolione moved toward the hall that led to the offices. "Only a minute."

It was obvious that the giant lizards hadn't fazed him. Nor did the gunfight, the sudden return of the woman he may or may not have blamed for his son's death, or the humongous beast in the streets. The only thing that dented Cantolione's façade was the idea that he'd been taken. It showed on his face that he was hurt by the misplaced trust in Thomas Preston. Or maybe it was the idea that he was robbed and now nearly destitute.

"You can check your accounts later," Cyrus yelled.

"Only a moment, I'll catch up. Go." Cantolione waved Cyrus on with dainty fingers like an old woman shooing a cat off her porch. "There's a door just like the one I padlocked down the hall. The others will be headed through there. If the men lose their wits, you may want to close it behind them."

Cyrus didn't wait around to argue further. He ran down to the lobby and slid to a stop on its marble surface. The direction he and Cantolione had come was the short way—Lucinda and the others would have to make their way around curves and angled halls, but their trip shouldn't take long, considering their speed and the elements persuading them to keep moving. The ground rumbled and a framed show poster fell off the wall, shattering the glass. Cyrus stepped to the front of the lobby and peered out the front doors. He could see the giant beast was only a few blocks away and nearing the airship tower. He wondered who was having a worse time of it, but he was sure the men in the tower couldn't top what was going on in the menagerie.

Just then, the two assistants that were helping Cantolione with the lizards came running out of the hall and made a mad dash through the lobby toward the front door.

"Where are the others?" Cyrus reached for one of the men but missed.

They didn't stop or answer him in any way.

"Hey," he yelled after them. "Where are the other people?"

79

About the time Lowell and the others heard the airship's engines roar, they discerned voices from below them on the stairs and the unmistakable sound of the elevator rising.

"This isn't looking good," Lowell said. "We're outnumbered, possibly surrounded, and we can't shoot anyone for fear of blowing everything up."

Jennings and Dex nodded. Riley was still grappling with the soldier, but the tide had turned and Riley seemed close to finishing the other man off.

"Dex, you watch the guys coming up the stairs," Jennings said. "If they pose a threat, shoot them. *They* aren't filled with explosive gas, I'll bet."

"Finally, something to shoot at." Dex checked his rifle and leaned as close to the wall as he could get for cover.

With a roar, the airship began to pull away.

One of the Sons of Grant ran toward the ship's berth and leapt. As the ship gained altitude, Lowell could see the man had managed to grab the ship's deck and held on by one arm for a moment before his arm slipped and he fell from sight.

Riley popped up from his freshly won hand-to-hand fight and looked toward the ship. "Hell, no," he said. He ran for the bay where *The Sky Climber* had just taken off and unstrapped the launcher from his back as he went.

"Riley, no," Jennings yelled.

In the next instant, several Sons began firing at Dex. Both Lowell and Jennings targeted them.

"Riley, take cover," Lowell said, but the man was oblivious. "Dammit, Riley."

Riley moved faster, at least having the presence of mind to hunch over as he sprinted, using benches and crates for cover, rather than just running straight on. By the time he got to the empty bay area, he had his launcher loaded and leveled it at the ship.

Lowell watched as Riley fired one of the highly explosive rounds at the airship before reloading and firing another. The shots were followed quickly by thuds and the crash of explosions outside.

Back at the stairwell, Lowell heard the reports of a carbine and he turned to see Dex shooting down the stairs at a half dozen advancing Sons of Grant. The men scattered for cover, but Lowell was sure it wouldn't keep them for long. Next to him, Jennings still covered Riley.

Lowell seized the opportunity to add his gun to the din and shot the first Son he saw. Then he ran and jumped over obstacles to catch up with Riley, to see what the man had done.

80

Tom Preston fired several shots toward the man with the explosives launcher, but they went wide. *The Sky Climber* was careening to get altitude, and its overloaded cargo bay made it difficult for the ship to do anything well. It was built for tourists, not heavy munitions.

Seconds after he heard the first shot, Tom felt the ship do more than careen— there was a deafening explosion from one of the engines that sent everyone falling to the deck or against the wall.

"That's the port engine," someone pointed in the direction of the explosion. "If we lose that, no way we'll stay up with all this cargo."

Another man squatted down and started pushing a crate toward the open door. "Dump the crates or we're done for."

Tom grabbed the man by the shoulder and shoved him away. "Don't be ridiculous. We can't panic yet." As he spoke, a small, dark object flew through the air between him and the man. It landed toward the front of the ship, closer to the control room. Tom ran in the opposite direction, toward the still-open rear hatch.

A second later, a new explosion rocked *The Sky Climber* and it began to drop.

Tom stopped at Dr. Poley's device and tore the cover back. He stared at it and swallowed hard. "If this is as far as I go, I'll not waste this chance." He grabbed the lever and pulled, listening to the bubbling and grinding sounds within. He jabbed at the activation button, but it hadn't popped up yet. The sounds within grew louder and faster and he stared at the button for his chance to push it.

A sudden wave of heat and flame tore through the ship and cut his opportunity short.

81

Aboard the *Polk*, Cashe watched as *The Sky Climber's* port engine burst into flames, quickly followed by a massive blast that blew out a part of the ship's cabin.

"Christ, get us clear. Hard to port, hard to port." He held on to the arm of the chair and winced. The pain was terrible, and the rough ride was doing nothing for him.

"I've got it," Corrigan said. "I'm going to port and attempting to increase speed. We should be clear of the ship's path, but if it explodes, there's no telling what the shock might do."

The Sky Climber careened to port and began to dive. Directly in front of it and below, the monster looked up. Its palsied lip dropped more as the beast roared and bared its teeth.

There was another explosion in the cabin of *The Sky Climber*. It shuddered—the gas bladder and the length of its frame rippled with the force. The airship descended quickly then, dropping some thirty feet in a second.

"Get us moving faster," Cashe said. He'd seen the death throes of airships over and over in his years with the military. This was it. "It's going to blow sky high any second."

"We're not exactly in tip top shape," Corrigan said. "We're building up to best speed, but it's not quick."

82

Lowell and Riley watched *The Sky Climber* explode nearly one hundred yards from the great beast in the street. The resulting fireball enveloped both the ship and animal until neither was visible. A tangled mass of ship frame and lizard toppled, falling over onto the buildings perpendicular to the street. At that point, it was impossible to even make out what was beast and what was ship. Buildings nearby shook and fell from the blast that occurred just above them. Those that weren't leveled caught fire from the explosion or the debris.

The blast shook the building and nearly everyone fell to the floor. As the roar of the explosion and the crash of the beast subsided, Lowell looked around the waiting room of the airship station. Aside from the soldiers that he'd met up with, three men from the Sons of Grant were still standing. Everyone seemed to be recovering from the sights and events of the last few minutes.

All eyes were on Riley as he turned around and eyed everyone in the room. "I'm going to say this one more time," he said. "Drop your weapons and lay down on the floor or some shit, before I get mad."

The three Sons did as they were asked without hesitation and dropped to the ground. As Lowell looked around, Jennings gave a smile and a look that asked jokingly if maybe they should get down just in case. The barrage of fire that had been sounding from the stairs ceased as the explosion outside erupted.

"They're gone," Dex said. "Presumably to see the carnage outside, but I can't be sure. Maybe they just ran like hell to avoid the wrath of Riley."

"We'll just have to take our chances, I guess." Lowell stood in the center of the room, taking it all in. He wasn't sure what they were going to do with prisoners. They didn't really have a base of operations or a prison where they could be kept. The O.M.O. rarely had to take anyone to jail. They had the small jail cells onboard the *Polk*, but that was it.

"All right, let's clean this up and get out of here," Lowell said.

"The only thing on my list of duties is soldiering. It doesn't say anything about scrubbing streets." Jennings wrinkled his nose. "Are we supposed to pick up that flaming pile of meat down there?"

Lowell looked at the mess below and shook his head. Like his nesting dolls, this mess had layer upon layer of ugliness to it. "Let's pick up our prisoners and meet up with our people. Someone will have an idea of what to do. I'd say you're right. We can leave this mess for the local military to deal with." He generally believed in handling a mess himself, but today had been a long day.

83

Everyone onboard the *Polk* held on as the waves of the explosion shook the ship. Corrigan had managed to get them away from the worst of the blast, turning the ship so its profile didn't have to take much damage. The ship's sheer size and mass also helped keep it on an even keel. The most they had to worry about was the equivalent of a heavy turbulence.

"Good work," Cashe said to Corrigan. "We'll make a pilot out of you yet."

"What now?" Corrigan asked.

Cashe was having a hard time keeping his eyes open and an even harder time thinking straight. "Do you see anywhere we can set down and collect everyone we need to account for?" He could see Corrigan and Bethy looking around, but didn't hear their reply. He could feel the ship descending a few minutes later and nodded as he watched their lips move.

Bethy got very close to Cashe's face and spoke loudly to his ear. "We're going to collect the men in the tower before the fire spreads to them. Do you understand?"

Cashe nodded weakly.

He was fading again, but clearly heard Bethy speak to Corrigan. "If he goes out again, have someone take him to the infirmary. He's not doing himself any good now sitting up here like this."

Cashe firmly believed he hadn't been doing anyone any good before that, either.

84

Lowell watched the *Polk* approach and waited patiently as it took extra time to maneuver into place. He could see the ship had been through a lot in the last few battles. It was riddled with bullet holes and scorch marks—panels were missing and windows were shattered. It would take considerable time to get it back into shape.

As the nearest ramp lowered, Bethy came running down, rifle in hand.

"Everyone all right?" She leapt the last few steps from the plank to the tower landing with ease.

"We're all scattered to the winds," Lowell said. "I ended up with these guys from the Northern army. We did our best." He waved around to the mess of the waiting room that was strewn with bodies, crates and their three prisoners.

He was dismayed when Bethy barely gave the scene a second glance.

"I'm going to go and check on Alek and the tank," she said. "I want to make sure everyone got clear of that explosion down there."

With a flourish, Riley stepped forward. "I did that. I made that thing explode real good."

"I'm not sure you should be braggin'," Jennings said.

It was obvious to Lowell what she was actually worried about. "Cyrus met up with us briefly and then took off for some reason," he said. "No idea where he ended up."

"Did he join Lucy?"

Lowell turned to her. "Lucy?"

"She left in a Goose mid-way through the battle," Bethy said. "She had a talk with Cashe and took off." Bethy started for the stairs. "I hope to hell that's where Cyrus ended up."

"If they aren't here, then maybe we can check Cantolione's business. They might've gone there if they thought it would help somehow," Lowell said. While the man wasn't involved directly, maybe there was a tangent that Lucinda and Cyrus might have pursued. He hoped that was the case, and not that something terrible had befallen them.

The Sons of Grant on the stairs had taken off, but Lowell worried Bethy might need help. And so might Lucinda. He patted Jennings on the shoulder as he passed. "Put these guys onboard and then get on yourselves. We'll meet up in a few minutes."

Lowell saw Daniel on the ramp and waved to him. "We'll meet you someplace safer in a few. I'll collect any wayward sheep on the way."

He bounded for the stairs and yelled to Bethy, "Wait for me. There could be more men down there."

She was already one flight ahead of him.

85

After the men ran out the door, Cyrus took off down the hall they'd just left. "Lucy?" he shouted.

No answer.

His slow stride became more hurried as he turned a corner and found it empty. He followed the signs indicating the direction to the animal cages, hoping he was retracing the men's steps. It paid off as he heard a rattling and shouts just ahead. Cyrus turned another corner and followed a T-junction to the right. Ahead of him was a reinforced barred gate just like the one he'd gone through with Cantolione. Someone was pounding on it from the other side.

"Lucy?"

The response was muffled. "Yes! Can you get the door open? We're trapped here and we're both out of ammo."

"One second." Cyrus stared at the metal bar across the door and found the bolting mechanism. He gripped it and tugged until it clicked. "Got it, push."

As he pulled the door handle, he could feel someone applying pressure to the other side. Simultaneously he heard the crack of a whip. When there was adequate space, Lucinda slid through and helped Cyrus pull it open just a little more for the clown that came with her. All three pushed to get it closed again. Cyrus caught just a glimpse of the leathery things that were chasing the two of them. He shuddered, thankful that he hadn't been the one to have to look back at those melon-sized eyes following him down the corridors in a desperate run for his life. He dropped the bar back into place and bolted it. Immediately, there were scratching sounds from the other side of the door and it shook slightly as the beasts tried to make it through.

"Jesus, are you two all right?" Cyrus asked. "I saw the keepers run past me and into the street, but they didn't tell me what happened to you."

Leaning against the door to catch her breath, Lucinda shook her head. "They got ahead of us and slammed the door shut to save their own hides."

"Probably smart they didn't tell me, I'd have put a bullet in their heads for that." Cyrus looked at Lucinda. Aside from being winded she didn't look the worse for wear. "You hurt?"

"No." She looked herself over for cuts and teeth marks, but had none to show.

"Good," Cyrus replied. "I'm glad."

After a long moment Cappy Marks spoke up. "I'm well, thanks for asking."

Cyrus looked over at the man who'd just shown up and claimed to be an O.M.O. agent. The big red smile painted over his mouth made Cyrus Spencer laugh for the first time in a long time.

"You look happy with the outcome," Cyrus said to Cappy.

"Hilarious," Cappy said.

A shout stopped their nervous laughter. "All of you just turn around."

Behind them, Cantolione stood with a pistol. "Keep your hands off your guns," he said. "I checked my safe and all the money that was there is gone. I suspect the same'll be true of my bank accounts." He looked agitated and shaky. A nervous twitch made his gun jump a little. "Thomas Preston wouldn't do this. Thomas Preston is loyal to me and this company."

"Look, Mr. Cantolione," Cyrus said. "We are here to help. We're trying to catch him. You'll see. He took your fortune from you." He moved slowly to put himself between the gun and Lucinda.

"Stay where you are, all of you." Cantolione pointed the gun at Cappy. "You double crossed me, not Tom. You work for the government. You've been working against me."

"You've got it all wrong." Cyrus put his hands out to calm Cantolione.

There were shots then, the reports of which filled the enclosed corridor. Cyrus wheeled, trying to clear his pistol from the holster and protect the others.

Still, Lucinda sank to the floor, clutching her side. Cyrus put his hand over Lucinda's wound in a desperate attempt to push the blood back in.

Where Cantolione was in a desperate frenzy moments before, his face had now gone blank and he appeared in a fog. "That wasn't meant for her."

"She had nothing to do with your money going missing," Cyrus yelled, "and she made an effort to come here and make things right for you."

Cappy Marks stared at Cyrus until he caught his eye and then nodded almost imperceptibly. He took two steps away from the pair and pulled his gun, pointing it at Cantolione. As Cantolione shot at Cappy, Cyrus drew his own gun and fired two shots, never letting go of Lucinda.

Both Cappy and Cantolione fell to the floor.

86

Lowell and Bethy ran down Waterline Street toward the circus. They stayed close to the eastern side of the street to avoid the flames on the west side. The fire was rapidly spreading down the block thanks to all the wooden buildings. Behind them they heard the *Polk*'s engines race. They turned to see it pull away from the tower. The flames were growing dangerously close to the berth. As he and Lucinda ran again, Lowell saw figures moving through the smoke-filled street. It was soon obvious that the shadows were not ordinary citizens or soldiers, but chewers.

"Something must have broken a section of the containment fence." Bethy raised her rifle and fired at the nearest walking corpse.

They continued to move forward, destroying a chewer as they went. There weren't many, but enough to slow down the duo's progress. There were a couple of times when both of them stopped and looked around, the grinding sound of the raucous tank filled the street, but neither of them could see it. They did however, see and hear the *Polk* as it revved and pulled farther away. The flames had jumped the street and were making their way to the airship base. It was smart for them to move when they did, before any further danger befell the crew.

As Lowell and Bethy got within a block of the zoo, they raised their rifles. Two men ran out the front doors and skidded to a halt in the street. They definitely weren't undead. The men looked at Lowell and Bethy and the destruction behind them and quickly decided to run in the opposite direction—down the boardwalk, past the empty stalls and booths.

"Hey, stop!" Lowell yelled. He and Bethy ran after them for a block, but the men didn't slow or look back.

Gun shots sounded from the zoo.

"Dammit." Lowell cursed at himself for being distracted from his goal. There was so much going on that he couldn't focus on a single objective for more than a minute. He and Bethy headed for the zoo entrance.

There was more gunfire when they entered the lobby. Cantolione lay on the floor—blood pooling beneath him on the stone.

"Help, someone help." The voice was Cyrus's, calling weakly from the darkness.

Bethy ran to him immediately and then saw he was cradling Lucinda on his lap. Another man slumped against the wall near them.

Bethy went to Cyrus and Lucinda while Lowell checked the other man.

"He distracted Cantolione from us," Cyrus said. "His gun wasn't even loaded."

Lowell recognized the man—Cappy Marks. The O.M.O. informant who had been feeding them information on the Sons of Grant. He could tell that Cappy was breathing, but that was about it. Lowell couldn't find a pulse easily. He looked over at Bethy, who was doing a similar check on Lucinda. She shook her head slowly.

There was movement behind them. Lowell turned to see two chewers shambling into the building. He pulled his pistol and opened up on both of them. The shots echoed in the lobby. "I got them."

"Ok, Cyrus," Bethy said. "Help me lay her out. I need to find the bullet and see how much damage it did." She tried to pull Lucinda from Cyrus, but he didn't answer. When she couldn't wrest the woman away, Bethy started tearing clothing from the areas where Lucinda'd been shot.

"Someone go signal the *Polk*," Bethy said. "We need to get to the surgeon's equipment in the infirmary."

"I've got a flare," Lowell said. "I'll light it and come back for Cappy." He ran out with his pistol drawn.

87

Cyrus felt numb as he stood in the hall.

"Cyrus? Listen to me. I need your help now to get her out of here," Bethy said.

The words registered with Cyrus, but he couldn't take his eyes off Lucinda.

"She could have stayed on the *Polk*, Cyrus," Bethy said. "There was no way for you to protect her."

His own breath was shallow and Cyrus felt like he was going to pass out as his head swam with the thoughts of the last week and the last couple of years.

He'd worked to make sure this didn't happen, and yet his work was never quite enough.

"I said I need you to carry her, so we can find some way to get her out of here." Bethy was shoving his arm to get him to focus on what was happening now.

Cyrus stooped and picked Lucinda up easily—following where Bethy led.

88

There was a roar of gunfire as Lowell shot two more chewers in the street and lit the flare. He ran back in to gather the others. He stopped at the bend in the hall where Cantolione lay motionless and bent to check for breathing, but the man was still— the life had seeped out of him.

"Jesus, Lowell. Get Cappy," Bethy yelled.

As he stood, Lowell steadied himself on the wall and nearly knocked one of the show posters onto the ground. He glimpsed it briefly and started to leave, but something made him look back. There was something familiar about the faces. The big letters across the top read "The Confounding Cantolione Family" in fiery red. A figure at the bottom was obviously Umberto Cantolione himself, dressed as a ringmaster, arms outstretched, welcoming the masses. Toward the top, two men held hands with a beautiful young lady who could only be Lucinda. The trio were outfitted in silvery sequined outfits and standing at the top of an acrobat's pole.

"It was an accident," Cyrus said. He was carrying Lucinda now, and his face was pale with concern for the woman. "She told me it was an accident. She was married to Cantolione's son and they had an act in his little show. High wire, swings, whatever." Cyrus started walking toward Lowell, but Lowell could tell he wasn't looking at anything but the poster. "There was some incident, bad timing on one of the stunts, nobody's fault, really."

"And you knew all along?" Lowell said.

Cyrus moved toward the entrance. "She never said. I heard it second hand."

Lowell thought about some sort of response, but decided instead to go without another word. On Waterline Street they slid to a halt. The opposite line of buildings, shacks and game booths were in flames—engulfed nearly top to bottom. The smoke was thick and blotted out the sky momentarily until the sleek form of *The Moon* came barreling through, dangerously close to the buildings lining the streets. The *Polk* was so immense, it wouldn't have been able to land anywhere near Lowell's position.

Lowell waved his arms frantically at the ship and it drifted low in response. Once it landed, Lowell shouted back to the others and ran onboard.

"I'm going to piss about you flying this thing without me later, but for now, set a course for Outpost Two Thirteen," Lowell said, dashing onto the bridge and leaning over to Daniel to see if he had any trouble. "Everything responding like it should?"

"Little sluggish, but not bad. When we get to the outpost, we can knock things into shape, I think."

"Well, until then, do your best." Lowell tried to smile. "But fly fast."

"I will," Daniel said.

Lowell went down to the cargo hold and helped pull Lucinda and Cappy onboard. Once inside, Bethy and Cyrus went about making the injured as comfortable as they could. Lowell saw a large group of chewers heading their way. He grabbed a rifle, firing as fast as he could. The ship rose just as three were close enough to touch him. He swung his rifle around and smashed at them with the butt of the gun. One of the things grabbed his ankle but couldn't get a grip and fell to the street as the craft got higher.

As they cleared the city, the *Polk* limped into view. They exchanged information via their signal lights and then they parted company. *The Moon and the Stars* pulled away toward the mountains and desert.

89

In the main observation room of *The Moon and the Stars*, Cyrus lay on the floor with his head near the big glass wall. He stared out at the clouds and sky, watching it all go by. He'd wanted to get out of the tin cans he'd been stuck in on the ground as he tried to make the money he needed to get overseas. He liked Cashe and the O.M.O., but it occurred to him that the *Polk* was just another confining box and that the dream of heading to Europe was beyond his reach.

There were no other craft in the sky and they were too high for many birds to make an appearance. There were just wisps of cloud and smoke. When he sat up, he could still see the fires that were producing the billowing smoke. Their fight with the dragon tore apart Santa Rosa and the reconstruction would take years to accomplish, if ever. The governments weren't exactly in any position to offer money for repairs to help the townspeople get back on their feet.

In the harbor, most of the ships were on fire, or half underwater. The attack had left the better part of the area's naval vessels devastated—another cost the governments would be hard-pressed to absorb. It was unbelievable to Cyrus that one strange creature could make life so difficult for so many people. He sat up and wiped the sweat from his brow.

"Nice view, huh?" Bethy entered the room. "I'm not sure how much of that damage the dragon did, and how much was our fault."

"No telling." Cyrus didn't turn around.

"I don't know what you want to do next, but we're heading to Two Thirteen for medical attention," Bethy said. "If you want to leave, you can arrange some sort of transportation from there. We may be able to drop you at a train station or rustle up a horse for you."

He could tell she was fishing for information, but he didn't have any answers for her or for himself. "Don't know. But I'll keep that in mind."

Bethy sat down a few feet away from him. She stayed quiet and stared with him for a few minutes.

"What're you going to do?" Cyrus asked.

"What can I do? This is my home. This is where I belong," she said. "Besides, were you not paying attention? This sorry bunch of males can't get along without me."

"I noticed."

The ship rocked slightly and one engine clunked loudly before returning to normal.

Cyrus could see his question reflected in her face. "I didn't fight in the war. I was making money and I didn't care."

She didn't respond.

"Maybe this is the way I make up for it?" He waved around himself and pointed to the O.M.O. on the shirt he was wearing. "I don't know."

"You don't have to figure it all out just yet."

He nodded in agreement, but in the back of his head he wondered where he would've ended up had he been a soldier back then. Would he have died, deserted or ended up on a ship like the Turtle, chasing his fate somewhere else?

Out the window, he saw the larger airship behind them shudder and dip slightly. "Are we sure the *Polk* is going to make it?"

"Sure it is. I helped fix it." Bethy smiled. "Like I said, they can't do anything without me around here."

90

They all stood around Lucinda's bed in Two Thirteen's infirmary waiting for her to wake up. Cyrus stayed toward the back and let Cashe and Bethy claim the closest spots. Lucinda had been in and out of consciousness since the surgery but the doctors called them all around when he thought she was waking.

Cyrus wondered how she would get on after this. Not just the wound, but the experience. She'd surely only wanted to join the O.M.O. for safety and refuge, much as she'd only joined with him for the same. Where would she go next and what would she want to do with her life? Cyrus half hoped she didn't want him to be a part of it.

She stirred with a low moan and the assembled spectators took a breath.

"Lucy?" Bethy asked.

"Let the girl wake up on her own," Cashe said.

"Yes, I'm sure six people staring at her wouldn't be frightening enough," Bethy said.

Lucinda stretched her right arm and arched her back. "No, I'm fine. You didn't startle me or nothin'."

"How do you feel?" Dr. Hastings asked.

"I'm sore and pretty tired," Lucinda replied.

"You feel like trying the arm again?" Dr. Hastings asked.

"Not really."

Cantolione's bullets had shattered her arm and Hastings wasn't able to save it. His only alternative was one of Dr. Poley's inventions.

"Just a little," Hastings said. "See if you can raise it and grip the glass by your table."

"Please?" Bethy added. "We can help you make it work."

Lucinda scowled at the younger girl and Bethy leaned back to avoid her wrath.

"Take your time," Cyrus said. "We can try it again tomorrow, right?" He didn't want to see everyone badger her on the issue. It was either something she could get used to, or she couldn't.

"I think it's better to get it moving now and make sure the body doesn't reject it. If it does, we may have to try another surgery to reset it," Hastings said.

"It can wait a day." Cyrus pushed forward to Lucinda's side.

When he'd wedged himself as close as he could, Lucinda reached out and touched Cyrus's chest. "No. It's fine. I'm sure he's right. I'll get it over with and that'll be that."

"You don't have to."

"You going to fight all of them, just so I don't have to try to raise my arm?"

Cyrus looked around at the assemblage. "Might do. I've seen them all in action. Wouldn't be much of a fight."

The group chuckled uneasily.

She didn't seem happy about it, but Lucinda pulled aside the covers on her left side revealing her new arm. It was a series of brass and steel parts that at least resembled a human arm—maybe the skeleton of one. There were dozens of tiny gears and pulleys visible just beneath the outer structure. The limb gleamed in the harsh light of the infirmary.

Cyrus grabbed her good hand, which was still touching his chest, and held it in his own. When she looked at him he nodded slightly. She strained as if she were lifting a heavy load, which could be the truth considering the heft of the parts used to make the arm. There was the faintest of sounds as the limb came up off the bed. It sounded almost like bees trapped in a jar as she lifted it higher.

"The sound will dissipate as you break the arm in," Hastings said.

Lucinda's lip curled up a bit at the idea. "Sure it will." She strained to lift her arm higher and a bead of sweat erupted on her forehead. She slowly moved it left toward the side table and with much effort, she wrapped the mechanical hand around the glass of water there.

"Marvelous!" Cashe said.

The sudden noise seemed to startle her and her hand closed, smashing the glass and splattering water all over the table and a number of the people nearby. She opened the hand and shards of glass fell to the table and floor. "I'd call this a successful first test. Anyone want to bring me something else to break?"

The gathered friends laughed. Cashe excused himself.

In the hall, Cashe rolled slowly along in his wheelchair until he came to a large window that let him see out into the parade grounds of Outpost Two Thirteen. From there, he could see the repair efforts that were taking place on the *Leonidas Polk*. Things looked pretty bad on the outside, and he was sure the inside wasn't much better. The battle with the Sons of Grant here earlier had left the fort in tatters as well, and the men stationed at Two Thirteen were going about the business of making it whole and defensible again.

"She'll be up and flying again," Cyrus said. "Just a little cosmetic damage, I think."

Cashe chuckled. "Not entirely reassuring, considering you, yourself, professed to know absolutely nothing about airships just a few short days ago."

"Let's just say I have a good feeling."

"That's better, I suppose."

Cyrus stepped beside Cashe and his wheelchair to look out at the ship. "How're you?" Cyrus asked.

"I'll be in this chair a spell, I understand. Then—" Cashe hit his legs with his fist and they made a metallic sound. "These things are supposed to help me walk when I'm ready. Least that's what Hastings says."

"Much pain?" Cyrus asked.

Cashe lied to just about everyone that asked the question, but he felt compelled to share his condition with Cyrus. "Like hell, my friend. Like hell." He changed the subject quickly, feeling he should've kept his mouth shut. He looked at Cyrus's bruises and scrapes. "How about you? How are you feeling?"

Without pause Cyrus answered him. "Like hell, my friend. Like hell."

Before either man had the chance to bring up the subject of Lucinda, or find a way to artfully dodge it, Dr. Hastings approached with two soldiers. "I told you if you wanted to get out and about you needed to let the nurse know, so she could take you. You're still pretty weak."

"Don't want to be a burden to anyone," Cashe said. "Besides, I'm fine. I wasn't going far." He'd been awake in his room for the last five days and no one would let him leave. They told him he'd been unconscious for nearly a week before that. He slipped into a deep sleep on the way back from Santa Rosa and hadn't stirred since. He joked that he'd just been getting all his sleep out of the way for the next year. In truth, they made it very clear that he'd narrowly missed death. The blood loss and internal damage had been that bad.

"You've been nothing but a burden up until now, why should that change?" Bethy walked up behind the doctor and his men. She pushed past them and squeezed Cashe's hand.

He was grateful to have one of his own people so close, though he was trying to get used to being able to call Cyrus one of his people. He'd proven himself to the unit, but at the moment, it was hard to tell if the man would stay.

"Thanks, that makes me feel missed," Cashe said.

"We've all decided you're milking this injury just to get out of repairing things," Bethy said. "Alek is stuck rebuilding the master controls by himself. Daniel and Corrigan are reattaching the port propeller, and I'm attempting to weld some structural damage to the frame. Everyone else is busy as all get out as well. The air bladders haven't even been patched yet." She put her hands on her hips and scowled at him. "Frankly this little sojourn is pretty ill-timed."

Cashe and Cyrus laughed until Cyrus stopped in mid-laugh. "Wait. Alek isn't working alone, I've been helping out."

"Like I said, he's on his own." Bethy wrapped her arms around Cyrus and gave him a squeeze.

Cyrus smiled, which was something that Cashe hadn't seen the man do before. Or Bethy for that matter.

"Doesn't talk shit," Cyrus said. "I'm good with that kind of thing."

Everyone laughed at that until Cashe realized the doctor and his men were still standing next to him, expectantly. "I'm sorry, Dr. Hastings. Was there something you wanted to say?"

He was sheepish at first but Hastings spoke up. "We were going to wait until you were feeling better, but you seem to be up for talking now."

Cashe nodded to them. He had no idea what they could want, considering the chaos around them of building and rebuilding. "Please, go on."

"Well, as you know. We've had an absence of contact from anyone in the O.M.O. or the U.N. for quite some time," Hastings said. "Sgt. Hersh here has led the soldiers for the most part, but the mantle of leadership over the post as a whole has fallen to me, since the outpost is mostly a scientific facility. I've been in charge of everything for the better part of a year now. And it's not that I mind, but the day to day administration of the place cuts into my ability to effectively conduct any research or experiments."

Cashe wasn't sure how he felt about where this was going.

"And really, my policy has been to stay the course and protect what's ours here at Two Thirteen. On Sgt. Hersh's recommendation, I've allowed them to strike out and help nearby towns when they needed it, but we've done little else."

"Sometimes doing nothing can be a strategy," Cashe said.

Hastings nodded. "You're too kind. But we're here to ask you to stay on and lead the West Coast arm of the O.M.O. After you recover, of course."

Cashe thought they were coming to ask him to watch over the base, not cover half the country. "I don't know, that's a lot of territory. Surely there are other bases with brighter military minds." He tried to read Hastings's expression. After their talk, the man should have misgivings about turning over command to Cashe, seeing as how he was a fraud and all.

"We've sent every kind of message we could think of off to other depots and outposts," Hastings said. "But never got anything back.

"We even sent riders off to see what they could find, but they never returned," Sgt Hersh said. "We have to assume we are the last O.M.O. or UN post out here, unless some of your men can take the *Polk* and check into it."

"There are other military posts, though?" Bethy asked. "We got help from a number of units in the fight in Santa Rosa."

"Yes, there are Northern and Southern troops up and down the coast, but they aren't interested in joining up with us; they're busy protecting borders, shooting chewers and watching each other."

Cashe rubbed his legs, but barely felt the touch. It was good news—having some feeling rather than none. He realized the doctors were right, it would be a long road to standing, let alone to walking. It would be a far stretch to running again. "Let's talk about it." It was as close to a yes as he wanted to venture. But it was as far from a no as he'd ever been.

91

The *Polk* and *The Moon* hovered over the Sacramento River, spotlighted by the rising sun. Daniel guided the hooks dangling from the airships' winches onto strategic spots on the Turtle and tested each for steadfastness before waving a signal to Alek and the others above. The engines whined on both crafts and they began backing up toward the west bank, dragging the Turtle through the water slowly.

On the shore, Cyrus stood with Bethy next to him and Cashe in his wheelchair nearby. Cyrus watched as his old craft became more visible the closer it got. It had been due in large part to Bethy's pushing that they'd returned to dredge the river. She told him about the effect it would have on his conscience. He didn't see the need for it and told her over and over again in the last few months that he'd rather leave it alone, but she was relentless. Once Lucinda joined in the badgering, it was all over for him and he gave in. Cashe was gracious and quite happy to help. Cyrus hadn't expected the man to actually come out in his condition, but he had progressed in great strides in the two months since his injury.

Bethy squeezed Cyrus's hand, and a little of the tension subsided.

On shore, a number of men from Two Thirteen waved the ships on to guide the pilots in their efforts. They all backed up a good distance when the Turtle finally got dragged ashore. Its legs were still touching water when the airships gave up and the men released the hooks. It was too heavy and bogged down to drag any further.

Water streamed from a thousand places on the Turtle's hull and the crowd stood back and let it drain out. The *Polk* and *The Moon and the Stars* came to rest in a nearby clearing. Once they were secured, crewmembers disembarked to come take a look.

While they were waiting, Cyrus grabbed a shovel that had been propped against a tree and started toward the clearing where the ships had landed.

"Are you seriously going to dig a hole and bury each and every one of those people?" Cashe asked.

"It sounds like a lot of work when you say it out loud, but yessir, I plan to."

Bethy walked to the tree and picked up another shovel and followed him.

"And then what do you plan to do after that?" Cashe asked.

They'd remained mute on the subject since they got back to the fort. Technically, he and Lucinda had joined up not long after they'd been brought aboard. He didn't have a crew to take anymore but he still had kin across the ocean. The dream of leaving the States seemed far too distant, though not unattainable. The work with the O.M.O. wasn't going to make him rich, but for now the good he could do was enough to satisfy him. He'd felt like an odd man out just as soon as he'd gone aboard the *Polk* for the first time. It seemed only right that it be something he truly committed to.

Cyrus looked around at the group, and up toward the airships circling in the sky. "Whatever you need me to, sir. Whatever you need."

About the Author

Matt Betts was born in Lima, Ohio, some years ago. Lima is just a stone's throw away from several other towns with excellent throwing stones. During and after college, Matt worked for a number of years in radio as an on-air personality, anchor and reporter. He has written for *Blood, Blade and Thruster Magazine* and *Shock Totem*. His fiction and poetry have appeared in numerous magazines, journals and anthologies.

Matt currently lives in Columbus, Ohio, with his wife and sons. He is hard at work on the next adventure of the crew of the airship *Leonidas Polk*. And watching old horror movies. And maybe reading comic books. He can feel you silently judging him and doesn't like it one bit. For more info visit: www.MattBetts.com.